A STRONG HAND GRABBED
THE BACK OF HER SHIRT

"Renata, stop!"

"No!" She surged forward. "Let me go!"

Adam tightened his grip, yanking her backwards. The wet fabric of her shirt ripped, costing him his hold.

The unexpected momentum of being released made Renata lose her balance. She pitched forward awkwardly, grasping her ruined shirt with one hand as she struggled to regain her footing. Staggering, she leaped away.

He tackled her, hugging her close as they hit the ground and rolled down the embankment toward the ditch. They stopped just short of the water, Adam on top, Renata trapped beneath his large frame.

She sank into the wet ground, her scraped side burning. The disappointment over not getting away cut to the bone, crushing her tenuous hold on her temper.

She drew back and punched him. "Let me go, damn you!"

He caught her wrists, yanking them over her head and pinning them.

"Give it up," he shouted hoarsely. "You don't stand a chance against me. You never did."

BOOK YOUR PLACE ON OUR WEBSITE AND MAKE THE READING CONNECTION!

We've created a customized website just for our very special readers, where you can get the inside scoop on everything that's going on with Zebra, Pinnacle and Kensington books.

When you come online, you'll have the exciting opportunity to:

- View covers of upcoming books
- Read sample chapters
- Learn about our future publishing schedule (listed by publication month *and author*)
- Find out when your favorite authors will be visiting a city near you
- Search for and order backlist books from our online catalog
- Check out author bios and background information
- Send e-mail to your favorite authors
- Meet the Kensington staff online
- Join us in weekly chats with authors, readers and other guests
- Get writing guidelines
- AND MUCH MORE!

**Visit our website at
http://www.kensingtonbooks.com**

PURE DYNAMITE

Lauren Bach

ZEBRA BOOKS
KENSINGTON PUBLISHING CORP.
http://www.kensingtonbooks.com

ZEBRA BOOKS are published by

Kensington Publishing Corp.
850 Third Avenue
New York, NY 10022

All Kensington titles, imprints and distributed lines are available at special quantity discounts for bulk purchases for sales
promotion, premiums, fund-raising, educational or institu-
tional use.

Special book excerpts or customized printings can also be
created to fit specific needs. For details, write or phone the
office of the Kensington Special Sales Manager: Kensington
Publishing Corp., 850 Third Avenue, New York, NY 10022.
Attn. Special Sales Department. Phone: 1-800-221-2647.

Zebra and the Z logo Reg. U.S. Pat. & TM Off.

First Printing: October 2004
10 9 8 7 6 5 4 3 2 1

Printed in the United States of America

ACKNOWLEDGMENTS

The author wishes to thank the following for their time and assistance. All errors are mine, not theirs. I tend to bend/break/ignore rules . . .

Rosale Lobo, R.N., M.S.N., C.L.N.C., Lobo Consulting Group, for medical expertise, friendship, and encouragement.

Karen Tapp, M.D., U.N.C. Hospital, Chapel Hill, for answering questions and being so cool.

FBI Special Agent Bret Kirby, for help on C-4, and other stuff, like not laughing.

WO1 Michael Desmond, U.S. Army, for helicopter information.

Heartfelt thanks, also, to:

Lori Harris, Karen Kearney, and Jean McManis, for reading drafts and giving valuable feedback. Nolen Holzapfel, for evil ideas. All the folks at Kensington Publishing, particularly Kate Duffy and Creative Director Janice Rossi Schaus. And two special friends: Carly Phillips and Janelle Denison.

Chapter One

The tan-colored bus—INMATE TRANSPORTATION stenciled crudely on its sides—skidded to a stop in the center of the rutted gravel road. The driver, one of two armed prison guards, set the hand brake and climbed out.

Adam Duval strained against his shackles, unable to see anything beyond the windshield. That they had stopped before reaching their designated work site was a bad sign.

Shoulders hunched, he tried peering between the dirty metal slats welded across the side windows. He saw little. Just eye-blistering-blue skies, a tobacco field, and a gray squirrel. Typical central North Carolina flora and fauna, except that the squirrel was dead, its bloated carcass floating in an ocean of scummy water that left only the tops of the tallest tobacco stalks visible.

Earlier in the week, a tropical weather system had stalled and dumped a record-breaking eighteen inches of rain on the state, spawning catastrophic flooding. Thousands were homeless, few had electricity, and transportation was at a standstill.

With the state's emergency resources stretched to the max, the governor had pledged the entire prison work force to recovery efforts. While Adam had been assigned to a road gang three days ago, this was the first time the busses had actually made it off the flood-ravaged prison grounds. If they were forced to turn back it could be days before they got out again as more rain was predicted later that night, courtesy of a second system creeping in from the Midwest.

Frustrated, he waited. And watched. Then waited some more. What was taking the driver so damn long?

"Ten bucks says we turn around and head back," Franklin Potter, one of the three other inmates, whispered.

The senior guard, Irv Wallace, who'd ignored them up till now, turned. "Who said that? McEdwin?"

When no one responded, the guard swung his black club in the air. "Y'all better shut your traps or somebody's going to be working with a cracked skull."

Adam narrowed his gaze to the back of Potter's head, willing him to keep quiet. The last thing they needed was grief from the guard.

Tempers on both sides of the bars shortened as the heat index inside the bus topped a suffocating one hundred degrees. Not that the lack of air movement bothered anyone but the prisoners. The guards had a small fan mounted on the cracked dashboard. They didn't care that the back of the bus felt like the inside of a sealed fifty-five gallon drum. Or that the exhaust system leaked.

The greasy sausage and biscuit Adam had for breakfast burned a hole in his gut. Perspiration trickled down his neck. He shook his head, realized he'd actually been praying—a habit he'd abandoned in childhood. Desperation did strange things to a man.

Finally, the driver returned and motioned for Wallace to climb off. Adam shifted, watching the guards confer outside. Neither man looked happy.

With no guards on the bus, Potter, the inmate with

ten dollars, grew vocal again. "Leaving a dog locked in a vehicle this hot is against the law. Damn dogs got more rights than we do."

"Shut the fuck up," Lyle McEdwin, the prisoner seated behind Adam hissed. "I already owe you for letting me take the heat earlier."

"Hey, can I help it if Wallace has a hard-on for you?" Potter sneered. "The man is always riding your ass."

"Yeah? Well, when we get outside, I'm gonna—"

The doors banged open, signaling the guards' return. A lethal silence fell over the prisoners. Adam shot Lyle a scowl, prayed it registered. Unfortunately, hints the size of a B-52 routinely went right over the kid's head.

The youngest man on the road gang, Lyle McEdwin's immaturity was legendary. He had a big mouth and a reputation for making stupid moves. He was also Adam's cellmate.

Irv Wallace cleared his throat and removed his sunglasses. The guard's right eye was slightly off plumb, giving him a harsh look that matched his attitude. "Listen up. Bus can't go any further. Roadbed's washed out. We'll have to walk to the site. With the equipment."

The inmates grumbled, but not too loud. Working a road gang—even under miserable conditions—beat being locked up in a prison cell. Anything beat that.

Especially today. Christ, Adam would belly crawl across razor blades with all the equipment strapped on his back to get to the work site.

The grumbling grew louder, which set Wallace off yet again. He clanged his metal clipboard against the interior bars.

"North Carolina statute 148-26 says all able-bodied prison inmates are required to perform diligently all work assignments provided for them," the guard recited from memory. "Diligently means doing whatever I tell you. Got that? It also says 'failure to perform such work assignments may result in disciplinary action.' Anybody need a demonstration of disciplinary action?"

When no one volunteered, Wallace locked his good eye on Adam before continuing in a drawl as thick and annoying as the late-July heat. "You're awfully quiet, Hollywood. Was there any part of that statute you didn't understand?"

Wallace dragged the slur out. *Holl-Leee-Wood.*

Adam knew what was whispered behind his back. Movie star face, Frankenstein body. He also knew the guard was spoiling for a fight. Part of him ached to oblige. But not now.

Stifling the urge, Adam looked away.

"I didn't think so." Pleased with his imagined victory, Wallace hiked up his pants and puffed his chest before speaking into the two-way radio clipped near his shoulder.

The driver moved to unshackle the inmates, an easy process since there were only four. Prison road crews were usually composed of eight men, but under the governor's emergency disaster plan, they'd been split into smaller groups to cover a larger geographic area. Two armed guards still accompanied each squad manned with medium-risk inmates.

As the inmates disembarked, Adam positioned himself between Potter and Lyle, who still swapped venomous glares.

"You prisoners turn and put your hands on the bus. Any unauthorized movement will be interpreted as intent to flee." Wallace motioned with his shotgun, while quoting yet another statute granting use of deadly force.

Flee? Adam eyed the flooded fields surrounding them. With no place to hide, no cover, it was a giant kill zone. A suicide run. Hell, there was scarcely enough ground on the raised access road for the men to stand beside the bus.

Tuning out the guard's sermon, Adam put his hands just above shoulder height and eased his head back. It felt good to be off the bus. Off prison grounds.

Squinting against the searing sun, he drew a deep breath. Free air. He'd missed it. God, he missed a lot. He'd only been incarcerated three months—nothing, compared to some others—but it still had felt like a life sentence.

He thought of what he'd like to do to the man responsible for putting him behind bars. The double-dealing bastard had a lot to answer for.

"Y'all turn around and pay attention!" Wallace pointed to a line of trees about a half-mile to the west. "Tarheel Creek runs behind those woods. There are ten ditches that empty into it. Every one of 'em is blocked with trash from the storm so they can't drain. And that's keeping the interstate flooded. Department of Transportation wants 'em cleared fast. Which means no slacking. You got that, McEdwin?"

Adam slanted his eyes toward Lyle. The younger man had been about to say something—probably a smart-ass retort—but stopped. Maybe there was hope for the kid after all.

"Then grab a wheelbarrow," Wallace shouted after each man had donned an orange safety vest emblazoned front and back with the word INMATE. "Daylight's a-wasting."

An hour later, Adam waded knee-deep in water swirling with the run-off from a nearby hog farm. He squashed a hungry insect buzzing near his neck.

Two more flew in to take its place. The putrid flood-water provided perfect breeding conditions for mosquitoes and biting flies. As annoying as they were, the insects were the least of his worries.

Now that they were actually getting on with the task, a new qualm surfaced with each step. The first two landmarks Adam had been instructed to watch for hadn't been there. The fact that they'd taken a slightly different route was probably to blame. At least that's what he hoped.

They cut across a pasture, heading south. The land rolled and dipped, much of it underwater, but finally he spotted a stretch of split-rail fence. A hundred yards beyond it sat a red barn. *Bright red, you can't miss it.* He hoisted the shovels he carried higher on his shoulder. For the first time in months he felt a spark of optimism.

Which died when they arrived at the first ditch.

"Well I'll be a—" The driver held up a hand, indicating they should halt. "Hey Irv! Look at that!"

On the opposite bank, the runoff had carved a steep ravine in the hill. A muddy chute formed, allowing garbage from an illegal dumpsite to slip down and obstruct the drainage ditch.

This was no small blockage; there was everything from rusted washing machines to yellow bats of insulation. But the *coup de grace*: a mountain of black rubber tires. While the landslide looked recent, a virtual lake of floodwater already gurgled behind the well-packed dam, growing larger by the minute.

Adam located the prearranged landmarks once again. The fence. The barn. Where the hell was the other?

A sickening feeling of *déjà vu* settled in his stomach. This had happened twice before. A dry run, he'd been told. But he'd been promised this time was it. God help him, someone would pay if it wasn't.

Scanning the area one more time, Adam finally spotted his last marker. It was buried under some debris, barely visible. That it hadn't been lost in the landslide was a miracle. He released a pent-up breath, relieved he wasn't facing failure this soon.

"Hold up while he checks this mess." Wallace pointed to the driver.

"Me?" The driver glanced up at the hill. "I don't need to check it out. Any idiot can see there's a ton of garbage still perched up there. If I sneeze wrong it will fall."

"Then don't sneeze. *Idiot*." Wallace didn't like having his authority questioned. "And hurry back."

Adam clenched his jaw as the driver kicked at a large blue coffee can before disappearing from sight. Seconds stretched without end as they stood, broiling beneath the unrelenting sun. Potter mumbled threats under his breath, low enough so that Wallace couldn't hear, yet loud enough Adam wanted to deck him.

The driver returned, dour faced. "It's worse than I thought. There's twice as much crap piled up behind this."

Wallace shrugged. "So they have to work twice as hard. Big deal."

"You don't understand. This is too big for four men and shovels. It'll take dynamite. Maybe a crane. We need to forget this ditch and move on."

"Dynamite? It don't look that bad to me," Wallace said. "Now you sound like them. Always wanting to skip the shitty jobs."

"That's bull—" The driver launched into defense mode, arguing his point.

As much as he disliked the senior guard, Adam

silently sided with Wallace on this one. Skipping this ditch was out of the question.

"Five minute break," Wallace finally shouted. "You can sit down, just don't get too comfy."

As Wallace turned his back to talk into his radio, the driver shifted away, more intent on eavesdropping on Wallace's conversation than watching the inmates.

Lyle lowered himself to the ground beside Adam and picked at his fingernails. "What's going on?"

"Not sure. A lot depends on him." He nodded toward Wallace, mentally measuring distances and weighing alternatives. One thing was absolutely certain: Adam was not going to return to prison.

"Follow my lead if we're ordered to move to the next site," he said.

"What if I—"

"*My* lead." Adam noticed Potter watching them. He met the inmate's gaze, held it until the other man looked away. "And let me handle Potter."

"I can take him." Lyle flexed his arm.

"Sure you can. The point is: Don't. Brawling with him could blow everything."

Wallace's radio crackled as the voice on the other end instructed him to stand by while they checked with the D.O.T.

"Stand by? Right." The driver spat and shifted his weight from one foot to the other. "Sounds like we'll be here a while."

Wallace mopped his brow with a bandanna, then lit a cigarette. He frowned at the prisoners. "Well, what are you waiting for? The friggin' trash fairy? Start bagging that crap on the bank. Just don't touch anything near the water."

"Be ready." Adam climbed to his feet, thankful their

original plan was still operable. Lyle was not the type
he'd want to ad-lib with.

Grabbing a garbage bag, Adam moved across the sod-
den ground and claimed an area by stopping to pick up
an empty soda bottle. Lyle moved off to the right leaving behind Potter and the other inmate who were just
pushing up from the ground.

"See there?" Wallace pointed to Adam. "That's the
kind of attitude I expect. Show 'em how to do it, Hollywood." Grinning, the guard walked off to respond to
a radio call.

Pretending to pick up a piece of garbage, Potter
bumped into Adam as soon as the guard's back was
turned. "You trying to make the rest of us look bad,
Hollywood?"

Adam drew up his full height. At six-four, two-thirty,
he towered over most men. So did his reputation. Inside
the prison walls, he'd carved out his own niche, made his
own rules. Most people gave him a wide berth. But he
still had enemies. Everybody did. And Potter was everyone's enemy; a trouble-making prick who never thought
beyond the moment.

Adam wanted to end this before it started. "You
don't want to go there. Not today. I'll pound you into
sand."

Potter glanced sideways, nervous, noticed the other
inmates watching. Straightening, he tried to save face.
"I don't care how many people they say you killed, you
don't scare me."

"Then maybe I need to try harder."

Potter backed down. "We'll finish this later."

Later meant back at prison, where the ultimate jury
of peers presided. There was an unwritten rule that
inmates were supposed to look out for each other. No
matter what. The old Us against Them. Except the

rules shifted with the wind, often pitting inmate against inmate. Ultimately it was about power. Some had it, some didn't. Most abused it.

I won't miss that either.

Adam bent to pick up the trash in front of him: a soggy newspaper half covering a blue, three-pound coffee can. He grabbed the can, its top covered by a snap-on plastic lid. It was heavy, full, but not with coffee.

He lowered the can into his bag, adrenaline kicking up as he checked the contents. There was no turning back now. Apprehension sank fangs into his spine as he thought of what was at stake, of what could go wrong. And how easily the line between right and wrong blurred.

He glanced at Lyle, nodding once. This was it. If the kid blew this, he'd strangle him.

Lyle moved, then stumbled and fell. Rolling onto his back, he grasped his ankle, yelping in pain.

"On your feet, you little wimp!" Wallace ordered.

"I . . . I can't. I think I broke it." Lyle grimaced. "In that goddamned gopher hole."

Wallace motioned to the driver. "Check McEdwin. The rest of you men: Down."

Careful to keep a safe distance away, the driver eased closer and nodded toward Lyle's ankle. "Let me see."

Biting his lip, Lyle reached for the hem of his pants. But instead of raising it, he twisted and sprang forward, clearing the distance to take the unsuspecting driver out at the knees.

The driver's shotgun dropped. The two men rolled around in the muddy clay as each man struggled to retrieve it.

Wallace's response was immediate, as if he'd ex-

pected it. Almost gleefully, the senior guard raised his
shotgun, trained it on Lyle and the driver as they wres-
tled. His finger moved to the trigger. "Prisoner, freeze!
Or I'll shoot!"

Behind his back, Adam yanked out the Beretta nine-
millimeter that had been planted in the coffee can. He
pointed it at Wallace. "Drop it."

The look on Wallace's face shifted from Kodak-mo-
ment to Stephen-King-nightmare. He swayed slightly,
uncertain whether to keep his weapon trained on Lyle,
or to come about and face Adam.

The guard clearly had difficulty comprehending two
facts: first, that Adam had a weapon, and, second, that
Lyle—of all people—was his accomplice.

At that moment, Lyle leaped to his feet, leaving the
driver sprawled on the ground, face down and unmoving. Triumphant, he scooped up the shotgun, jacking a
round into the chamber before swinging it toward Wallace.

Wallace opened and closed his mouth, then shouted
the driver's name. "Get up, damn you. I need help!"

The driver didn't respond.

"Lay your weapon on the ground and step back,"
Adam ordered.

"Easy, there." Wallace's voice remained surprisingly
calm as he slowly lowered his weapon and moved
away. "You don't want to do this, Duval. He's made
you an accessory to murder. They'll fry you."

"Murder? Bite me." Lyle moved in and kicked Wallace's shotgun out of reach. "He ain't dead. Just out
cold thanks to my special sleeper hold."

Unable to hide his irritation, Adam glared at Lyle
before nodding toward the driver. "You forgot to secure him." Sleeper hold or not, the driver could regain
consciousness at any time. "And hurry."

Red-faced, Lyle stepped back and quickly cuffed the driver's hands using the handcuffs from the man's own belt.

"You won't make it far. Not with that dipshit for a partner." Wallace eyed his voice-activated radio, smug. "Besides, they've heard every word. Probably got back up coming already. You're both gonna regret this. I guar-an-fucking-tee it."

"Afraid not." Adam held up a wafer-thin transmitter that had been taped to the Beretta's grip. "Radio's jammed. They're only hearing static. By the time they send someone to check, we'll be long gone."

"Yeah. So hit the ground and kiss dirt," Lyle added.

Wallace's self-righteous smirk melted as it dawned on him that no help was coming, no rescue was imminent. The balance of power had shifted, leaving him trapped in a guard's worst nightmare. He was probably recalling every wrong act he'd committed against a prisoner.

And while he wasn't as barbaric as some, Adam knew first hand how the man misused authority.

Once the guard was flat on his stomach, Lyle leaned close and knocked Wallace's hat off before securing his hands. Then he drew back and kicked the guard hard, in the ribs.

"How does it feel to know nothing can stop me from blowing you away?" Lyle dropped to one knee and shoved the end of the barrel into the guard's right ear as he ran his hand along the shotgun's stock. "Bet you never figured I'd be the one to off you."

"Leave him," Adam ordered.

When Lyle made no move to comply, Adam shifted closer. So far no one had been injured. He damn sure wanted to keep it that way.

"I said—"

"I heard you." Lyle withdrew the shotgun, then bent down and snatched the guard's cigarettes from his back pocket. "Guess I'll catch you next time. And give Huggins this message for me: Tell him to watch his back."

Ned Huggins was another guard, known for being exceptionally cruel, especially to the prisoners he considered weak. It was no secret that Lyle had been Ned's favorite target.

Adam turned to the other two inmates who were on their feet now. "It's every man for himself. You don't have much of a head start so I'd think twice before wasting time with them." He nodded toward the guards.

Potter moved forward. "Fuck that. I'm going with you."

"No, you're not." Adam raised the nine-millimeter. "And I'll shoot anyone who tries to follow us."

Potter stepped sideways. "I'm taking his gun, then."

Adam moved closer to Wallace's shotgun, blocking Potter's access. "You heard me. It's every man for himself."

Snarling, Potter raised his fist, shook it. "We'll meet again, Duval. And remember: payback's a bitch." Spitting, he turned away and took off running with the other inmate.

"Shoot him," Lyle urged. "Show him who's boss."

Adam stooped to pick up Wallace's shotgun. "I already did. Let's go."

Motioning for Lyle to lead, Adam threw one last look at the guards, then took his first step toward the woods.

Toward freedom, justice . . . and retribution.

* * *

Adam didn't stop running until they'd reached the car—a stolen Ford Taurus—hidden in a dense copse of hickory trees a mile away.

Letting the shotgun slide to the ground, Lyle collapsed against the car's hood, panting. "Did you see the look on Wallace's face? He thought he was seconds away from getting his head blown off. By me! What a fucking rush!"

"Rush? You think killing people is a joke?" Adam yanked the younger man to his feet, and spun him around. He wanted to throttle Lyle, shake some sense into him. Except there wasn't time for that much shaking. "We agreed up front—no shooting unless absolutely necessary."

"Hey, back off! I wasn't really going to shoot him. Just fire a warning shot next to his head. Make him piss in his pants. He did it to me plenty of times."

"We weren't that far from the main road. Someone could have heard." Adam released him. "I ought to leave your ass right here, right now. I didn't want company to begin with and I don't need someone who can't stay focused on the big picture."

Lyle straightened his shirt. "I thought the big picture included settling old scores. Hell, I've heard you talk about it plenty of times."

"That comes later. The first priority is to get away. Which means sticking with the plan until we're safe."

"Well, this couldn't wait," Lyle defended. "Wallace has been on my case since I got there. Circling like a buzzard, hoping to collect the reward on my kin. I hope he's shaking in his boots wondering what my pa will do to get even."

"Fine. Once we part ways, you and your family can do whatever you want." Disgusted, Adam stepped away.

"Wait." Lyle's brow wrinkled. "Ah, hell. I'm sorry. You're right. And I swear, after we hook up with my family, you'll forget all this talk about parting ways."

"I doubt that." Adam's snort was authentic. "You place too much stock in your family, kid. Family will screw you just as easily as a stranger off the street."

"Mine won't. Mark my words. Besides, you need me—my connections. Remember?"

Adam stared at the ground, pretended he was weighing options he didn't have. Lyle's connections were indeed vital.

The two men had shared a cell from the first day Adam landed in prison. Initially wary, they forged an uneasy alliance when Lyle hid contraband for Adam during a search.

Adam repaid the favor by showing the younger man several effective self-defense moves, which improved Lyle's fate with the other prisoners if not with the guards. This last act also elevated Adam's status to hero.

When Lyle guessed Adam planned an escape, he begged, pleaded, to be included. Adam flat out refused. Until Lyle promised that his family would hide them once they were on the outside.

His offer had been impossible to refuse. Willy McEdwin, Lyle's father—and his three older brothers, Nevin, Tristin, and Burt—held the top four spots on the FBI's most-wanted list. Dubbed the Four Horsemen in the right-wing press, they were responsible for the deaths of more law enforcement officials than anyone in history—a number they had sworn to double.

If anyone could hide two fugitives, it was Willy McEdwin and sons. Famous for striking and disappearing without a trace—and despite rumors of family rifts—they had eluded capture for over four years. And while Lyle had had no contact with his family in the nine months he'd been incarcerated, Adam doubted Willy would leave his youngest out in the cold once he'd escaped.

However . . . until they connected with the McEdwin clan, Adam wanted to make damn sure Lyle played by the rules. *His rules.* "We also agreed: I'm in charge until we part ways."

"Whatever. You da man."

Lyle lit a cigarette, then blew smoke rings and tried to poke a finger through one, reminding Adam that he was barely twenty years old. Still a kid—albeit a stupid one.

At thirty-four, Adam felt ancient.

"Now can we celebrate?" Lyle asked.

"Not yet. If the guard doesn't check in soon, they'll dispatch someone to investigate. We need to vanish. And I cashed in all my chips making arrangements for *two.*" He looked pointedly at Lyle. "Which means the ball's in your court. I held up my end, got us out, got us wheels. But we need a destination. As soon as we're on the road, you need to contact your family."

Unloading the shotguns, Adam pocketed the shells and tossed both twelve-gauges into the brush.

"Are you crazy?" Lyle started after them.

"We don't need them. And I damn sure don't want any souvenirs from that hell hole."

Adam moved to the back of the car and opened the trunk. Inside were civilian clothes, non-perishable food, a few hundred in cash, a handheld police scanner, a cell phone with charger, and a second handgun, this one a Smith & Wesson.

Eyes wide, Lyle made a grab for the gun. "You're right, we don't need their stinking shotguns."

"Cut the John Wayne act, kid. I mean it. We're stowing both weapons under the seat." Where Adam could keep track of them. "Let's change up and go. I want to put some miles on this car—fast."

"You won't regret this," Lyle said. "I promise, by nightfall, we'll be somewhere safe and sound."

"Yep, like the county jail."

Both men jumped and turned at the new voice.

About thirty feet away, Adam spotted a man crouched beneath a tree, an old double-barrel propped at shoulder level.

The man's overalls and worn John Deere cap indicated he was a farmer, probably the owner of the submerged fields surrounding them. And judging by the comfortable way he held the shotgun, he wasn't fond of trespassers.

Adam raised his hands. "Easy, Mister. We don't mean you any harm."

"You can tell that to the sheriff when he gets here," the farmer said. "Now tell your friend to get his hands where I can see 'em."

Chapter Two

The Bay Meadow Urgent Care Clinic in Durham, North Carolina, was one of the few smaller medical facilities open and operating. The widespread flooding had paralyzed the eastern half of the state, shutting down schools, shops, and most businesses.

As utility companies scrambled to get water systems and power plants back on line, the Red Cross shelters filled as fast as they opened. After three days, most basic resources like food, drinking water, and batteries were scarce as dodo birds.

Government officials urged everyone to stay home and off the roads, especially because more rain—and inevitably more flooding—were forecast.

Dr. Renata Curtis, who had just finished her third year of residency, was in charge of the facility's Disaster Response Program. She tackled the job enthusiastically, grateful to be in a position to help others—versus needing help herself.

While the clinic was running with only a skeleton crew, they were prepared to field excess traffic from the emergency room, which at times like this could expand tenfold because people couldn't get in to see their regular doctors for minor medical problems.

They were also prepared to handle requests for provisional refills of common prescriptions—insulin, blood pressure medication, inhalers, and so on—that people couldn't get because local pharmacies were closed. Likewise, over-the-counter drugs—aspirin, decongestants, anti-diarrhea aids—were in high demand, too.

Renata's morning had started off hectic with the delivery of a baby in the backseat of a car in the clinic's parking lot. Afterwards, the mother and her new daughter were transported by ambulance to the hospital along with the father, who suffered a concussion after fainting and striking his head on the car door.

"First baby?" the paramedic had asked.

"Last baby," the mother responded.

In contrast, the late afternoon had been surprisingly quiet. Except, of course, for the regulars, the ones they saw weekly, such as the patient Renata dictated notes on: Caucasian male, age unknown. She had guessed by his prepubescent build that he was thirteen. Fourteen, tops.

He'd had a broken wrist, multiple contusions, two bruised eyes and a long, shallow laceration across his chest that was consistent with a knife slash. The boy claimed he fell off his bicycle.

Renata suspected his injuries had been received in a gang-related dispute. She had recognized the scar on his right wrist. A small circle of cigarette burns. Skin graffiti—body tags—marked local gang members. Colors were passé; tattoos expensive.

The Bay Meadow Urgent Care Clinic was located near one of Durham's roughest neighborhoods. Consequently, they saw an above average number of *regulars* with injuries linked to unlawful activities.

In conformity with the clinic's policy on crime victims and unaccompanied minors, Renata had called the police, but the young man slipped out before they arrived, a scenario she saw all too often.

"Soon," she muttered, "that's going to change."

Thanks to a study Renata had worked on over the past two years, the clinic had been awarded a landmark grant targeting health care issues for preteen gang members and their families. Treatment and follow-up would be coupled with preventive education aimed at disrupting the patterns of physical violence.

And she'd just been offered a key position in establishing the pilot program. To see her long hours—most of them volunteered—bear fruit was gratifying. She had accepted on the spot.

A voice from the hallway broke into her thoughts. "Mrs. Bolton, you need to give me the pepper spray."

Renata frowned. Mrs. Bolton was another of the clinic's regulars. But what on earth was she doing with pepper spray?

Besides being old enough to be Moses' great grandma, Mrs. Bolton was diabetic and half blind. She lived a block away and came into the clinic several times a week after misreading her blood sugar or forgetting to take her insulin. Or when she got lonely.

Renata stepped into the hall and found Mrs. Bolton arguing with their receptionist, Janet.

"It's mace, not pepper spray," Mrs. Bolton was saying. "And my nephew said I should bring the can up like so—"

Renata moved forward before the older woman's finger found the spray button. Gently but quickly, she took the canister.

"Why don't we let Janet hold this while I examine you?"

Mrs. Bolton looked dubious. "I'd feel safer if I could keep it in my pocket. Bad enough we got flooding, but now with those escaped prisoners on the loose . . ."

Renata looked questioningly at Janet. "What escaped prisoners?"

"Is that what this is about?" Janet grinned and patted the old woman's hand. *"Pfft.* I just heard a blip on the news. They captured them. You don't have a thing to worry about, Mrs. Bolton."

Dusk had fallen on the City of Medicine, Durham, North Carolina. Home to several famous hospitals, nationally recognized medical teaching facilities, pharmaceutical conglomerates, and Research Triangle Park, the largest university-related research park in the world.

Or at least that was what the last radio commercial had claimed. But Adam wasn't in town to play tourist. He snapped the radio off.

He and Lyle had managed to outmaneuver the farmer after luring him closer by pretending to surrender. Adam had blindsided him before he could fire a shot.

In the end, the farmer had been more furious at Adam for throwing his shotgun in a nearby creek than for tying him up. That he could have been injured—or killed—didn't seem to faze the old fart.

Adam and Lyle had sped off, driving due north. If the farmer had indeed called the sheriff's department, they wouldn't have much of a head start.

They had to backtrack twice. Driving was treacherous, as many secondary roads remained under water, forcing them onto the main routes, where cops were concentrated. And if that wasn't bad enough they had problems getting a clear cell phone signal. They got through briefly once, but the signal dropped before Lyle's brother, Nevin, gave them instructions.

Uncertain of which direction they were to head to meet Lyle's family, and wary of traveling in broad daylight, Adam pulled into a state campground. Though most of the park was high and dry, it was closed because of the flooding.

After hiding the car in the woods, he broke into one of the bathhouses. They showered and changed clothes, which made Adam feel almost human.

When Lyle finally reached Nevin, he was given directions to a commercial storage lot in Durham. They had headed south and were now less than fifty miles from where they'd escaped, which the cops probably wouldn't expect.

A light rain started as Adam pulled up to the afterhours gate at the storage lot. He and Lyle had watched the place for nearly an hour, keeping an eye open for anything or anyone out of place.

They couldn't wait any longer. The radio had just broadcast a news alert of their escape that included a report of the nondescript Taurus. No license plate number was given. With what seemed like every third car on the road being a Taurus, it wasn't much for law enforcement to go on, but it was more than Adam was comfortable with.

It was also safe to assume their mug shots had been flashed on the evening news. Not that many people would be watching. Over half the area remained without electricity.

A cheap neon CLOSED sign flickered in the window of the lot's office, proof that the place had power. Adam punched in the four-digit security code Lyle rattled off. The electric gate took forever to open, shuddering and stalling twice before slowly heaving sideways an inch at a time.

The storage lot had five long buildings crowded on

it with each building holding thirty or so units. Adam passed the first building. They were looking for 18C.

"God, we're almost home free," Lyle said. "I don't know what I want more. A piece of ass or a decent meal. I know I want a beer with either one. What about you?"

Adam snorted at the irony. Lyle wasn't even old enough to buy alcohol. "I'll settle for a safe place to sleep."

"Then what? You haven't said what you're doing beyond this."

"That's right."

"I know you wanted out of prison before they got something else on you. Something big," Lyle continued. "I couldn't figure it out until I saw that high-tech radio jammer. That had to be military. Stolen?"

"Borrowed." Adam slowed the car. "What's your point, kid?"

Lyle tried to act nonchalant and failed. "A guy with that kind of access could make a lot of money—provided he hooked up with the right buyer."

"Who says I'm not?"

"Nobody. But you did say your old partner is hesitant."

"For now. He knows the cops will put two and two together and come looking for him when they investigate our escape."

"See? That's exactly what I mean. Being a fugitive can put a crimp in things; might scare off your customers, too."

"Temporarily, maybe. Long term it won't matter."

"But what about short term, man? I know several buyers who'd pay top dollar for hardware like that jammer."

"You? Or your daddy?" Adam didn't hide his skepticism. "If half of what you told me about your family is true, I doubt they need another supplier."

"More than half of it's true," Lyle defended. "And for the record, I was asking for myself. I've been thinking about striking out on my own."

Adam glanced sideways. "Back up a minute. Which half of what you've told me isn't true?"

"Not much."

"Define much."

"Well, fuck-a-duck. I was going to tell you later." Lyle shifted in his seat. "My old man didn't want me breaking out. Can you believe that? He's been in prison before. He knows what it's like."

Lyle's admission shocked Adam. Family was religion to the McEdwins. In fact, the theme of Lyle's life was *blood is thicker*. His incessant chatter about family, loyalty, and ties binding father to son, brother to brother, drove Adam nuts. That and all his talk about his brothers' blood oath to not be captured alive.

"Are you saying your father wanted you to stay in the pen?"

"Not exactly. He just wanted me to wait before making a move. But I knew you were my only chance to get out. Those guards would have killed me."

Several things struck Adam. Lyle *had* been in contact with his father somehow. At least enough to communicate his intent to escape. Which meant the McEdwins had a better, more secret system of communication than he'd been led to believe.

It also meant Lyle was expert at playing dumb when it came to his family. Adam hadn't suspected a thing. So what else was the kid hiding?

"Did he say why he wanted you to wait?"

"He's, uh, busy," Lyle hedged.

Too busy for his son? Adam wondered. Or too busy

planning his next big event? Maybe family—or just
Lyle—wasn't as important as Willy's other priorities.
Or maybe there was more truth to the rumors of dis-
sension in the McEdwin family than Lyle would admit.

"Truth is, I've only talked with Nevin," Lyle continued. "But he's probably contacted Pa by now."

"Probably? I thought your family was this close?"
Adam held up crossed fingers.

"They are, most days. And we'll be fine with Nevin.
He's got as many connections as my Pa does. Maybe
more."

But it wasn't the McEdwins' *connections* Adam was
interested in. Lyle had sworn his father would help
them, hide them, once they escaped. Now it seemed
his brother alone was aiding them. How safe would
they be?

Lyle sat forward. "Building C is right there."

Adam turned and stopped in front of unit 18. He
killed the headlights, but left the engine running.

A single dim bulb burned in a rusted fixture, casting
uneven shadows. "Unscrew that light."

Lyle climbed out and loosened the bulb before re-
trieving a key hidden in the rainspout.

"This will only take a sec." Lyle opened the unit's
overhead door then flicked the interior light on and off.

In the flash of light, Adam saw a black Toyota sedan.
Stuck on the windshield was a note. Lyle read it, then
passed it to Adam.

> HEAD NORTH ON I-85. WHEN YOU
> REACH RICHMOND CALL 555-0856.

He tossed the paper back. "What kind of dim-witted
game is this? Richmond's a couple hundred miles
away. We could have been there hours ago. And the

longer we're on the road the greater the chances of getting stopped."

"Hey, Nevin knows what he's doing. He's a fugitive, too, remember? Besides, once we dump this Taurus, they won't have a clue what we're driving."

"I still don't like it." Having no other choice, Adam put the car in gear. The vehicle was a definite liability now that the police were searching for it. "Get the Toyota out of there, so I can stash this one."

After swapping cars, Lyle got out of the Toyota to secure the storage unit's door. He paused to light a cigarette, hanging back to take a couple of deep drags.

Adam took advantage of the delay and climbed in the driver's side. If they got into a high-speed chase, he wanted to be the one behind the wheel. Especially with the rain steadily increasing.

He put the police scanner on the dashboard. Thus far it had yielded little useful information on their escape as most law enforcement agencies continued to be inundated with flood-related problems.

Headlights flashed behind them as another car pulled around the building and slowed.

Adam lowered the window, his eyes glued to the rearview mirror. "Get in. Now!"

Instead of moving away, Lyle turned and studied the car creeping toward them. "Wait. Maybe it's my brother."

"If it's not, you just gave someone a good look at your face. Come on!"

"Shit!" Lyle dropped his cigarette and turned back to the overhead door, fumbling with the keys.

"Leave the damn door!"

By now the car had pulled in close and stopped. Once the headlights shut off, Adam was able to make out its profile. It wasn't a patrol car but that didn't rule out an unmarked unit or even an outside security company making a check, though this place didn't look like the kind to spring for that type of service.

The car's interior light came on as a man climbed out. "Hey!" he called. "What do you think you're doing there?"

Lyle turned. "What I'm doing is none of your business."

"Oh, yeah?" the man snapped. "You're parked right in front of my unit and I've been broken into twice."

"Big fucking deal. Call someone who cares."

The man swung a flashlight forward, spotlighting Lyle. Immediately, the man straightened and drew a pistol. "Hold it right there. Your mug shot has been all over the news, buddy."

"I ain't your buddy," Lyle sneered, spreading his hands only slightly above waist level.

Inside the car, the hairs on Adam's arm lifted. The man brandished the gun and the flashlight like a cop.

Damn Lyle for not getting in the car sooner! Adam reached for one of the handguns tucked beneath the seat as he quickly debated the best way to defuse the situation without anyone getting hurt.

"I bet that's your cellmate inside the car." The man bent slightly, trying to see Adam through the window as he directed his flashlight toward the Toyota. "You. Climb out nice and slow. And don't do anything stupid."

The man stepped closer to the car. As he did, Lyle pulled a handgun and fired two shots.

Adam shifted the car in gear. Where in the hell had Lyle gotten another weapon? The answer was obvious: Nevin must have left one in the Toyota.

Dropping back to use his car door as a shield, the man returned fire. Lyle dashed around the Toyota pausing to squeeze off another shot. As he opened the passenger door the side mirror shattered in a hail of bullets.

Swearing, Lyle fell into the front seat. "Go, god-damn it!"

Adam punched the gas. The car fishtailed, tires squealing. "Stay down!"

At the end of the row he headed toward the first building. He turned right but immediately stopped. Dead-end. Wheeling around, he tried another route, only to find it blocked as well. That meant there was only one way to get back to the gate: the same way they'd come in.

In the distance, sirens wailed. Had someone, per-haps even the other man, called the police? If the fellow was indeed a cop it was likely he had a radio in his car.

Lyle, who had for once listened to Adam and stayed down, now moved to sit up. "Are we clear yet?"

"No." Adam retraced their original route, surprised to find the way wide open.

But just as they shot past the unit, the man stepped out of the shadows and opened fire again.

"Look out!" Adam had barely shouted a warning be-fore the windshield shattered. He swerved, struggling to see through the damaged glass.

Sparks flew as they sideswiped the building. Metal screeched against concrete as Adam fought to regain control of the car.

"You okay?" Lyle shouted.

"Fine." Adam eyed the closed gate, knew it would take too long to enter the code and wait for it to open. "Hang on. I'm going through it."

Gunning the engine, he shot forward, crashing into the chain link. While the car had quick acceleration for short sprints, it lacked bulk. The rusted gate bowed, but held. The police sirens grew louder, leaving no doubt where the cruiser was headed.

Slamming the Toyota into reverse, Adam backed up then sped forward once again, tires smoking. He didn't let up.

This time, the gate gave way just as the rear window exploded from another bullet. Adam ducked, then glanced back. The man chased them on foot.

"Crazy bastard! I'll fix him." Grunting, Lyle leaned halfway out the window and fired three more rounds.

Driving with one hand, Adam grabbed Lyle's shirt and tried to stop him. "Now you're giving him a perfect target."

Lyle slumped against the seat, breathing heavy. "Too late. But at least I got him."

Automatically Adam hit the brakes. "You shot him?"

"Winged him, I think . . . The jackass didn't even go down!"

They were on the main road. Already flashing blue lights were speeding up the highway behind them.

"Go!" Lyle shrieked.

Cursing, Adam floored it, but the patrol car closed in. It was over. They were circling the drain. A choking rage burned in his throat.

At the last second, the patrol car turned sharply and disappeared into the storage lot. Adam looked twice in disbelief then jammed the gas pedal to the floor. The cop turning off only bought them a few minutes, because backup units would undoubtedly be en route.

At the first intersection, he turned into a residential neighborhood. The car hit a water-filled pothole so deep it scraped the undercarriage.

Slowing, Adam vented his temper. "What were you

doing back there? Why the hell didn't you just get in the car like I told you?"

"I was trying to . . . help."

"Help?" Without taking his eyes off the road, Adam held out his right hand. "You can start by handing me that gun. Or I pull over and throw you out."

When Lyle hesitated, Adam hit the brakes. "Have it your way."

"Wait, man. Here." Lyle passed the gun.

The grip was wet, sticky, and nearly slid from Adam's hand.

"What the—?" With an escalating sense of disaster, he glanced at the other man. "Is that what I think it is?"

"Yeah." Lyle let out a low moan. "That son of a bitch shot me!"

It was late when Renata finished her last patient. Janet, a nursing student who worked part-time at the clinic, was still at the reception desk talking with Beth Gianno, a first-year resident.

"Looks like we may close on time tonight after all," Janet said. "It's quarter till ten and the lobby is empty. And I expected to be here half the night with standing-room-only crowds."

Renata nodded. "Me, too. But when I spoke to the hospital earlier, they said people weren't expecting us to be open. They posted a notice in the emergency room, but most folks don't want to venture back out once they get there."

"Can't blame them." Janet shrugged. "Road conditions aren't great and now it's raining again. Tomorrow will be a disaster."

"You can say that again," Beth said. "Mercury went retrograde today. Everything that can go wrong will—

for the next two weeks. Mark my words. Tonight's rain is only the beginning."

"Is a retrograde like a full moon when all the freaks and weirdos climb out from under their rocks?" Janet yawned. "It's usually the only time I get asked out anymore."

Beth rolled her eyes. "Retrogrades are astrological occurrences, reported to be fairly accurate. You should read the statistics on surgical recovery times during retrogrades. A group of French doctors did a study."

"French doctors? *Oo, la, la.*" Janet perked up and sat forward. "You know, I read a study, too. It claimed Frenchmen make the greatest lovers because they're strong-willed, yet charming."

"Funny, I heard the same thing about Italians," Renata said. "And Swedes."

Beth peered over the rim of her glasses. *"Ahem.* We were discussing retrogrades. As in planets, astrology."

"Then I plead ignorance. I can't make sense of the newspaper horoscopes." Renata held up her hands palms out. "I was looking for Richard. Has he left already?" Richard was the clinic's senior staff member and her mentor.

"He's writing 'scrips for his last patient," Janet said. "Then we're all going to my place for frozen pizza since I have electricity. Want to come?"

"Can't. Too much paperwork." Renata pointed to her overflowing IN box. Seemed like a never-ending pile. "It'll take me half the night just to sort it."

"Oops! Almost forgot these." Janet held up four pink phone message slips. As always, when the clinic was shorthanded, calls went to the answering machine. "I just retrieved them off voice mail."

Renata frowned at the first message. CALL DAVID MED-

DARD AT WORK. The next read DAVID MEDDARD AT HOME. The third was his cell phone.

"Let me guess. Number four is his pager," she mumbled, dropping them in the trash. Maybe there was something to this retrograde stuff after all.

"Actually, one's from your mom," Janet hissed in a stage whisper.

"Great." Renata rifled through the trash and retrieved one of the slips. CALL YOUR MOTHER—NO MATTER HOW LATE.

Renata checked the beeper clipped to her waistband. The display blinked with only the date and time. No calls. That meant it wasn't urgent—her mother had her pager number for emergencies.

But the fact that her mother had called her at work instead of at home was telling. As telling as David leaving three messages.

Janet escorted Richard's patient to the door and locked it behind him. "There went the last one. Sure we can't talk you into joining us?" She looked at Renata and batted her eyes. "I want to hear more about your experiences with Italians and Swedes. Like who's hung better? And who has better staying power?"

Renata opened her mouth to reply then closed it. Could she honestly remember? Back in her younger days—she'd be thirty in three months—she used to know. She used to have an active sex life. But then she entered med school. And married. Divorced.

Crap—how long *had* it been?

Richard, who had joined them, frowned at Renata. "Penny for your thoughts?"

Not on your life. Renata cleared her throat. "I was just telling Janet I can't make it tonight."

"Why not? You are entitled to a social life, you know.

In fact I wanted to tell you about a colleague who's in town."

"He isn't by chance Italian or Swedish is he?" Janet teased.

Richard looked from one woman to the next. "I'm afraid to ask why. Actually, he's the all American type who—"

Janet laughed. "Save your breath, Rich. I've been trying to tempt Renata with men for months. But apparently you can't have a social life and save the world too."

"I'm not trying to save the world. Just a few city blocks," Renata defended. "And I have one last report to finish for this grant. Then I'll get a social life."

"I want a sex life," Beth chimed in. "I've heard we're allowed to reclaim our libido after our second year of residency."

"Which is why I opted for nursing. I couldn't go that long," Janet said.

"Sounds like I just missed another stimulating discussion," Richard deadpanned.

"Nah. We'll pick it back up over pizza. Come on." Janet grabbed her backpack, fished out car keys. "By the way, the drug cabinet's ready for pickup."

"Wait up," Richard called to Beth and Janet. He turned back to Renata. "If you still want me to look over your report, leave it on my desk. I'll look at it first thing."

"Thanks. I owe you one."

Richard grinned and shrugged into his raincoat. "Good. Because my friend is in town for another two weeks."

"Ugh. I hate blind dates."

"Then let me assure you his vision is fine. Seriously, this guy may surprise you. He's a research fellow. Brilliant. Witty. And before you write him off as a nerd, call my wife. She swoons around him. In fact, Vicky's told him all about you. He's eager to meet you."

"Oh swell. Tell Vicky thanks."

"Then it's a date."

Renata made a face and was rewarded with deep laughter. She heard a series of beeps as Richard set the alarm before ducking out the back exit.

The sound of the door closing rang hollow in the deserted clinic.

God, she was tempted. To call it a night. To join her friends for food, laughter. Maybe even a glass of wine. Or three. It was bad enough she couldn't remember the last time she'd had an orgasm. But to not remember the last time she just plain had fun.

She glanced from her stack of work to the phone message in her hand, mind made up. *Screw work.* She could save the world tomorrow. Richard was right. She was entitled to a night off.

Right after she called her mother . . .

Adam used torn pieces of Lyle's shirt to fashion a makeshift compress. Lyle took a hit in the lower left groin, just as he had been climbing into the car.

At the time, Adam had been so intent on escape he hadn't noticed. And Lyle had been in shocked denial until the pain registered. The bullet had obviously severed a major vein. It took heavy pressure to stem the blood flow.

"You need a doctor, kid."

"I'd rather die than go back to prison." Lyle shook his head, swallowed a cry. "If you're gonna dump me, do it where I have half a chance. Not here."

Here was a dark alley near the hospital emergency

room where a police car had sped by moments ago. Did the police realize Lyle had taken a bullet and anticipated his showing up at a hospital?

Somewhere along the way, probably while switching cars a second time, they'd lost the police scanner and Lyle's handgun. As bad as Adam wanted to retrieve both, they didn't dare go look for them.

"Though you damn sure deserve it, I wasn't planning to dump you." It wasn't exactly the truth. While Adam shared the younger man's opinion of returning to prison—he couldn't stand by and let the kid die.

"I had hoped to find a doctor or nurse hanging around outside," he continued. "Someone I could coerce into helping."

"We ain't that lucky." Lyle grimaced at the cell phone he had clutched in one hand. "Damn it, if I can just get a hold of my brother. Nevin will know what to do."

"Provided you haven't bled to death by the time he calls back." Adam checked the wound. "It's stopped bleeding for the moment. But it's critical you don't move until I return."

"Where are you going?"

Standing, Adam tucked his gun beneath his shirt. "I'll see if I can slip in the ER, at least get some clean gauze and bandages."

"Something for pain, too."

Adam grunted. He'd been shot before, knew it hurt like hell. "We also need another car."

They had abandoned the shot-up Toyota, but the one they'd stolen was overheating. The owner had probably left the key in it on purpose, praying someone would take the piece of shit.

Careful not to trigger any alarms, he hurried along a dark row of parked cars, checking for unlocked doors as he went. He paused beside an old rusted Volkswagen, did a double take. He wasn't interested in the car as transportation; however, on the passenger's seat was a white lab coat.

He backed up. The rear window, a pop-out vent, had been left ajar. He forced it open and reached in to unlock the door.

Snatching the coat, he slipped it on. It was snug across the shoulders. If he moved the wrong way it would rip. He ran his hands through his hair, tucked the length beneath the collar before checking his reflection in the side mirror. In bad light, he could pass for a grungy med student.

An employee badge hung from the pocket. Turning it so the photo didn't show, he grabbed the foam coffee cup from the drink holder and strode toward the emergency room entrance, whistling. Acting as if he belonged.

The lobby was jammed. He paused inside the glass anteroom, pretending to sip coffee while feigning interest in the paper-covered bulletin board. Twisting his head slightly, he scanned the waiting room. Two uniformed police officers huddled near the reception desk, their backs to the door.

Adam stepped away and quickly searched the opposite side of the lobby, looking for an alternate way in. He saw none. Now what? Should he check for another entrance? Try another hospital? Surrender? Whatever his choice, he had to act quickly.

He turned to leave. A sheet of paper taped haphazardly to the door caught his attention.

BAY MEADOW URGENT CARE CLINIC
OPEN UNTIL 10 P.M.
NON-LIFE THREATENING CASES ONLY

A map detailed the clinic's location. Adam glanced at the clock in the lobby: 9:45.

He tore the note down and stuffed it in his pocket. Perhaps their luck was improving, after all.

Chapter Three

Renata's mother lived in Denver. With the two-hour time difference, it was only eight o'clock there.

Her mother answered on the first ring. "Thank God! I've been worried."

"What's wrong?" She pressed the phone closer. "Are you okay?"

"Yes, I'm fine. I was just surprised to get the answering machine at the clinic."

"We've been short-handed, Mama. The roads are still flooded from the big storm and most of our staff couldn't get in."

"Then what are you doing there?"

"A few roads are still navigable. And the clinic's one of the few locations that's accessible on this side of town."

"Oh." Her mother grew silent, then, "David asked if you were still working *there.*"

Renata released a puff of air. She should have guessed. "You talked to David?"

"He was having trouble reaching you. He sounded quite . . . concerned. Have you called him?"

"I have no desire to talk to the man. Except to tell him where to go and not to call you." Which of course would accomplish his mission of getting her to call.

"He said you always expect the worst from him."

"He rarely disappoints."

"I think he's changed this time."

David change? Renata took the phone from her ear and stared at it. Had her mother gone senile? Had she forgotten their disastrous marriage?

Renata had met David her first year of med school, had been flattered by his attention and awed by his status as a surgeon. She'd been willing to overlook a lot. Like the way he pressed her to pursue a career in surgery because the money and prestige were better. Or the remarks he made about her being gorgeous and smart, as if they were mutually exclusive. She had been in love. Or thought she had.

A week after their honeymoon, the late night hangups started. They'd been married two months when she caught him cheating; learned it hadn't been the first time. Nor had it been the last. In the four years since their divorce David had remarried numerous times. The man was a gifted orthopedic surgeon; he was equally gifted when it came to adultery.

"Let me guess." Renata made no attempt to disguise her sarcasm. "He and Lisa broke up."

"It's Shawna," her mother corrected. "He and Shawna broke up."

"So let him call Shawna. Or Karen. Or Jean. Or one of the others. God, you'd think even Nevada would have a per capita limit on divorces."

Her mother ignored the remark. "David says he's finally realized you're the only one who's ever been right for him. And there's an opening at his clinic you'd be perfect for."

So that's what this was about.

She sighed again, only louder. She'd heard through the grapevine about David's latest disaster. The woman, a staff practitioner, had threatened a sexual harassment lawsuit.

This wasn't the first complaint. Or the second. And to pacify his business partners, David needed to come up with a replacement physician. Fast. Did he figure Renata would be safe? Or fair game?

"I've already accepted a position that's perfect for me."

Her mother took a deep breath. "But—"

Renata cut her off. "No buts. Look, I've asked David not to call me. And I'll make sure he gets the message not to call you."

"He doesn't call that often."

"That often?" Exactly how frequently did they talk? She rubbed her forehead, determined to ward off a headache. "He shouldn't call ever."

"He thought I could help persuade you. Do you know how much closer Nevada is to Denver?"

The muscle above Renata's left eye ticked. Twice. "I need to go. We'll talk about it this weekend, okay?"

Her mother's voice raised. "You're off this weekend? You could fly home."

"I work Saturday but I'll call Sunday. I promise."

"You work too much. How will you ever meet someone?"

"Mama, please."

"Or give me grandchildren?"

Renata heard her stepfather intervene, warning her mother to mind her own business. Bless him.

It did little to deter her mother, though. When Renata finally hung up she was in an awful mood. *Blast David.* Now it would take half of Sunday to convince her mother to drop the subject.

It seemed all their conversations ended off-key. No matter what her accomplishments, her mother saw a half-empty glass. Renata lived too far away, pursued her career too aggressively, studied too hard, earned too little. Especially when compared to her older brother and sister.

Her prior desire to join her friends had waned, but she didn't want to go home and stew alone in her tiny apartment. She had a theory that anger dissipated more quickly in larger spaces. Better to stay and work.

She headed to the lobby where the television still aired twenty-four hour news. But instead of shutting it off, she switched channels—to MTV—and punched up the volume to test yet another theory: If music truly soothed the savage beast, then livid beasts needed even louder music.

From his hiding spot, Adam watched a group of employees dash into the light rain as they left the Bay Meadow clinic. There were three of them—more than he cared to confront.

He listened, catching a name. *Richard.* He waited, hoping the man would linger in the parking lot, but they took off in unison.

Adam circled back to the front. Only one car remained now, in a spot marked RESERVED FOR PHYSICIANS. Lights still burned inside and the blinds were open. A woman sat at the front desk. A receptionist?

He narrowed his eyes. The woman wore a white lab coat. A doctor? Or a nurse?

Headlights swept into the parking lot as a yellow van pulled up in front of the clinic. HOSPITAL SECURITY.

Cursing, Adam ducked around the side of the building and watched as a uniformed man climbed out.

The man rapped loudly on the door. When the

woman answered, he smiled and tugged the brim of his hat. "Evening, Dr. Curtis. Working late again?"

Adam couldn't hear the woman's response as she held the door open. The man had barely stepped in before backing out, this time hauling a metal cabinet on wheels. He loaded the cabinet in the van, then returned to collect her signature.

Their voices dropped, inaudible. Adam heard a brief guitar riff, laughter, then the man started toward the van. Halfway there he stopped and turned back.

"Hey Doc! Don't forget to close those blinds. No sense advertising you're here alone."

"Thanks, Clarence," she called.

"Yeah, thanks," Adam whispered as he watched the taillights disappear.

He didn't like what he was about to do, but he was out of viable options. There was a lot hanging in the balance. Lyle had been adamant about not going to a hospital. Short of physically forcing him—or surrendering and letting the cops force him—Adam could do little. He had to make some tough decisions.

And time was running out. Adam wasn't a doctor, but he knew Lyle had lost a lot of blood, knew he needed treatment.

Straightening the stolen lab coat, he hurried to the front entrance. Through the window, he watched the woman wrestle with a tangle of cords hanging from the blinds.

She was teeny, barely over five feet, with a sleek ponytail of hair that was nearly as dark as his own. He frowned, eyeing the stethoscope tucked in her pocket. She looked too young to be a doctor. Too . . . perky. She was also very pretty, though pretty didn't matter right now. All he wanted was her medical expertise.

Squaring his shoulders, he stepped up to the door and knocked. "Dr. Curtis."

Inside, Renata paused, cocked her head.

She heard the knock, heard someone call her name. She peeked out the blinds she'd just closed, but with the lights on inside, she couldn't see beyond the glass.

The knocking repeated, more urgent.

Automatically her hand went to the pager at her waist, sliding it forward. In her dash to close the blinds, she had forgotten to reset the alarm after Clarence left. But no matter. The pager had a red panic button that remotely triggered the alarm. While she had never had to use it, it did make her feel more secure when she stayed late.

Keeping the security chain in place, she unlocked the door and opened it an inch, before peering out the crack. The man standing on the step was a doctor, but not anyone she recognized.

She opened the door a little more, to get a better look at him. Immediately her eyes widened in appreciation. Whoever he was, the man was gorgeous. A bit disheveled, but gorgeous all the same.

"Dr. Curtis?" The man bowed. A polite, disarming gesture.

"Do I know you?"

He shook his head. "We've never met. I'm a friend of Richard's. He's mentioned you before."

Ohmigod. Was this the friend Richard had wanted her to meet?

"Hold on." She stepped back and quickly smoothed her clothes. Perhaps it was just as well she didn't have time to check her hair and makeup. Ignorance was bliss.

She released the security chain and opened the door

fully. The move earned her a dazzling smile as the man stepped closer, into the spill of light.

Renata's gaze traveled slowly over him. She melted, her bad mood evaporating. She'd been wrong. He was not gorgeous. He was *breathtaking*. With that androgynous Madison Avenue kind of beauty: high cheekbones, strong jaw, patrician nose.

Michelangelo would have taken one look at the man and scurried off to find a sledgehammer to destroy his David. Janet, the receptionist, would have helped.

The man's ebony hair was long, brushing his shoulders, and a little wavy from the rain. Tousled—as if he'd run his hands through it too many times.

But it was his eyes that intrigued Renata. In the half-shadows, they appeared black. Secretive. Haunted, she decided. Which suited his dark charisma.

She scrambled to recall what Richard had said about the man. He was a research fellow? Gifted? He had slight circles under his eyes. Did he work too hard, with no one to hurry home to at night?

Renata understood that. Her work was her life, her passion. She couldn't not be a doctor. But sometimes, it wasn't enough. Sometimes she couldn't bear to go home, to the emptiness. The long nights . . .

When he ran a hand through his hair she realized she'd been staring. Probably drooling.

God, she needed a life. If he hadn't been standing there she'd have smacked her own forehead.

Still flustered by her sensual thoughts, she quickly straightened and slid on her professional persona to cover her adolescent gaffe.

"I'm sorry, but you just missed Richard."

The man glanced at his wrist then looked back at her. "Could I use the phone to call him?"

"Certainly." She held the door open and stepped back.

When he crossed the threshold, she found he was even taller than she'd thought. He had to be at least six-four or five, with a physique to match. And in the light she saw that his eyes were actually deep blue with little flecks of gold above the irises.

He winked and smiled, sending her pulse to a dangerous elevation. "I'm glad to meet you, by the way. Richard speaks highly of you."

"He does?" Renata fought the urge to stammer. "Uh, the phone's right there. He was stopping at Janet's for pizza, though, so I'd try his cell."

"Thanks." The man shifted closer.

Again she caught her breath, her knees shaky. "Had . . . had he invited you to join them? I could drive us there."

"Are you sure it's no trouble?"

She grinned, and tried to flirt. "None. But if I drive, you have to tell me what Richard said."

"About you? Deal."

He extended his hand. When she went to shake it, he tugged her close. The move threw her off balance, levering her against his chest. His arms circled, one at her waist, one at her back, steadying her as he held her gaze.

"He said you were beautiful. So forgive me," he whispered. "But I'll die if I don't do this."

His mouth lowered, sweeping across hers in a hard, fast kiss. Renata jumped at the intensity, the unexpectedness of it, her senses overwhelmed.

She had a brief thought that she didn't know this man, followed by a rush of desire *to* know him. Intimately. Raw sexuality spilled from him, overpowering her sensibilities. No man had ever claimed he'd die if he didn't kiss her. And likewise no man had ever held her as if she were the most precious thing on earth. This was the stuff of fairy tales, midnight fantasies. Kinky singles ads: *Warrior god seeks single princess*.

His arms tightened slightly, drawing her attention back to his kiss. She parted her lips to breathe and felt his tongue sweep forward. Instinctively her mouth opened wider. He made a low noise, in approval, as he deepened the kiss.

Renata reveled in the moment, feeling secure in his embrace. Part of her realized that while this man was a stranger, he was highly recommended by Richard. Which allowed her to relax.

Then he straightened, breaking off the kiss. The abruptness left her unsteady. She blushed, uncertain of what to say. The thoughts she'd been thinking . . . This had never happened to her before. And now that it ended, she felt awkward. Embarrassed. *Turned on*.

She pointed to the television. "I'll shut it off while you use the phone."

As she went to move past him, he raised his arm, blocking her. She stopped, half expecting another kiss.

Then she noticed the gun in his hand.

The fantasy developing in her head imploded. She searched his face for a clue this was a bad joke. But the eyes that minutes ago seduced her now looked grim.

"What is this?" she demanded.

"I won't hurt you as long as you do exactly as I say."

"Who are you? Richard said—"

"Richard and I have never met."

His blunt admission bewildered her. She eyed his jacket again. In the light, she could see the badge had been tampered with, the photo torn off. Stolen. She had simply looked at his white jacket and assumed.

Her fingers went for the alarm button on the pager

and found it missing. Her cell phone was gone too. He'd taken both while kissing her.

What a fool.

She took another step backwards and quickly reassessed his appearance, zeroing in on details. His cheeks were shadowed with stubble but what she had thought was grunge was grubby. His face and neck were sunburned.

He didn't look like a junkie. His hands were steady; his eyes clear. Which didn't rule out drugs. He could be a dealer. Certain prescription drugs had tremendous black market value.

Her mind stumbled as she fought to remain calm. *Keep him talking.*

"If you're after narcotics," she began, "there are none here. A guard picks them up after hours."

"I know. I watched him leave."

Too late she realized her mistake. "He'll be back."

The man shrugged. "I won't be here long."

Renata shook her head, struggling against a rising panic. If he wasn't after drugs or money . . . She pivoted and ran down the hall. If she could reach an exam room, barricade herself in, and call for help—

The man caught her before she made it ten feet. Hooking her shoulder, he spun her back, forcing her up against his chest as he twisted her arm behind her. But where she expected pain there was instead brute strength—a physical reminder that he could break her in half with ease. That he could do anything he wanted. Rape. Assault. Murder.

She started to struggle, but stopped when he raised his gun. "Don't. Please."

He didn't respond. His eyes drifted slowly over her, the same way hers had done earlier, his gaze fastening to the exact spot where her breasts were smashed against his chest.

She stiffened, tried to pull away. He tightened his grip, holding her in place.

"You have my word, *Renata*. You won't be harmed," he said. "I need your medical skills."

Relief that he'd merely read her name embroidered on her jacket overwhelmed her. "My medical skills? Are you hurt?"

He stepped away, releasing her, but keeping the gun trained forward. "A friend of mine is. He's just outside."

She hung back, afraid. Disbelieving. "How do I know this isn't another trick?"

"You don't. But when I bring you back inside—unharmed—you'll know you can believe me. Let's go."

Go? That the man's intentions included kidnapping hadn't dawned on her until now. "I'm not going anywhere with you."

"Want to bet?" He grabbed her elbow and tugged, leaving no doubt he'd simply drag her.

Play along, she thought. *Watch for a chance to escape.*

Outside, the rain had lessened to a mist, the air a damp shroud. Eerie. Evil. He walked fast, his stride much longer, but slowed after she tripped trying to keep up.

He rounded the building. When she saw they were headed into a dark, isolated niche, she tried to jerk free, terrified. "No!"

"Renata!" He swung her around in a sharp semi-circle, catching her by the waist and pinning her against his frame. She kicked, but he tightened his hold, crushing her. Pain lanced up her spine, stealing her breath.

She stopped struggling.

He eased his grip and dropped his head to hers in a move that was almost intimate. Frightening.

"Shhhh," he soothed. "Just ahead, to the left, is my car. Do you see it?"

Reluctant, she turned, narrowed her eyes. She saw the car, the open door.

"There's a man inside," he continued. "And he's hurt."

"I don't believe it. And I'm not leaving with you."

He sighed, tugged her forward again. "Suit yourself."

As they drew close, she saw a man in the back, head reclined. He jerked upright when they approached.

"Damn it, Adam! Make some noise."

Adam. Renata tucked the name into memory. It probably wasn't his real name but—

"Who's she?" the man asked.

"A doctor."

"Good." The man grimaced, groaning as he tried to climb out of the car.

"Don't move," Adam warned.

Unsteady, the man pitched forward. Adam caught him with one arm, while keeping the gun on her.

"Help me," he ordered. "Let's get him inside."

Renata bent to lend support, instinctively trying to see the injured man better. "What happened?"

"Gunshot," Adam said. "Left groin."

She straightened, her outrage overcoming her trepidation. "I can't treat this kind of injury here. This man needs a hospital and—"

"No hospitals!" The injured man cut her off. "It's you or nothing. Go!"

In the clinic's lobby, Renata got a clear look at the injured man. In spite of the pain contorting his face, she could tell he was younger than Adam. Early twenties perhaps. Not very tall; maybe five-seven, with a slight build. He had a small nose, uneven from being broken long ago, and pale, thin, lips.

His shirt was gone, dried blood smeared on his abdomen and arms. Blood had drenched the front of his jeans, down the legs, to his shoes.

"How long ago did this happen?" she asked.

"Maybe twenty minutes," Adam said.

She tried to gauge how much blood he'd lost. *Too much.* She touched the injured man's shoulder. "Let me call an ambulance. You need—"

"No! I will not—" The man passed out before finishing his sentence.

"Shit!" Adam caught him before he hit the ground. "Where can I put him?"

"First room on the left. Get him up on the table." Renata snatched a pair of latex gloves from the open box atop the cabinet, pulled them on. "Get his pants off. Scissors are on the cart."

She slid a nasal cannula over the man's face and adjusted the oxygen flow. Grabbing a blood pressure cuff, she secured it around his arm, clipped an oxygen sensor to his finger, and quickly collected vital signs.

"His pressure's low, pulse is elevated and weak." She checked his pupils, noted he was panting. "He's going into shock. He needs fluids. Fast."

She glanced at the saturated cloth covering his wound. "We have to get this bleeding stopped, too." She picked up a thick stack of gauze squares and placed them over the wound, then motioned to Adam. "Come here and press down on these, firmly."

Moving to the opposite side of the table, Renata straightened the injured man's right arm. His loss of blood would make it hard, maybe impossible, to find a vein.

She ripped open an IV kit, tied a tourniquet around his upper arm. There was a sharp smell of alcohol as she prepped the skin on his arm.

The man flailed when she stuck him, dislodging the IV needle. It fell to the floor, rolled beneath the table.

"Hold him!" She grabbed another IV kit, then flicked his hand, searching for another vein. Adam leaned across the younger man, holding him in place as she took another stab at his wrist.

"Got it. But don't let go of him until I get it taped down." Working quickly she connected the clear tubing to a bag of normal saline and adjusted the flow. She glanced up, saw the question on Adam's face. "I need to increase his volume of fluids, make up for what he's lost. He could probably use a couple units of blood, which we don't have here."

She moved to where Adam stood, waved him aside. "Let me take a look."

He backed away as she lifted the gauze. For now the bleeding had stopped. It would restart when the wound was cleaned, though.

Turning to the cabinet beside her, she opened a drawer. Adam raised his gun.

She glared at him. "I need supplies."

Unapologetic, he leaned forward, inspecting the contents of the open drawer before nodding.

Taking a pair of scissors, she quickly cut away the rest of the makeshift bandages, noticing the extra layers of cloth.

"Were you trying to make a pressure dressing?"

"Trying."

She wondered briefly at Adam's background. The steps he'd taken had prevented the other man from bleeding to death. It was obvious he'd had experience with gunshot wounds before, but how? Military? Paramedic? Career criminal?

She examined the wound, grateful it wasn't a shotgun blast. They were the worst, especially at close range, blowing away whole sections of flesh and vital organs. Some bullets could be equally damaging, though, shattering on impact and sending deadly fragments to ricochet through organs.

"Any idea what he was shot with?" Knowing the caliber and type of ammunition would help her assess the potential damage.

"Handgun. I'm guessing three-fifty-seven," Adam said.

She started to ask how it happened, but stopped. Given the way they'd shown up here tonight, it was unlikely they'd tell her the truth.

During her rotations in the ER, she'd seen people shot for a lot of different reasons. Intentional or accidental, there was nothing good about a gunshot. Knowing how or why it happened didn't change the treatment. Or the chances for survival.

And in this case, perhaps the less she knew the better. Too much knowledge could make them think twice about leaving her alive.

"I need to check for an exit wound. Can you turn him?"

The man's left buttock was bloody, making the exit wound easy to locate. More slit shaped than round, it wasn't bleeding as badly. She pressed on it, then irrigated it with saline to clean it before grabbing another thick stack of gauze to cover the wound so Adam could ease the man back down.

She checked his blood pressure again, keenly aware that being on her own in a critical situation reduced her effectiveness. If they had come in when the clinic was fully staffed, there would be two or three others assisting. A nurse would monitor his vitals, get a medical history. Someone else would draw blood, start an IV, while the front desk called for an ambulance. They would take whatever life-saving steps they could, but mainly they'd stabilize the patient for transport to the closest hospital.

Perhaps while the man was unconscious she could talk Adam into letting her call for help. But before she could speak, the injured man's eyelids fluttered open.

His complexion looked ashen. Unhealthy. He moaned back to consciousness, his voice hoarse and tinged with fear. "How long was I out?"

Renata glanced at the clock. "Seven minutes."

"God . . . I feel like shit."

"You should. You've been shot."

"Did it . . . go straight through?"

"That's hard to verify without X-rays, but it appears so."

The injured man seemed relieved. "That's good, right, Doc?"

"There's nothing good about a gunshot."

"But it could have been worse," the man pressed. "If it . . . had hit my heart or lungs . . . I'd be a goner."

"It doesn't have to hit a vital organ to prove fatal." Renata moved her stethoscope around on his thin, hairless chest. "Are you allergic to any medications? Penicillin or other antibiotics?"

The man took a shallow breath. "No. I'm not allergic to pain medication either."

"Our narcotics are taken to the hospital each night. Too many break-ins."

"Great." He coughed, looked at Adam. "What now?"

Adam glanced at her. "What's the course of treatment?"

"If we were at a hospital, I'd order X-rays, blood work, and ship him to the OR for surgery to repair that vein."

"Yeah, well, we're not at the hospital, are we?" The injured man interrupted. "What can you do besides bandage me up?"

"Not much."

"That's what I figured."

She realized she may have spoken too soon again. If there was nothing more she could do, would they get rid of her?

"Actually, I was going to add an antibiotic to the IV to help fight infection," she rushed on. "You're definitely at a greater risk for that."

"How long before he's stable?" Adam asked.

She swallowed the urge to lie, to tell them he was fine so they'd leave. "I'm not sure. He'll need at least another liter of saline intravenously. And the bleeding has stopped for the moment, but that could change if he moves too much. With the amount of blood he's lost he could go into shock rapidly."

The two men exchanged glances. Lyle shook his head. "Get on with it then."

She grabbed a bag of antibiotics and moved to connect it to the IV. She fingered the control, realized her hands were shaking.

"Don't do anything stupid, Renata." Adam was right behind her. She hadn't even heard him move. "Once he's stable enough to travel, we'll leave. You won't be harmed."

"What guarantee do I have of that?"

"My word. Now finish up."

His word? Oh, that made a big difference. Biting back a retort, Renata turned to the injured man.

Uncovering his wound, she began cleaning it with

saline. When she examined it more closely she saw bits of threads protruding. There were probably pieces of cloth inside the wound that needed to be removed as well. Her probing would start the bleeding again. There was also a jagged piece of flesh that needed to be cut away to ward off complications and promote healing. Both would also be extremely painful. Typically a patient was heavily sedated first.

She opened the drawer, grabbed several small forceps and disposable scalpels. Adam hovered close, watching.

"This will hurt." She picked up a scalpel.

"I'm already in pain, lady." The man curled his lip back. "It can't get much worse."

"It will."

"That's just fucking great."

She leaned close to offer an alternative. "If I call an ambulance, they'll have morphine—"

Without warning, the man grabbed her hand, bent it backwards and snatched the scalpel. Renata screamed at the intense pain.

"If I hear you say ambulance or hospital one more time, I swear I'll take this scalpel to your face and—"

Adam knocked the younger man's hand aside, breaking his grasp. "She got the message."

For long seconds, Renata stared at the floor, fighting for composure. If Adam hadn't interfered the man would have broken her wrist. Or worse. The thought of what he might have done with the scalpel terrified her.

It also fanned her anger, made her want to shout every vulgarity she could think of. More, she wanted to turn and walk out, refuse to treat him further. Except . . . she didn't have a choice. They were armed. And they had a physical advantage. The unfairness of the situation only incensed her further.

She picked up another scalpel and straightened before staring coldly at the man on the table. "Touch me again and I'll—"

"You'll what?"

Adam stepped between the two. "Enough. We're going out to the lobby while you try to get hold of your brother again. When we come back, she's going to finish dressing this wound. And you're going to let her."

Renata noticed the younger man didn't question Adam's authority though she sensed he wanted to.

"We need a closer meeting point." Adam handed him a cell phone, then tugged her out of the exam room.

He steered her toward the front lobby where MTV still roared. The only source of light, from the television, cast the waiting room in flickering shadow.

"Sit there." He pointed to the chair closest to the set. "What station has eleven o'clock news? Local stuff?"

His question was unexpected. She was also surprised to realize the men had been there less than an hour. It felt like a week. "Channel six is local. So is twenty-two."

"Just find one. And turn it down."

She grabbed the remote and nervously lowered the volume. From the corner of her eye she saw Adam glance down the hall. What had he meant about a closer rendezvous spot? Were they really planning to leave soon?

She heard Lyle murmuring on the phone, but couldn't make out what was being said. She shifted sideways.

Adam caught her eavesdropping and scowled. "Hurry up."

Straightening, she punched the remote again. Since

he was so concerned about her overhearing the phone call, maybe he did intend to leave her unharmed.

It wasn't quite eleven o'clock, so the credits for one of the popular reality series scrolled. Trying to calm her nerves, she sank deeper into the chair.

The headache she'd tried to ward off earlier had landed like a Harrier jet, and throbbed with each beat of her heart. *I have to get away.* She peeked toward the front door, wondered how many steps to reach it? How long it would take to get it open?

She glanced toward Adam, wondering if at any point she would be left alone. Ten seconds was all she needed.

Just then the news came on, the screen emblazoned with the words PRISON ESCAPE. Beneath it were two mug shots. It felt as if she were being smothered as the camera panned from the mug shots to the serious-faced anchorman.

"A door-to-door search is underway in Durham County as police search for two armed and dangerous convicts."

Chapter Four

Renata stared at the mug shots, recognizing the injured man immediately. Lyle McEdwin. The name rang a bell.

But she had to look twice at the second photo. It barely resembled Adam. The photo showed him with a full beard and shorter hair, which made him look sinister. Ruthless.

"Four prisoners fled a road gang earlier today, after overpowering guards in a daring escape," the anchorman continued. "Police in Alamance County quickly apprehended two of the inmates but the other two remain at large."

Renata recalled Janet reassuring Mrs. Bolton the prisoners had been captured. Clearly she hadn't realized not all had been caught.

The screen blinked as they replayed the video of an earlier Department of Corrections news conference. "Inmate Adam Duval was serving a five-year sentence for possession of stolen property. The second man, Lyle McEdwin, was serving time for armed robbery and assault."

Renata felt a shudder creep up her side. It wasn't hard to imagine Lyle assaulting someone. By comparison, Adam's crime seemed tame. Except . . . he was the one who kept flashing the gun.

"McEdwin is the youngest son of Willy McEdwin, who is wanted by the FBI in connection with bombings in Omaha, Chicago, and Des Moines."

Hope faded as she realized why Lyle's name had sounded familiar. The McEdwins were notorious criminals.

Like most of the country, she could recall their saga. Years ago, Willy McEdwin had joined an antigovernment group after losing his farm. He ended up imprisoned for the murder of his own wife—who died in an explosion prosecutors claimed Willy had rigged to take out a federal marshal serving a warrant.

In a shameful twist, Willy's sentence was overturned ten years later when new evidence surfaced proving two police officers had actually rigged the explosives in an attempt to prevent him from testifying in court. Willy and his wife had both been victims.

Once his name had been cleared, Willy was released from prison and eventually realized millions from wrongful death and false imprisonment suits. He was lauded as a folk hero when he promised to testify about government extortion regarding farmlands, but then he and his three eldest sons disappeared.

Overnight, the public's sympathy turned to outrage as a string of explosions in the Midwest were linked to the McEdwins.

Renata's hands trembled as she continued to watch the grim television report.

"There are unconfirmed reports that one of the prison guards was taken hostage. And in what may be a related case, Durham police are investigating a shooting that occurred this evening involving an off-duty deputy."

The deputy's photo flashed on the screen. "Sheriff's Deputy Jim Acton is currently in surgery at Duke

Medical Center. No word on his condition. It is believed Acton was shot at a commercial storage facility trying to apprehend the two fugitives. Police are mounting a massive manhunt—"

She lurched to her feet. "Oh, God! Not Jim."

"A friend of yours?"

She barely nodded. "He's engaged to one of the nurses at the hospital." She covered her mouth. "Poor Mary-Ellen."

Adam's gut tightened over the news that the man Lyle had shot was indeed a law enforcement officer. Equally alarming was the mention of the missing guard. Wallace? Or the driver?

While he hadn't been fond of either guard, he hadn't wanted them harmed. He thought back to their escape. Had one of the other prisoners returned after Adam and Lyle fled? The handcuffed guards would have been easy prey.

What should have been a precisely executed prison break was spinning out of control. Lyle had been shot, a deputy had been shot, a guard was missing and they'd broken into a clinic, forced a doctor to treat Lyle. It couldn't get much worse.

The news coverage switched to the flooding, the backdrop changing to a montage of water-covered roads and dire predictions of more rain. Adam yanked the plug from the wall, killing the broadcast.

Renata spun to face him. She jabbed a finger in the direction of the exam room. "That slimy bastard in there shot Jim, didn't he?"

Adam didn't bother to deny the obvious.

"And what about the missing guard? Did he shoot him too?" She made a strangled sound. "Please tell me you didn't leave that poor guard to bleed to death somewhere? You miserable—" She broke off when he made a move toward her.

"Both guards were alive and unharmed when I last saw them," he said.

Lyle interrupted, calling out.

"We're coming." Adam reached for her arm.

She stepped back, eyes flaring. "You don't really expect me to go in there and help him, do you?"

"Sometimes you have to do things you'd rather not." *For the higher good.* He tried to grasp her by the arm again.

"I can find my own way." She stuffed her fists in her pockets and moved sideways, avoiding his touch. Hard plastic brushed against her knuckles: the handle of a disposable scalpel, the ultra sharp blade still covered.

In the confusion earlier, she must have dropped it in her pocket. She tried to draw comfort from the thought that she had means to defend herself.

Adam pressed closer. "Come on."

Leaving the scalpel in her pocket, she pretended to give in and followed along.

In the exam room, they found Lyle fumbling awkwardly with a match as he tried to light a cigarette.

Renata ripped the cigarette out of his mouth and tossed it into the sink. Next went the match from his fingers. "No smoking."

"Bitch! What'd you do that for? Worry about the hole in my groin, not my lungs."

"I could care less about your lungs." She pointed to the posted warning on the wall. "We're running oxygen in here. Highly flammable—though personally, I don't care if either of you get blown to kingdom come."

"Fuck off, lady." Lyle tapped out another cigarette. "You're not in charge here."

"That's right. I am. Remember?" Adam took the cigarette from between Lyle's lips and tossed it after the other.

Renata saw resentment flash in Lyle's eyes. Did Adam realize how unhappy his accomplice was about taking orders? Or had the gratitude for saving his life already worn thin? Perhaps the two men weren't as close as she'd assumed.

Adam leaned in. "Tell me what your brother said."

"We sit tight until he calls back," Lyle said.

"That's it? Sit tight?" He shook his head. "That's not good enough."

"He's doing the best he can. Getting another set of wheels takes time."

"We don't have time." Adam updated Lyle on the news report. "Durham police are starting a manhunt. And they've got blood in their eyes now that one of their own's been shot."

Lyle didn't blink over the news that he'd shot a deputy. "Now what?"

"We need to get the hell out of town."

Lyle curled his lip in Renata's direction. "Then if she has any more doctoring to do, she better do it fast."

Reluctantly, she moved forward. While the news they'd be leaving soon should have relieved her, the idea of giving aide to this punk really tested her Hippocratic oath. First, do no harm . . . Drat. Look how much harm he'd caused others.

Just treat the injury and ignore the man, she told herself.

Grabbing a handful of sponges, she began cleaning the area around Lyle's wound. There was dried blood everywhere, making her wonder again how much blood he'd lost.

She swiped the skin across his lower abdomen, then

paused. The man bore signs of other injuries—burns, cuts. Some were healed, some more recent. All were purposely inflicted. Neatly. Methodically.

She glanced at Lyle, confused. "You sustained these in prison?"

"The guards call it 'rehabilitation.' I flunked." Lyle closed his eyes, his breathing labored.

Adam watched her face as the realization that the prison guards had tortured Lyle dawned on her. That was a facet of life she hadn't been exposed to.

He had seen the scars before. Most were faded, since it had been going on for most of the nine months Lyle had been in prison. Adam also knew who was behind it—two guards, Wallace and Huggins—and what they were after: the location of Lyle's father and brothers. Or rather, the million-dollar reward for the capture of the infamous Four Horsemen.

Small wonder the kid had been near rabid in his desire to escape. Adam recalled how Lyle had promised Wallace he'd get even, making him wonder whether Lyle or his family had anything to do with the missing prison guard.

The cell phone rang. Lyle winced as he answered.

"Nevin! The doc's bandaging me up now."

Lyle grew quiet, saying only "yes" or "no." Several times, he looked at Adam but said nothing. Adam knew they were discussing him, wished he knew what was being said.

Finally Lyle held out the phone. "He wants to talk to you."

Skeptical, Adam pressed the phone to his ear. "Yes?"

"You know who this is?"

"Of course."

"Listen, I know this hasn't gone like it should, but

I'm going to fix that. In the meantime I need your help with something."

Adam snorted. "You're not in a position to ask much."

"Maybe not. But right now I figure you need me as much as I need you. Especially since the cops are combing that area. Wouldn't take much for them to find you."

"You picked the wrong person to threaten."

"Wait!" Nevin's voice turned cajoling. "You're right. Actually, I have a proposition. You make sure my brother gets to me safely, and I'll make it more than worth your while. I'll have a car for you within two hours. Directions for safe passage will be in it."

"Where are we headed?"

"I'll tell you when you're on the road," Nevin promised. "And plan on bringing that doctor along."

Adam hesitated. Forcing Renata to care for Lyle was one thing. Kidnapping her . . . "That's not necessary."

"I don't give a damn if you think it's necessary. I won't take chances with my brother's life. Not when we're this close to getting him back to the family."

This piqued Adam's interest. "You're in this vicinity?"

Nevin sighed, impatient. "Not any more—thanks to your little fiasco with the deputy."

"Fiasco?" His grip on the phone tightened. "Let's get clear on a few things: It wasn't my screwup that produced this mess. If I had been alone, I'd have been out of the country by now."

The implication was plain: Adam wasn't to blame. Nor was he pleased with the current situation.

"Look, I know my brother can fuck things up big time. And I know you're not happy to involve anyone else. But you have to bring the doctor along now,"

Nevin said. "If Lyle gets worse on the road, are you going to risk busting into another clinic?"

"We both know the cops would expect that."

Nevin lowered his voice. "Where you're going, you'll be miles from a hospital. I'd rather be safe than sorry. And it won't be for long. Then you can turn her loose on a country road, no worse for the wear. It'll be like dumping a stray animal."

Adam briefly shifted his eyes to Renata, hoped she couldn't guess what they discussed. "The stray will be one-hundred percent unharmed?"

"Absolutely. You should know that I don't hold with killing innocent people."

Unless it suits your purpose, Adam thought. He was familiar with the crimes attributed to the McEdwins. Willy made a point of taking out innocent people along with his targeted objective. All in the name of vengeance for a wrong that could never be righted: the death of Willy's wife.

"Don't forget she could also have value as a hostage," Nevin continued. "The cops always claim they won't negotiate, but it's a different ballgame when you're holding a gun to someone's head. Just be ready. I'll get back to you with details."

The phone went dead. Adam looked at Lyle. "He's calling back. Chill out while I get supplies."

Grasping Renata's arm, he dragged her out of the exam room and down the hall. "Do you have coffee?"

The question surprised her. "What?"

"Coffee? An employee kitchen?" It didn't sound like he'd get much sleep tonight. And Nevin's remark that they'd be miles from a hospital was telling. It was clear they were no longer headed toward Richmond.

She pointed to an open doorway. "There's the employee break room."

He made her enter first. "Make a pot. Extra strong."

She opened a drawer and once again felt Adam peer over her shoulder. She grabbed two foil packages of coffee, held them up. "You're welcome to do this yourself."

"Just checking." He turned away.

While she drew water, he studied the photographs pinned on the bulletin board. A hand-written index card noted the photos were from a group hike the clinic staff had done at the start of summer.

He pointed to a snapshot of her with three other people. "These are people you work with? Other doctors?"

At her nod, Adam re-examined the photo. They looked more like a band of gypsies than professionals. The group appeared to be laughing over some private joke. Renata wore a tank top, shorts and hiking boots, showing off legs that were muscular and tanned. Runner's legs.

His eyes took in her figure. The shapeless white jacket she wore now hid a lot. In the photo, her hair was loose, a dark silky spill that hung just below her shoulders. She had big brown, expressive eyes that twinkled behind long lashes. He studied her mouth, her full lips. Very kissable lips, he recalled.

He pointed to the background. "Is that the bridge at Laurel Fork Gorge?" Laurel Fork was on the Appalachian Trail. "That bridge was built using nothing but primitive skills and native material."

Renata squinted at the picture. "I'm afraid to ask how you know that."

He grunted. "Having a hard time imagining me hiking?"

She nodded. "It seems a little wholesome. Unless of course you were burying a body."

Adam moved to where the coffee had finished brewing, helped himself to a white foam cup. "Have you hiked much of the Trail?"

"Some." His questions made Renata suspicious. "Why the small talk?"

He took a sip of coffee, savored it, then shrugged. "Thought I'd get to know you since you'll be coming with us."

"With you?" She shook her head and took a step backwards. Away from the man. Away from his words. "I am not going anywhere with you."

"You'll be released, unharmed, later."

His unperturbed manner upset her even more. "You think I believe that? You're escaped convicts. You already shot one man." What was one woman?

"I've kept my word. You haven't been hurt, have you?"

Renata started to remind him of Lyle grabbing her wrist earlier. Except Adam had sort of rescued her then by knocking Lyle's hand away. She didn't want to hear him claim chivalry. Fugitives had no chivalry. They acted solely in self-preservation.

She tried a different tact. "I'd be a hindrance. And you really don't need me. If he won't go to the hospital, there's not a lot I can do that you couldn't. You've obviously had some experience. You can change his dressings—"

He cut her off. "We both know he'll need more fluid by IV. What if he requires a blood transfusion?"

"And no weasels are available as donors? Gee, you'll have to take him to the hospital. You don't need me for that either."

He scowled. "There's plenty of other things that can go wrong: What if the needle dislodges again? Or he starts going into shock?"

"He'll still require a hospital. Can't you get that

through your thick head? That doesn't change, damn it!"

Adam wondered if she even realized she swore. Her bottom lip quivered as she struggled to contain her emotions, her distress palpable. He could imagine what was going through her mind, knew she feared the worst. He wished he could offer assurance.

He pinched the bridge of his nose. Lyle's condition needed close monitoring. Adam knew basic first aid— field stuff. Lyle's wound was beyond that.

There was also the question of crossing Lyle's brother this early in the game. While Adam had no intention of playing patsy, he needed to gain Nevin's trust. If Adam took Renata along for just a short time and then set her free, it would appear he'd attempted to comply with Nevin's decree.

Mind made up, he drained his coffee cup, refilled it. "Where do you keep your medical supplies?"

"There's a closet in the hall."

"Show me."

Inside the supply closet, he grabbed an empty cardboard box. He scanned the shelves, pulling out unopened packages. Basic provisions: gauze, tape, peroxide, a thermometer, blood pressure cuff. He grabbed one of the green scrub suits for Lyle to wear, then turned to her.

"What else will we need? Think worst-case scenario because you won't have access to more once we're on the road."

"I am *not* going with you."

"We've established that you don't want to. But you will. Now either help me or be stuck with whatever I've got here."

Renata slowly unfolded her arms. Arguing with the man was futile. There was no reasoning with the unreasonable. She'd have to wait for the right opportunity and make a move.

She shot him a dirty look then checked the supplies he'd taken.

"You've got enough gauze for a small army. How long will I be held? Or are you anticipating more casualties?"

"Worst case, remember?"

She scanned the contents again, then added a box of latex gloves, bags of antibiotics, and suture kits. "There's IV kits and tubing to your left. Grab them. We'll need a case of saline, too." She reached for a general-purpose first aid kit.

Adam surveyed the box. "That's it?"

"Short of splints, we have a little of everything. If he's not showing marked improvement within forty-eight hours, nothing I've got here will keep him alive."

That wasn't exactly the truth. Problems like infection or blood clots could still show up a week from now. And there was an entire universe of potential complications, particularly since she didn't know if bullet fragments had caused any internal damage. A miniscule nick on his intestine could slowly leak poison into his system. In a truly worst-case scenario, nothing in the box would replace a surgeon and trauma facility.

A knock echoed from the front door. That quick, Adam hauled Renata back against his chest. His hand covered her mouth as the knocking repeated, louder.

"Dr. Curtis? You in there?"

"Is that the security guard who was here earlier?" Adam whispered.

She nodded.

Lyle's voice drifted down the hall. "Adam! What the hell's going on?"

Renata felt the hard press of his gun against her ribs as they hurried to the doorway of the exam room. Adam motioned for Lyle to remain quiet, then pushed her to the lobby, his hand still covering her mouth.

"You need to get rid of him. Fast. Without arousing suspicion." Stepping behind the door, he pointed the gun at it. If he fired, he'd hit Clarence. "Think about his well-being."

She nodded and cracked the door. His hand dropped to her elbow, out of sight, but still controlling her. The security chain seemed to mock her. Clarence stood outside.

In spite of the lump in her throat, she tried to smile. She'd worked with Clarence for almost two years, had met his family at the annual Christmas party. He had three kids. Right now she felt responsible for them.

"Yes?"

"Sorry to bother you, Doctor Curtis." Clarence shook his head. "We got a couple convicts on the loose. Thought I'd check on you."

She forced a neutral look to her face. "I saw the news earlier. Is there any word on how Deputy Acton's doing?"

She felt Adam's fingers press into her arm, knew he wasn't pleased with her query. Too bad, she thought.

Clarence frowned. "Last I heard, he was still in surgery. Bad stuff. It might be a good idea for me to see you to your car. Follow you home. Weather's supposed to get worse, too. Lord knows we don't need more rain."

She felt a slight panic. "But I can't leave yet. I still have work to do."

"Well, then, if the police come by, don't let it surprise you. They've started a street-by-street sweep. Of course, they may have already nabbed them by now.

They got an APB out on the car; know exactly what they're driving."

"That's encouraging," she said. "I'm sure they'll find them."

"I have a few more pick-ups." Clarence checked his watch. "How about I swing back by in thirty minutes, walk you out then?"

Adam squeezed her arm once again.

"It might take a little longer," she said. "Why don't you give me your beeper number and I'll page you when I'm ready to leave."

"Sounds good. I'm on duty till five."

Grabbing a small notebook from her pocket, Renata pretended to write his number. Instead she scribbled: H-E-L-P.

Adam's gun bit sharply into her side. She glanced sideways, noticed he had moved closer. With his height advantage he could see exactly what she wrote.

She pocketed the notebook and nodded. "I'll call you."

As soon as she closed the door, Adam forced her to face him. His eyes glittered perilously. She thought about screaming, to catch Clarence's attention, but if Adam harmed him . . .

"You played the part perfectly," he gritted between clenched teeth. "Except for the note at the end. That was stupid."

Shifting, Adam blocked her, pressed her back against the door reminding her that he was a foot taller. He let his full weight rest against her as he leisurely tucked the gun into his waistband behind him, freeing both his hands.

If he meant to intimidate, he succeeded. She could feel every ounce of muscle, sensed the tension wound up within him. He placed a hand on either side of her head and leaned even closer. The gold flecks in his eyes sparked.

"I know this isn't nice or fun," he said. "But if you cooperate, it will be a lot easier on you."

Her right hand, which was still clenched inside her pocket, brushed against plastic.

The scalpel. Her fist closed over it like a lifeline.

"What do you say?" he whispered.

Her pulse pounded in her skull. Loud. Scary. She pretended to consider his words, while she summoned her courage.

"Fine," she said at last. "I'll cooperate."

But the moment Adam stepped away Renata yanked the scalpel from her pocket and raised it in the air. "When hell freezes over!"

Chapter Five

Willy McEdwin had a look that would make God nervous. And right now that unholy gleam was directed at his twin sons.

Tristin, older by eight minutes, looked nervously at his brother, Burt.

"Don't kill the messenger, Pa," Tristin blurted.

It was the second time that night Willy had been awakened with bad news. First an irate business associate had threatened to dump his C-4 in the ocean; make fish bait of his plastic explosives.

Now this.

Willy's fist hammered the table. "Just tell me the SOB who shot your little brother is dead."

"The SOB's a deputy," Burt said.

"Doesn't matter. Is he dead?"

"Last we heard he was still in surgery."

"Pray he doesn't survive," Willy said. "Where's Lyle now?"

"Holed up in some emergency clinic in North Carolina. His partner forced some lady doctor to treat him. Lyle's pretty lucky."

"Lucky? You mean stupid," Willy spat. "He goes off all brash-assed and gets himself shot. Damn impatient kid!"

"It's not like he did it on purpose, Pa, he—"

"Stop right there. I'm tired of excuses. Lyle's gotten too used to you boys cleaning up after him. Wiping his butt. I had hoped a little time behind bars would toughen him up. That's why I told him to stay put."

That was one of the reasons anyway. Willy grabbed a bottle of antacid tablets, shook a couple into his hand.

Only a few weeks old when his mother died, Lyle had been a sickly infant who'd been spoiled rotten by his brothers and a maternal aunt while Willy was imprisoned. By the time Willy was released, the mold was set.

Lyle had been in and out of trouble since junior high. In the beginning it was easy to get him off the hook. A bribe here, a favor there, and charges were dropped; evidence disappeared.

But instead of learning his lesson, Lyle grew cockier. On his eighteenth birthday he was charged with attempted rape when a police chief's daughter got caught with her panties down. The little whore died in a car accident before the case ever went to trial, but consequently the chief's men made damn sure Lyle went down for something else. Framed him, with an ironclad case.

Willy popped the chalky antacids in his mouth before shaking out a few more.

"He was desperate, Pa," Burt continued. "Nevin said those two guards were threatening to castrate Lyle if he didn't start talking. Shaved his nuts and everything."

"What makes you so sure he didn't talk already?"

Tristin leaned forward. "Lyle's done a lot of stupid things, but he'd never betray us. In the nine months he's been behind bars, the guards couldn't break him— but this castration stuff. What would you have done?"

An ominous quiet settled over Willy. "I want those guards taken care of. Everything they did to Lyle, give back in spades."

"One guard's already missing," Burt said. "Chicken shit probably ran off."

"Find him. I assume Lyle's well enough to travel?"

"He doesn't have a choice. Police have kicked off a manhunt in the Carolinas. Nevin told them to bring that doctor along until they're sure Lyle's out of the woods."

Willy disagreed. "Dragging another person around will only hamper them."

"Nevin says Lyle's wound is bad."

"Has Nevin seen it himself?"

"No, and I know what you're thinking—"

"Then cut the bullshit. We all know your little brother has a tendency to blow things out of proportion. So where are they headed?"

"Nevin's working on that now," Tristin piped in. "The cops set up roadblocks at the state line, so getting them out is tricky. The good news is they don't have the manpower to guard every single road, not with all that flooding."

"Good news?" Willy grabbed the antacids again. "I hate that term. What aren't you telling me?"

Once again the twins exchanged nervous glances. "The governor's asked for federal help with the search," Burt said.

"I'm sure it was the other way around, the FBI pressuring the governor to let them take over. The Feds will expect Lyle to run home to daddy. Mark my words, they'll give him a wide berth and try to follow."

Burt shrugged. "Yeah, so? We've made monkeys out of them time and time again. This won't be any different."

"The hell it won't! It gets harder each time. Don't ever forget that. You get overconfident, you hand them an opportunity." Willy stood and started pacing. "What's the story on the guy Lyle's with? What's his name again?"

"Adam Duval. He was Lyle's cellmate. He was busted for stolen property. Big shit, like tractor-trailers loaded with telephone switching equipment. His partner got away, but they nabbed Duval's girlfriend," Burt explained. "And get this: The girlfriend was never charged. She apparently cut a deal with the Feds; tipped them off that Duval and his partner were also hijacking military goods."

"Bet he'd like to strangle the bitch."

"She disappeared last month on her way to a deposition. I figure Duval's partner arranged it."

His heartburn under control, Willy lit a cigarette. "What do you know about his partner?"

"Not much. A name: Daniel Montague. He slipped out of the country, but I bet that's who helped Duval set up the escape."

"Something doesn't feel right," Willy said. "If Duval's got help on the outside, what does he need Lyle for?"

"He doesn't," Tristin grunted. "That's what's got Nevin worried. Duval didn't want Lyle along in the first place. But Lyle promised we'd provide sanctuary until the heat died down and Duval can get a fake ID and skip the country—probably to meet up with Montague."

"Yep. As it is, Nevin had to do some fast talking to keep Duval from dumping Lyle," Burt said. "Duval's not too happy with our little brother."

"Do you blame him?" Willy grew thoughtful, then sighed. "Tell Nevin to cover Duval's back, for now.

Offer whatever incentive he needs and make damn
sure he has nowhere to go but here. And get me more
background on Duval. His partner, Montague, too. I
want to know what makes Duval tick and how far he
can be trusted. I also want to know how their escape
was set up, how they got on the same road gang. Contact Kenny Ray—he'll know where to dig."

"I'm on it," Tristin said.

"And tell Nevin to call me ASAP. That wire transfer
he was supposed to handle didn't go through. He put
me in a bad spot." Willy blew out a streamer of smoke.

"I'll tell him."

"Emphasize that I don't want any more loose ends.
Like this doctor. Nevin needs to make damn sure she
doesn't show up on a witness stand some day. Women
are the worst. They start crying and the jury turns to
mush." Willy stubbed out his cigarette, indicating the
meeting had ended. "Make it real clear that as soon as
Lyle's out of the woods, she dies."

Chapter Six

Renata clenched the scalpel in her right fist, uneasy with its potential as a weapon. Light glinted off the razor-edged blade. Held like a weapon, the handle bit uncomfortably into her palm.

"Back off," she demanded.

Instead, Adam swung his arm in an arc toward her.

She ducked, remaining beyond his reach. Too late she saw the flaw in her strategy, realized he was purposely maneuvering her away from the door, away from her only avenue of escape.

Determined to regain lost ground, she stabbed the air between them. He retreated. Buoyed by the small gain, she darted to the side.

He rushed her, crushing her against the wall beside a large ceramic planter.

"Let me go!"

"Hold still."

"Never." She fought back, catching a frond of the potted palm. It tilted and crashed to the tile floor. Desperate to be free, she windmilled her arms, felt the blade stab him.

He grunted in pain. Lightning fast, he caught her hands and yanked them out to her sides. His fingers dug into her right wrist, pinching. Hurting. "Drop it, Renata!"

"No way!"

Ignoring the pain at her wrist, she refused to relinquish her weapon. She tried kicking, unable to land a blow where she wanted.

Cursing, Adam squeezed harder.

A nail-like, debilitating pain shot up her arm, clear to the shoulder. She cried out, her hand opening reflexively, releasing the scalpel. It hit the ground and skittered across the floor into the dirt from the planter.

Immediately the pressure on her wrist eased.

Renata braced for retaliation, fully expecting to be struck. She had cut him with the scalpel. Where and how badly she didn't know, nor did she let herself dwell on it as she battled a rising nausea, afraid of what would come next.

Her knees shook and she was hyperventilating. From exertion. From tension. From waiting. This had to be the end.

The silence roared.

She blinked.

That he hadn't moved to punish her made her even more edgy. She noticed his breathing matched hers: harried, heavy. Daring to glance up, she found him staring down, the look in his eyes unreadable. He took a deep breath, exhaled slowly. Automatically she did likewise.

"Again," he whispered. "That's right."

Confused, she looked away. That's when she saw the blood on his forearm. Even as she told herself he had deserved it, the knowledge that she had inflicted the injury left her unsettled. Damn it, he held her at gunpoint. It was self-defense, self-preservation.

So why did her knees feel rubbery? Why did she want to throw up?

The burning in her wrist where Adam pinched the

nerve had subsided. She shifted her eyes to his hands, which still braceleted her wrists. His hands were large. Powerful. She was very aware of their strength, their potential. He could crush her bones effortlessly. Which he didn't.

In fact the fingers that had wrought excruciating pain moments before, now stroked, easing the throb. This motion surprised her. Was he actually comforting her? Or was it a trick to throw her off guard? His actions were impossible to reconcile with her image of him as a cold-hearted criminal. Unless . . .

Did Adam have a conscience? Was he having second thoughts? And if so, could she play on that? She sought more proof of his lenience. While still guarded, he had relaxed his stance. Which didn't mean he was no longer a threat.

Raising her head, she found him studying her just as intensely. The only clue her attack had indeed riled him was those gold flecks in his blue eyes. They glinted dangerously, a reminder she wasn't out of peril.

"You hesitated," Adam said in a low tone. "That was your first mistake. Always move swiftly. With confidence. Your second mistake was your choice of weapons. To stab someone, you have to step in close, less than an arm's length away. Which isn't wise when your opponent's reach exceeds yours."

He extended an arm. It dwarfed hers.

Releasing her, he kicked aside the palm tree and retrieved the scalpel. "If you go for blood, make it count. The eyes. The groin. You'll only get one shot. This shit," he waved his bloody arm, "will only piss him off. Which puts you in greater danger."

"Thanks for the pointers," she snapped.

"Yeah? Here's one more." He held up the scalpel,

flipped it in midair, then caught it. "Once I overpowered you, I could have used this against you."

But you didn't, she thought. Which proved nothing. It also did nothing to alter the situation.

"Maybe next time I'll have a gun."

He snorted. "Think that would make a difference? You still couldn't do it. Shoot someone."

"Don't bet on it." She jutted her chin, not wanting him to see her distress.

If she got her hands on his gun could she really shoot him? Yes, if it was truly life or death. But, oddly, with Adam she didn't feel that degree of danger. Lyle, however, was a different story. He'd shot a man and showed no remorse; was only upset that he'd been hurt himself.

A calm realization settled over her. Adam was . . . different from Lyle.

"Everything under control out there?" Lyle called out.

"Fine." Grasping her upper arm, Adam tugged her toward the hall.

But instead of going into the exam room, he returned to the supply closet.

"I thought we were done in here," she said.

"Not quite." He grabbed a small adhesive bandage and handed it to her. Then he held out his arm.

She eyed the cut on top of his arm, steeling herself against the backlash of remorse. Grabbing a brown bottle, she cleaned the wound with peroxide, then pinched the edges closed with a butterfly strip before covering it with a bandage.

Adam looked amused. "I don't think it required all that. But thanks."

She scowled. "Actually, it could have used a suture or two."

"If it had needed stitches, I'd have done them myself."

He flexed his arm, then helped himself to another roll of gauze. Instead of loading it into the box with the other supplies, though, he caught her and jerked her close. Tethering both her wrists in one hand, he started wrapping the gauze tightly, binding her hands.

She struggled uselessly, the cotton strip biting into her skin. "How dare you!"

He ignored her protest, tying off the gauze.

"Do you have other weapons you want to voluntarily declare? Maybe a stray pair of scissors, or a bone saw?"

"Just the scalpel."

"You'll understand if I don't take your word on that?" He turned her around and forced her up against the counter. His hard body crowded her from behind as his knee urged her legs apart.

Renata stiffened as she realized he was going to frisk her. How stupid to think she was safe from reprisals for pulling the scalpel on him.

"This isn't necessary."

"We'll see."

He started at her neck and worked his way down. She held her breath as his hands cupped her breasts, then moved beneath and into the hollow between them, circling each completely, checking for more weapons.

"Don't worry. This is no more enjoyable for me than it is for you," he whispered.

It was the truth. Her revulsion at his touch was tangible. Not quite the reaction Adam was accustomed to getting from women when he fondled them. They normally begged for his touch, seduced him. *Used him, used his body.*

This also wasn't how he'd envisioned his first post-prison encounter with breasts. Mighty fine breasts, too.

He ran his hands down her arms, drew back her sleeve and examined her watch. It was a well-worn little Timex, a man's model that had been shortened for her wrist. He started to unfasten it. That's when he saw the bruise on her wrist. Guilt slit his stomach with a dull knife.

He swore under his breath. Although this was unintentional, he'd never marked a woman in his life. God knows he'd watched his father bruise his mother enough times.

Leaving the Timex, he lightened his touch as he continued moving down to her waist and lower. He quickly emptied the pockets of her jacket, inspecting her key ring with interest. "Is that white Honda out front yours?"

She nodded. "Leave me, and you can have it. I'll even give you my gas card."

"Thanks, but I prefer cash. No paper trail." He turned her around. "This way."

Adam led her back to the exam room. He pushed her into a chair, and quickly bound her ankles. When he glanced up he noticed that her blouse had come unbuttoned during the earlier search. He rebuttoned it.

Lyle watched with interest. "So that's what all the ruckus was about. Guess having a female doctor will come in handy in more than one way. When do I get a chance to check her out?"

"You don't." Adam saw loathing flash in Renata's eyes. She wouldn't know the kid was all mouth, no teeth. And with his injury even his mouth was weak. "Security guard came back to warn her about us. Said the cops have escalated their search." He held up her key ring, jingled it. "Call your brother and tell him we have new wheels."

Lyle frowned. "Hers? I'd rather wait."

"Me too, but we can't stay here another two hours. Tell Nevin we'll meet him somewhere. In the meantime, I'm going to see if I can hide our old car better."

"Fine. Leave me a gun."

Adam shook his head. After the shootout with the deputy, there was no way Adam would let Lyle have another weapon. He hoped Lyle didn't press it; he didn't want to debate the issue in front of Renata.

"Tied up she won't give you any trouble. And I'll be right back."

Lyle shrugged and closed his eyes, but his tone didn't match his cool response: "Whatever."

Adam turned back to Renata. He didn't like leaving her. He didn't trust her. He recalled her pulling the scalpel. It had been a surprise, but it let him know what she was made of. She had plenty of grit. He checked her bindings, then took off.

Outside, Adam checked her car. It had less than a quarter tank of gas. Christ, what was it with women and gas tanks?

He grabbed the dry cleaning she had hanging in the back and popped the trunk. Jumper cables were coiled next to a gray canvas car cover that was still in the box. He dumped the clothes and removed the cover.

Stopping just long enough to scan the street, he jogged back to where they'd left the stolen car and drove it to the run-down service station at the corner. He parked the car beside several others before throwing the cover he'd found in Renata's trunk over it. The station owner would eventually find the car and report it, but by then they'd be long gone.

Next, he circled the building, checking for a pay

phone. He needed to make a call where it couldn't
be overheard.

Unfortunately, the phone on the side wall had been
vandalized: the cord cut, the receiver gone. He considered using Renata's cell phone for one quick
call—except it would leave a record of whom he
called. And he knew from experience the smallest slip
could bring down the mountain. Adam had a lot riding
on this job, professionally and personally.

Before taking this assignment, he had worked undercover in Central America, trailing arms dealers
through Mexico to the U.S. border. The FBI's investigation had begun at the request of the foreign
government and had taken over a year to establish. A
single phone call by a rookie agent—to his girlfriend—had blown the operation. Worse, it had nearly
cost Adam and another FBI Special Agent their lives.

Adam was still dealing with the career-damaging
fallout. Even though he hadn't done anything wrong,
he suffered guilt through association: The rookie had
been his partner.

On the heels of that professional snafu, came another:
His brother—who Adam had thought was dead—turned
up alive and well in the Caribbean, as a person of interest in an Interpol investigation.

At that time, he hadn't seen his brother in twenty-
seven years. And while everyone at the Bureau agreed
Adam had done nothing wrong—hell, they weren't
even sure what his brother was accused of—it was another strike against him. He'd been relegated to a back
office, forgotten.

Headlights flashed on the street. Taking cover, he
watched as a beat-up station wagon, its muffler dragging, ran a stop sign and sped off, an empty beer can
flung out the window in its wake.

He waited until it disappeared, then sprinted across the street to the closed convenience store. When the car's lights had swept the store's parking lot, he'd spotted two pay phones. The first one worked.

Adam quickly punched in numbers. His partner, Stan Beckwith, answered on the second ring.

Stan sounded half asleep until he heard Adam's voice. "Halle-fucking-lu-jah!"

"I don't have long," Adam began. "I'm at a pay phone. And everything that can go wrong has."

"No shit. I've seen the news. How much of it's true?"

"Probably too much." He updated Stan on the shooting, Lyle's injury and Renata's involvement. "If I have to, I'll fold my hand. I don't want to endanger the woman and I won't be responsible for Lyle dying."

"I'm with you. But what's Ethan's take on it?"

Adam snorted. "I haven't talked with him yet."

"I'm not surprised. He's had more pressing matters. But then you probably haven't heard the latest political scuttlebutt. Ethan's name has been tossed in the ring as a potential running mate for presidential candidate Richard Barrington."

Now Adam swore. Ethan Falco, a former CIA and FBI honcho, was the man in charge of the top-secret task force assigned to capture Willy McEdwin and sons.

A high-level security advisor to the White House, Falco had handpicked the task force players from the ranks of FBI, CIA, and other federal agencies. The task force operated outside normal channels, which gave Ethan almost limitless authority. Most important, though, it avoided the leaks that plagued the system and helped Willy to evade arrest and continue his killing crusade.

In fact, part of the task force's agenda was to flush out those moles and spies that aided the McEdwins. *At any cost.*

Adam had discovered the hard way what that meant. When he'd first been approached for the assignment, he'd jumped at the chance to get back in action; back on track career-wise. Until he heard the job involved going undercover in prison.

His first instinct had been to refuse. Except Ethan had been persuasive, promising the job would only run a week or two, max. And more, he'd offered Adam a personal favor: information that would clear his brother's name.

Then Ethan had shown his true colors and left Adam inside the prison for three months. Was that because he'd been too busy glad-handing? Or had he been purposely delaying the bust to maximize publicity? While Falco was well known in political circles, he was unknown in the private sectors. Bringing the McEdwin clan to justice would make him a household name. The type of hero a presidential campaign needed.

"Well, when you talk with Ethan," Stan continued, "find out what the hell I'm supposed to do with all this intel I'm gathering. He gives me free access to every system in the world, then won't return my phone calls."

Adam knew Stan wasn't exaggerating by much. A computer genius and former CIA contract agent, Stan had helped Ethan create an extensive criminal background for Adam. If anyone checked, he looked like a genuine felon right down to the fingerprints. And Willy McEdwin would have him thoroughly checked.

If they ever connected with Willy, that is. Lyle's contact thus far had been only with Nevin.

"Does any of this intelligence hint at the McEdwins' whereabouts?"

"Mmm, maybe." Stan's voice dropped. "I'm trailing a large shipment of plastic explosives I think is destined for the McEdwins."

"How large?"

"Fifty kilos."

"That's over a hundred pounds." Adam gripped the phone tighter.

As part of his inducement to convince Adam to take the job, Ethan Falco had claimed to have inside knowledge that Willy McEdwin was planning another bombing. A big one to mark the twentieth anniversary of his wife's death. A hundred pounds of C-4 would more than fill the bill.

"How sure are you it's for McEdwin?" Adam asked.

"Right now, I'm not. The supplier is waiting on payment. I'm hoping to trace it and confirm."

"How the hell did you find this out?"

"Got lucky."

Lucky? Right. More likely Stan had been snooping in somebody's computer files. Adam knew the other man's background included a stint as a hacker. Stan was damn good at what he did because he had an insatiable appetite for boldly going where he wasn't supposed to.

"Listen, I've got a much tamer request for your abilities." Adam pulled Renata's cell phone from his pocket and gave Stan the number. "Can you reroute service so I have my own phone to use? And mask it so it can't be traced to her cell phone?"

"That's not exactly legal."

"Has that ever stopped you?"

"I'll see what I can do. In the meantime, keep the C-4 info under your hat. If I'm right and the shipment is for Willy, I want all the credit. If it's for someone else, I can still leverage the information with my other connections and get reassigned."

"Just don't jump ship until I'm clear." Outside of Ethan, Stan was his only contact on the task force.

Adam hung up, but just as he lifted the receiver a second time, he heard footsteps. Swearing, he turned and found two men had crept up close enough to grab him.

Renata watched the door, wishing Adam would return. She didn't like him; didn't like the situation she was in. But being left tied and helpless, with Lyle, was worse.

Once Adam left, Lyle's demeanor shifted, Hyde-like. He'd made several crude remarks and hinted his strength was greater than he'd let on.

She glanced back, found him still staring at her. She couldn't hide her shudder of revulsion.

He tried for a smile and failed. "You want to know how long it's been since I was alone with a woman? Nine months, fourteen days. Before I left, my girlfriend gave me a helluva blow job. But I bet you could do better."

Renata ignored him, turning her head.

"You do know what a blow job is, don't you? I drop my pants, you hit your knees and suck till I say stop. Really no blowing to it. 'Course you being a fancy-schmancy doctor, you probably never heard it called that before."

When she didn't respond, Lyle coughed. "Am I scaring you, Doc?"

She met his stare. That was the last thing she wanted him to think. Yes, she was quaking inside, but she didn't want him to know.

"Scaring me? No. Disgusting me? Yes. But then you don't sound any different from most of the other street punks we see in here."

"Punk?" Grimacing, Lyle rolled onto his side and slowly started to ease his good leg off the table. "Let me show you just how different I am. Do you have another scalpel?"

Adam nailed the first man squarely in the jaw. He went down. His partner leaped back and drew a handgun.

Adam didn't move. The men were cops. Feds, he guessed, but not FBI. He had two choices. Rush the guy with the gun and risk getting shot, or surrender and explain the situation before they radioed the collar in. Except what could he tell them? He was sworn to the highest level of secrecy. On paper, it appeared that Adam—under his real name—had resigned from the FBI. Stan was the only person besides Ethan who could even verify his story.

The man on the ground groaned and rolled onto his feet, holding his jaw. Adam noticed neither man made an attempt to call for backup.

"Ethan Falco sent us," the man with the gun said. He seemed in charge.

Adam felt a momentary relief. He should have known Ethan would keep his own men close. There would have been multiple tracking devices on the first car, which they'd been forced to abandon along with most of their supplies. Which meant there had to be a tracking device on the cell phone he'd left with Lyle. These men must have been watching the clinic and followed Adam to the pay phone.

Adam held up his palms. "I was just getting ready to call, but I'm out of change."

"Tell him that." The man thrust a cell phone forward. It was already ringing when Adam pressed it to his ear.

A man answered. "Falco here."

"I just nailed one of your men. Too bad it wasn't you."

"Look, I know you're pissed—"

"Pissed doesn't begin to cover three months in prison."

"Hey. *Whatever it takes,* remember? Now tell me what the hell's going on down there. Why haven't you called in before?"

"I haven't exactly had a lot of privacy. And I've had my hands full trying to make certain Lyle didn't die from the bullet he took."

Ethan let loose with a string of curses. "If that kid dies . . . we lose our shot at nailing Willy."

"I have no intention of letting Lyle die. And neither does his brother."

"You've made contact with the family already?"

Adam relayed his conversation with Nevin, including his insistence that they bring Renata along. "I don't want to involve the woman any further."

"Never thought I'd hear myself say it, but I have to agree with McEdwin on this one. Keeping Lyle alive is our top priority. Do what you have to and make the woman cooperate."

"Including abducting her at gun point?"

"With the right spin, no one will hold that against you."

I'll hold it against myself, Adam thought. "Spoken like a true politician."

Headlights flashed as a car approached.

"Someone's coming." The other man snatched his cell phone back. "Gotta go."

The men ducked to the side of the building. Adam dove behind them just as a car rolled up to the corner stop sign.

It was a patrol car. The black and white unit cruised slowly down the street then turned and disappeared from sight. A second unit followed.

"They're probably getting ready to search the area," Adam said. "I've got to go back."

"We'll be in touch."

Adam raced back to the clinic. Ethan's men being this close bothered him. If the McEdwins were nearby, too, and spotted Ethan's men, it would blow everything.

On the other hand, Ethan's men would be someone Adam could safely entrust Renata to when the time came to get her to safety.

Inside the clinic, he found Lyle struggling to sit up on the exam table.

"What the hell?" Adam snapped. "Are you trying to make your wound start bleeding again?"

Sweat beaded on Lyle's upper lip. "I was trying to make myself comfortable."

Adam looked briefly at Renata, noted her distress. Something had passed between these two while he was gone, but there was no time to pursue it.

"I just spotted two patrol cars. We need to get out of here fast."

"Damn!" Lyle made a phone call, left a message.

When the cell phone rang a few seconds later, he grabbed it, relief and panic evident in his voice. "Nevin! This place is crawling with cops. Adam wants to leave the clinic, using the doctor's car."

There was silence, then, "Got it. A white Buick

LeSabre. Jessup's Truck Stop, Yanceyville. Don't forget clothes and painkillers. Can't wait to see you, too."

Lyle ended the call. "He's leaving a car north of here."

"Where are we headed from there?"

"He won't say over the phone. Instructions will be in the car. He'll call again after a short black-out."

"A what?"

"Black-out," Lyle repeated. "It's a trick the old man taught us. He won't use the same phone number more than two or three times, then he waits twenty-four hours before activating a new one."

Which makes him hard to trace, Adam thought. And difficult to get in touch with on short notice. "Somebody must have hellacious connections at the phone company."

"He only does it . . ." Lyle's voice dropped, his eyes shifting to Renata, as if worried he'd said too much in front of her.

Adam was curious about what he left unsaid. *He only does it . . .* When? When they have a big job coming up? Adam thought back to his conversation with Stan and the shipment of plastic explosives he was tracking. Did Lyle know about his father's plans?

Grabbing scissors, Adam cut Renata's restraints. "Finish dressing his wound and get him ready for travel."

"But—"

"Now!"

Moving to the exam table, she disconnected the IV tube and put a med lock over the port. Then she covered it with gauze.

"Just yank the damn IV thing out," Lyle said.

She shook her head. "You will need more fluid and

antibiotics. And I had a hard enough time getting this one started."

While she helped Lyle into a scrub suit, Adam grabbed the trashcan and dumped as much as he could inside before pulling the liner out. Destroying every shred of evidence would take too much time. And would ultimately prove moot. However, not making an attempt to disguise their presence seemed too sloppy.

When he finished, he yanked Renata's cell phone from his pocket. He knew Stan hadn't had time to change it over yet, which was okay. "Does the hospital have a clinic in Fayetteville?"

Fayetteville was about seventy miles southeast of Durham. She nodded. "But this late, they're closed."

"Call Fayetteville police. Tell them your name is Nelly Bright and you work for the cleaning service. You just left that clinic and noticed two men who may have matched the mug shots you saw on TV. Tell them they were driving a brown Chevrolet Impala, with tag number 020936L. Then complain you're losing your signal."

"I won't help you create a diversion."

He pulled his gun. "You will."

Renata stared at the large handgun. She knew from a gun safety course it was a nine-millimeter. The clip easily held fifteen rounds, maybe more. She also knew from working the ER the gun was deadly even with one bullet. *But only if the safety was off.*

Her eyes flared. Did Adam realize the safety was on?

Did she want to test him?

"No tricks this time." Adam got the telephone number from directory assistance, then held the phone while she talked, his finger over the power button.

As soon as she said, "My signal is breaking up—" he switched it off.

"Let's go." He moved toward her, held out a hand.

Renata hung back. Leaving with them—not knowing if she'd ever return—was too terrifying to contemplate.

"Can't you just leave me here?"

Adam wished he could. He didn't want someone else to worry about. But he did need her for Lyle's sake. For now he had to play hard-ass.

He motioned toward the door. "Grab the box of supplies."

Keeping his gun on her, Adam helped Lyle outside. Lyle pulled out a cigarette. "I know we're in a hurry. Just let me get two quick puffs."

"Make it fast." Adam pulled Renata to the rear of the car.

She resisted. "Are you going to lock me in the trunk?"

Lyle groaned. "Right! If I need help what are we gonna do? Pull over and pop you out of the trunk? With cops looking for us?"

Ignoring Lyle, Adam stowed the supplies and slammed the trunk closed. Then he tucked his gun behind him into his pants and caught her chin, forcing her to meet his eyes.

She flinched, her gaze a mixture of wariness and revulsion. He knew it was more than the horror of being forced to give medical care to someone she loathed. Two escaped convicts were abducting her. Men who'd been in prison, locked up without social contact—without female contact. He could imagine the direction of her fears.

"You're riding in the front, but you do have to keep down," he said. "You also have to stay tied."

"Don't." She tried to dart away, but he stopped her. Catching her wrists, he bound them with a strip of gauze he'd stashed in his pocket earlier.

"Jumping from a moving car could mess you up," he warned dispassionately. "If it didn't kill you, that is."

"I won't jump." It was a lie. First chance she got, she would try to get away.

"Good." Tugging her upper arm, he pulled her to the passenger door. When she opened her mouth to complain, he cut her off. "I hope it won't be necessary to gag you."

Frustrated, Renata swallowed her protests and climbed into the car. *Bide your time, your moment will come,* she told herself.

As they pulled out, she looked back at the clinic. The lights were off, the door locked. With her car gone, nothing looked suspicious. If the police did go door-to-door they wouldn't suspect anything. And if Clarence returned, he'd simply think she'd gone home on her own.

Her hopes sank even further as she recalled that she worked second shift tomorrow. It could be late afternoon before anyone even missed her. How long after that before someone called the police? And unless they suspected foul play, what was the rule on reporting missing adults? Forty-eight hours?

She closed her eyes, offered a brief prayer for her own safety.

The trip to Yanceyville, a sleepy community about an hour north, was uneventful except for the gusty winds and rain that steadily increased. Between the flood and the false Fayetteville sighting Renata phoned in, the cops were busy elsewhere.

Adam watched the rearview mirror, wondered if Ethan's men were trailing them or simply monitoring the tracking device. He hoped the latter, not wanting to arouse suspicion.

Jessup's Truck Stop was the only business on that particular stretch of highway. Surrounded by dark woods and pastures, the parking lot was crowded with eighteen-wheelers in spite of the large spray-painted sign that read "NO GAS." Many of the trucks were probably stranded until road conditions cleared and fuel was available; others were waiting for businesses to reopen, or for instructions where to leave their freight.

In the back of the lot sat a white Buick LaSabre with dark tinted windows. Adam parked Renata's car and approached the Buick cautiously.

Inside was a sheet of paper with typed instructions. A handwritten postscript said SUPPLIES IN TRUNK. Adam read the directions, memorizing what he could. They were headed toward the Appalachian Mountains, to a rural area of northern Virginia. He hoped all the roads between here and there were passable.

He checked the contents of the Buick's trunk to make certain Nevin hadn't left another handgun. A cooler sat beside a flashlight and a coil of rope. A pair of handcuffs, key in the lock, was included along with some clothes for Lyle and a bottle of prescription painkillers.

Adam read the bottle's label. The powerful narcotic was familiar. It received a lot of press about its potential for abuse. The street demand for the drug was so high many small pharmacies refused to carry it after being targeted for break-ins.

The cooler held water, some peanut butter, crackers and a pocketknife. No ice. Judging by these supplies, they weren't expected to be on the road long. He slid the knife in his pocket along with the prescription.

Behind him, someone coughed.

Adam spun around, gun drawn. He scanned the shadowy tree line. While he couldn't see anyone, he sensed a person about twenty feet to his left. He raised his gun, finger on the trigger. If it was Ethan's men again, he'd shoot them.

"Come out, slowly."

"Easy there." A wiry man not much older than Lyle, stepped forward, a rifle in hand. "I'm a friend of Nevin's."

Adam lowered his weapon.

The man did likewise. "Just verifying it was you. We get our share of riffraff here, so I was reluctant to leave the car with the keys in it and all."

"Appreciate it." Adam tried to get a better look at the man without being obvious. How close a friend was he? "Is Nevin around? Lyle's eager to see him."

"Nobody sees him. Man's a ghost."

"Safer that way," He shrugged, faking indifference.

"Make sure you leave keys in your vehicle so we can drive it off."

Adam's ears perked at the word *we*. How many more friends did Nevin have tucked in the woods? "Will do. Anything else?"

"Yeah. Tell Lyle that Griz says to keep his eye to the sky."

"I'll give him the message."

But the man had already disappeared into the mist.

Adam closed the trunk and moved the Buick closer to Renata's car. He helped Lyle into the Buick.

The younger man moved slowly, cursing frequently. "Did Nevin leave anything for pain?"

Adam dug the pills out of his pocket. "Should I check with Renata before you take these?"

Lyle took the bottle, scanned the label. "Nah, I've taken this stuff before. And the doc would probably rather see me suffer without anything."

"By the way, I met a friend of yours."

"Who?"

"Griz." Adam repeated the message. "What the hell does that mean? Should we expect trouble?"

"It means they're planning a diversion."

"What kind?"

"Not sure. I'll have to check with Nevin."

While Lyle tried to get comfortable, Adam transferred the medical supplies. Then he went to get Renata. He briefly debated substituting handcuffs for the gauze but didn't want to waste any more time. Or risk Ethan's men coming in for a closer look.

Adam opened her car door and reached to help her.

She leaned away. "Let me stay in my car. Please! I swear I won't call the police or tell anyone."

He knew Griz and Company were still watching them; probably waiting to report to Nevin that they'd departed. Leaving her behind would place her in even greater danger: They wouldn't tolerate a witness. Adam tugged her out, helped her stand. She was trembling. Afraid. Until he'd touched her. Now her eyes flashed with boldness. In the face of her fear, she had spirit.

"Sorry, but I'm starting to like having you around," he said.

Chapter Seven

They drove for five hours, crossing into Virginia and then weaving north. Adam pressed hard, knowing it was critical to reach their destination while it was dark.

Their route had been well chosen. The roads had some traffic but no roadblocks. While Virginia didn't have the same degree of flooding that North Carolina had, parts of the state had received record rainfalls. And, according to the radio, as the new storm system brought more precipitation to the mid-Atlantic, flood warnings would soon be posted along the entire eastern seaboard.

Just before dawn, Adam made the last turn onto a rocky lane that led to a large barn near the edge of a recently mowed hayfield. He glanced at Renata. She hadn't said much since they'd left Yanceyville. Which made him wonder what she was thinking.

When they stopped, Lyle roused from a drug-induced slumber. "Are we there yet?"

"Afraid so." Adam reread the directions. *Follow lane to barn.* That was it? He grabbed the flashlight. "Let me check it out. I'll be right back."

Renata leaned forward, watched him disappear.

"What's he doing now?" Lyle asked.

"He went inside." She heard the back seat squeak as Lyle shifted.

"You sound nervous, Doc. Afraid?"

"No."

He started to laugh, then groaned, as if in pain. The sound was macabre. Practically nonhuman.

She glanced over her shoulder. In the dark, and with Lyle lying down, she wasn't able to see anything. "Are you okay?"

For a moment he didn't answer, then he rasped, "No. I need your help."

With her hands tied she couldn't do much. Concerned, she looked out the window, but saw no sign of Adam. "Tell me what's wrong," she said.

"What's wrong? I think I explained earlier. Nine months, fourteen days. I'm so horny, my dick hurts." Again that creepy, disembodied laughter followed.

The painkillers. Lyle was high.

When Adam mentioned the narcotic, she warned that Lyle shouldn't self-medicate. Besides altering his moods and perceptions, the drug could mask the severity of his injury, conceal the symptoms of other problems.

In Lyle's case, the drug seemed to amplify his innate nastiness. When she'd been left with him at the clinic, she'd learned that he wasn't nearly as strong as he'd acted, which made his remarks no less repulsive.

"Why don't you climb back here and sit with me," Lyle whispered. "And I'll show you what you can do to make me feel better."

Renata jerked as cold fingers brushed against her neck then tightened, pulling her hair.

The inside of the empty barn had enough room for several vehicles. Adam's curiosity about who owned the property and what connection they had to the McEdwins spiked. Did the owner realize he housed fugitives? The FBI had long suspected the McEdwins had others helping them—finally they'd have names.

A sagging bench was tacked against one wall. Beneath the bench were four five-gallon containers of gasoline, more than enough to fill the car.

On top of the bench was another cooler. A note and map were tucked under the edge. Adam read them, then returned to the Buick.

As soon as he climbed back in, he knew something had happened. Renata had her back pressed to the car door and was agitated.

"Everything okay?"

"Terrific." Lyle was sitting up now, his breathing labored. "Oow."

Adam turned. "You shouldn't move without help."

"The help's tied up. What did you find inside?"

"This." Adam passed Lyle the note and map before driving the car inside the barn. "We head to West Virginia next. Any of those places look familiar?"

Lyle tossed the map back over the seat. "Shit. To be honest, it's all familiar. I did a lot of deer hunting in that area when I was younger. Nevin mentioned using 'interim solutions' to hide us during daylight hours. But I expected more than a friggin' barn."

"Me, too, kid. But it hides the car and gives us a place to catch some shut-eye."

Adam just hoped their next destination wasn't another *interim solution*. Yes, he would expect the McEdwins to be extremely cautious about meeting Lyle, especially with a manhunt underway. However, the McEdwins weren't in Adam's shoes: fleeing police with a wounded man and a kidnapped doctor, in a car that would eventually be reported stolen to protect the owner.

Shutting off the engine, he climbed out and shut the barn doors. Then he opened Renata's car door, helped her stand. He noted the dark smudges beneath her eyes. She hadn't slept during the night, and had to be feeling tired and stressed.

Hell, he was exhausted. It had been over thirty-six hours since he'd slept. He withdrew the pocketknife and flipped the blade open.

"Raise your hands." He sliced through the gauze.

He knew she hated being tied. He empathized, remembered having his hands and feet shackled while being at the mercy of another. He had hated it, too.

He took her right wrist, examining it for signs of chafing. He trailed his fingers lightly over the bruises he'd caused when they'd fought over the scalpel. They bothered him.

"We're stuck here for the day. If you need to use the bathroom, we've got to do it now, before the sun rises."

She looked around the barn. "Where?"

"Outside."

Her cheeks flushed. "Can I go alone?"

From the back seat, Lyle snickered. "Hey man, I'll take her."

"No!" She pulled away, glancing over her shoulder.

Adam frowned. He suspected something had passed between these two earlier, and knowing Lyle, it hadn't been pleasant. He stepped closer to her. "Come on."

Outside, dawn lightened the veil across the sky. The ground surrounding the barn was muddy, saturated with rain.

"You know it's pointless to run," he said.

Renata looked at the empty fields and nodded. The urge to flee was strong, but as desperate as she felt, she wasn't stupid. She'd been able to wiggle free of Lyle's grip in the car after underestimating him; she wouldn't make the same mistake with Adam.

To her surprise, Adam turned his back, offering her

a modicum of privacy. She squinted, searching for a bush, a tree, but the landscape was barren. Semi-darkness was her only cover.

Resentful, she eyed his silhouette, knew his courteousness was merely an act. He was too close and the sky was growing light. If she tried to escape, it would be easy enough to shoot her.

But would he? She recalled his not retaliating for her stabbing him and his having the gun on safety earlier. Neither act made him a saint.

He seemed to know instinctively when to turn. That, or he peeked. Avoiding his eyes, Renata walked straight for the barn.

He hooked her arm as she passed, stopping her. "Anything you'd like to talk about?"

She looked at his hand. "Sure. When will I be released?"

"Soon. But—"

A dull *whoosh-whoosh* echoed in the distance, interrupting their conversation.

Renata recognized the sound. Spotting the helicopter, she twisted, tried to tug free. If she could just break away long enough to wave her arms and get the pilot's attention.

Adam pulled his gun. "Inside. Now!"

She resisted. "No! They might be looking for me."

Her five-foot-three was no match for his six-four. With ease he yanked her back into the barn. She stumbled, then righted herself.

Adam peered out the door. As the helicopter passed overhead, he stepped outside again. Renata tried to rush past, but he stopped her. She read the lettering on the chopper's underbelly as it disappeared.

"False alarm," he said, releasing her and closing the door. "Acme Timber—aerial survey."

From behind them, Lyle let out a noisy sigh. "Cripes. I thought we were fucking goners."

Renata turned. Lyle had the car door open, a cigarette in his hand. He could barely breathe yet he was smoking. The man was brainless.

He blew a streamer of smoke in her direction and coughed. "Yeah, I know. It'll kill me. But you're hoping I die anyway, right? Make your life simpler."

She opened her mouth, then closed it, as his barb struck too close to home. Did she really think that? Wish for his death so she could be freed? She mentally sidestepped the question. If Lyle died, there was no guarantee Adam would release her.

Adam moved in and held out a bottle of water and a package of crackers. "Eat, then you can check him."

He offered the same to Lyle, who took the water to swallow more pain pills, but set the crackers aside untouched.

"I'm too tired to eat."

"You should try anyway." Adam helped him back in the car. "It might help you regain some strength."

"I doubt a couple crackers will make much difference," Lyle said. "Right, Doc?"

Renata poked her last bite into her mouth, more hungry than she'd realized. She cleaned her hands before donning latex gloves.

"Everything helps. Especially the water. With the blood you've lost, fluids are vital."

"What the hell is that for then?" Lyle pointed to the IV she had reconnected.

"To keep your blood volume stable. And to get the antibiotic into your system quicker." She pointed to his bandage. Blood had seeped through the layers of gauze, staining them. "When you strain, you restart the bleeding."

But Lyle was already drifting to sleep. When she finished, Adam carried the supplies back to the trunk.

Renata took advantage of the moment to study her surroundings. Faint light seeped in from outside. The barn was quite old and weather-beaten, and had either been deserted for a long time or had been emptied just for them. The thick layer of straw strewn across the dirt appeared to be fresh and wouldn't show tire tracks or footprints. She didn't detect any animal smells, or see signs of any farm equipment, making her wonder if the barn was used solely as a safe haven for criminals.

She watched Adam refill the car's gas tank using the five-gallon cans. "Are we taking off again?"

He shook his head. "Just staying prepared."

"For a quick getaway?"

"If necessary."

When he finished, he came up behind her, herding her toward the open car door. "Climb back in. We need to get some sleep."

"I'm not tired."

"Fine. You still have to get in the car. And I still have to restrain you again."

Renata had mentally prepared herself for this; knew she wouldn't remain unbound. But unlike before when he'd tied her, she had a plan. She had spent part of the car ride discreetly loosening the old gauze. She was confident that given more time, she could work free of her new bonds.

The challenge was what to do, then. Timing was critical, as she'd only get one chance.

She got back in the front seat and watched as Adam knelt beside her. When he grasped her wrists, she pulled back, putting up token resistance so he wouldn't become suspicious.

Then she heard the *chink* of metal, and began struggling in earnest. "No handcuffs!"

"You'd loosen the gauze sooner or later, and I can't risk it." He depressed a lever to recline the seat before putting an arm to her shoulder, to force her backwards. "Just in case you change your mind about snoozing."

She scowled. They both knew reclining would make it even more difficult to move with her hands cuffed.

Adam climbed behind the wheel and slouched toward the doorframe. Ignoring her, he yawned and closed his eyes. Renata watched in amazement as he almost immediately fell asleep.

God, she hated him.

Adam watched her through slitted eyes, wondered what she was thinking. He knew the types of things that went through a hostage's mind, was familiar with the psychology of a prisoner. But that didn't tell him her personal slant on the situation.

Renata was a strong woman, a problem solver. Yes, she was scared but she wouldn't let fear stop her. First and foremost she'd try to escape. He needed to anticipate her; watch her closely. Which wouldn't be difficult. She was easy on the eyes.

Too easy. The pull of attraction surprised him. She wasn't his type. He preferred redheads. Tall ones. Short women were hard for men his height to kiss— unless you were in bed with them.

Of course he hadn't had any trouble kissing her the night before, when he'd needed to confiscate her pager. He'd damn near forgotten his mission.

He eyed her mouth, tried to analyze what about it fascinated him. It had to be those full, pouty lips. They looked swollen. Sexy. Just begging for a kiss.

His gaze drifted lower. He remembered the body search, how he'd tried to keep it impersonal. Hard to do when she was one hundred percent female: lush and curved in all the right places. The memory made Adam grow hard. *Not good.*

He tried to think of willing females who'd be available when this assignment wrapped. Several names came to mind; women who thought of him only in sexual terms. Like Lizzy Yale.

Lizzy had lived next door when Adam was in high school. She knew what he endured at home, had called the police once when his father had been on a particularly vicious rampage. She brought flowers to the hospital afterwards.

Lizzy was twice his age, divorced a handful of times. She was also the horniest woman Adam had ever met. Or at least that was how he'd thought of her when he was sixteen. Lizzy had let him crash on her couch a few times. Until she walked in on him in the bathroom one day. He'd been naked and she'd seen it all. Especially the bruises and scars he tried hard to hide.

But Lizzy had focused on his groin, had boldly touched him, cupped him. *There.* Told him that with his face and his penis no woman would care about anything else. *"And unlike love, great sex will never break your heart."* Her motto. Then she'd taken him to bed and taught him a thing or two about toe curling.

For a time that had been enough. Raw sex. Physical gratification. Lizzy had been right. Most women didn't care about anything else. When he was clothed, he looked fine and they clamored to be at his side. When he was naked, they turned their heads and clamored for him to get *inside.* He obliged.

He blinked, purposely squashing those memories. He'd long ago given up his libidinous ways. So why was it just now dawning on him that he'd also given up the dream of finding someone who'd care for *all* of him?

Morning turned to early afternoon. Except for the hum of soft rain, and Lyle's snoring, the barn remained quiet. No outside noise reached Renata's ears. No cars. No planes. It was as if the world beyond had ceased to exist.

She kept expecting—hoping—that the the doors would be thrown open as a SWAT team swept in and rescued her. It never happened. Minutes seemed to tick forward, then skip backward, as if time were as much a hostage as she.

It was impossible to close her eyes. She worried that in sleep she might miss an opportunity for escape.

Bored, she studied Adam as he slept. Grudgingly she admitted the man was in top physical condition. Even relaxed, his arms bulged and his abs rippled. That type of physique was only acquired with serious weight lifting, which he'd probably had plenty of time to do in prison.

A giant of a man, he was so tall he barely had room to lean back in the car. As it was, his head was tilted at an awkward angle against the door frame. The thought that he'd have a sore neck when he awoke gave her a small amount of comfort.

She started to turn away when her eye caught his denim-clad leg. Outlined perfectly in his pocket, was the handcuff key. Within reach, yet unattainable. She sighed, wished she had the nerve to go for it. But those jeans were just a little too tight; the key a little too close to that bulge beneath his fly.

She averted her eyes and fumbled with the cuffs,

testing them. She squeezed her fingers together. If she could just compress her knuckles slightly, slip her hand free—

She sensed Adam's eyes were open and looked up. The man was uncanny. He never said anything, just shook his head and went back to sleep. Damn him.

Angry and frustrated, Renata leaned back, determined to come up with a plan.

At some point she must have drifted off, because when she awoke, Adam was gone. Disoriented, she studied the patches of light shifting between boards. Judging by the shadows, it had to be late afternoon. She couldn't have slept more than an hour or two. Had they left her?

She scrambled to sit up.

"Relax, doll." Lyle's voice drifted across the seat. "I'm still here. Care to join me?"

"Drop dead."

Lyle coughed. "Your big, bad savior ain't here, so I suggest you watch your smart mouth."

"Where's—"

At that moment one of the barn doors opened and Adam stepped inside. Relief flashed over her.

"Speak of the devil," Lyle snorted. "Actually, his timing's perfect. I've got to piss. Bad."

Lyle started complaining as soon as Adam drew close. Adam helped him outside, then returned and unfastened the handcuffs.

Renata rubbed her wrists, her arms tingling from poor circulation. "Maybe next time you could leave them a bit looser."

"Sore?"

At her nod, he grasped her wrists and straightened her arms before lightly pressing his fingers into her forearms. The discomfort disappeared as he worked the flesh.

She marveled at how he knew which muscles were most tense and where to rub to ease the cramping. Was that because he'd spent so much time in handcuffs himself?

He dropped her wrists and stepped away. "The rain's stopped and we'll be leaving soon. So I'll take you outside now."

Renata would have loved to refuse his offer . . . but she couldn't.

Outside, the sun was getting ready to slip behind the trees, the sky muddy with clouds that promised more rain. It was hard to believe an entire day had passed. Once again Adam gave her privacy to relieve herself, while he remained nearby. His actions irritated her. Thoughtful or cruel, everything this man did would be wrong as long as he held her against her will.

Back inside the barn, he tossed her a bottle of water and another pack of crackers. For a moment, she debated refusing the food simply to exercise her right to defy him. Except that she knew her body needed every bit of fuel she could get. If the opportunity to run arose, she had to be ready.

Adam spread a map out on the hood of the car, studied it intently. He refolded it and turned to her. "You need to check Lyle before we hit the road. We'll be driving all night again."

She bristled over being given orders. "How much longer do you intend to keep me?"

"I haven't decided."

"That's not an answer—"

He cut her off and moved away. "You're alive. And uninjured. Like I promised. Some days, that's as good as it gets."

"At least tell me where we're going," she called after him.

Lyle began loosening his pants. "If you're real nice, maybe I'll tell you where we're headed."

"I don't want to know that badly."

"Snooty bitch."

Disregarding him, she took his vital signs and changed the bandages. Once again the gauze was saturated with fresh blood.

"This isn't good."

"No shit. But we both know there's not much you can do," Lyle's lip curled. "My brother will get me in to see a real doctor, so just throw a new bandage on it for now."

Renata had been about to snap back when Adam rejoined them, a serious look on his face.

"We need to hurry. I just heard on the radio that there are flood watches and tornado warnings all along the east coast. It'll be a bad night for driving."

Renata prayed for rain. Lots of it. In hopes it would slow them down enough to let the police catch up.

At first it seemed the weather couldn't make up its mind. Rain sputtered intermittently, then gradually grew steady and heavy. She fought to remain awake, casting her eyes to the side of the road when the hypnotic sweep of the windshield wipers made her eyelids feel they had weights attached.

Over and over, her thoughts returned to the clinic back in Durham. Had anyone discovered her missing? Noticed her briefcase still in her office? Or found clues in the exam room? She had purposely stuffed a section of bloody cloth in the supply drawer. Would someone recognize it as a clue and call the police?

Neither man had attempted to avoid leaving finger-prints behind. Arrogance or carelessness? She'd bet on the former. At least it wouldn't take the police long to confirm who had abducted her.

She bit her lip, worrying again about how her mother would react to the news. Her older sister and brother lived in Denver, so they'd be there for her. But Renata knew her mother; she'd make herself sick imagining the worst.

They had left Virginia, skipping across Maryland before entering Pennsylvania. It was a deceptive route; she knew their ultimate destination was West Virginia. But their route was convoluted because they bypassed most towns.

She watched Adam in her peripheral vision. Each time a car went by, his eyes drifted to the rearview mirror. *Please be a cop,* became her silent mantra.

They rounded yet another curve and this time, just a short distance ahead, she spotted flashing red and blue lights. The road was blocked by a patrol car.

Renata leaned forward in disbelief, her eyes wide with anticipation. "Finally!"

Adam hit the brakes. The car hydroplaned slightly on the slick roads as he slowed and pulled onto the shoulder.

He pointed to the luminous sign beyond the patrol car: BRIDGE OUT.

"Don't get your hopes up. Rain's washed out the bridge. We have to turn around." He reached over and unfastened her seat belt. "But just as a precaution, get down on the floorboard."

Adam put the car in reverse as a slicker-clad officer climbed out of the patrol car. Ducking his head against the wind and rain, he waved a flashlight as he made his way toward their car.

The cop probably wanted nothing more than to advise them which way to detour, but Adam couldn't let him near the car. If he recognized them, or swept his flashlight inside and saw Renata in handcuffs and an injured man hooked up to an IV, it was over.

Adam hit the gas. With a squeal of tires, he reversed, speeding backwards down the road before spinning into a three-point turn.

In the rearview mirror he saw the cop pivot and shine his light at the rear of the car, trying to get the tag number. Adam sped off, churning up mud.

Seconds later, flashing lights appeared on the horizon behind them. He floored it, grateful for the Buick's powerful V-8 engine and a full tank of gas.

With luck he could outrun the patrol car. But outrunning the radio was another story. The cop was undoubtedly broadcasting their location and would soon have help. The dark, the rain, and the fact that Adam was unfamiliar with the roads would add to the cop's advantage and erode their slight head start.

He spotted a sign, a junction for a main highway he was vaguely familiar with. Increasing his speed, he turned. The road was busier than he liked but he didn't dare cut down some dirt road and risk a dead end. He also needed help.

"Lyle!"

The younger man didn't respond.

"Damn it, wake up!"

"He took more painkillers," Renata said. "Even if he comes to, I doubt he'll be much help."

Adam glanced at her, then shoved the map and flashlight across the seat. "Fine. If you want to live, find a way to get us out of here!"

Chapter Eight

Adam thought he had lost the cop. Then he spotted the telltale flash of lights behind them. He punched it, eager to increase their lead.

"Well?" he prompted Renata.

"Turn left on Highway 56 and follow it to Highway 96," she said. "It will take us south."

At the intersection, Adam turned sharply, felt the tires lose traction and become useless against the wet pavement. The car skidded, started to spin. "Hold on."

Steering into the slide, he regained control, but instead of slowing he shot straight ahead, the gas pedal floored.

He spared a glance at Renata, saw her huddled on the floor, her knuckles bloodless from gripping the flashlight. He knew she was terrified, yet there was nothing he could do to reassure her.

He backed off the gas slightly and grabbed the flashlight. "You can get up now."

She awkwardly climbed back into the seat. "Damn you, Adam! You could have killed us driving like that!"

It was the first time she'd said his name aloud. That she'd used it swearing didn't bother him; it wasn't his real name. Still it had been a moment of personal connection. A lost moment.

"I had the car under control the entire time." He

reached over to refasten her seat belt and had to resist the urge to touch her cheek.

"Does the term 'too fast for conditions' mean anything?"

Her voice quavered, husky from restraint. Adam knew she covered her fear with anger. She'd been pushed beyond a reasonable point numerous times.

He squeezed her fingers briefly, released them. "Keep the map handy. The weather is getting worse and we have to get off the road as soon as possible. That means I'll need to find a short cut to our next stop."

That he even bothered explaining surprised Renata. He didn't have to. Even more surprising was the way he'd brushed her hand, as if offering silent comfort. It was one more clue that in small ways, perhaps even subconsciously, Adam seemed concerned about her well-being. She needed to play on that. Exploit—encourage even—any sign of softening.

"Where are we headed?" she asked. "And I'll start checking for alternate routes."

"You're volunteering to help?"

She didn't miss the sarcasm. "Actually, I'm helping myself. I'd rather look now instead of when we're being pursued. And with Lyle passed out, I'm your only navigator."

For a moment Adam remained quiet. Then he handed over the flashlight again.

"I need to end up on Highway 150, in the Yew Mountains."

"Then where?"

"The other roads won't be listed. Just get me to Highway 150. And we have to avoid all cities, so think rural."

She studied the West Virginia map, first found

where they were headed. After a few minutes, she rattled off an alternate route.

Adam slowed, not fully trusting her. "Show me."

Turning the map toward him, she held the flashlight and pointed to the route. He studied it, only taking his eyes from the road for brief seconds.

"Thanks," he said finally. "It'll take us a few hours to get there. Why don't you try to grab some shut-eye?"

She shook her head. "I'm used to not sleeping."

"In that case, you can talk to me. Keep me awake."

"If you're tired, pull over."

He laughed. "Nice try. Actually, I'm curious why you pursued medicine. Was your father a doctor and you decided to follow in his footsteps?"

Renata's first thought was to not answer. Then she remembered her earlier resolve to draw Adam out. This was an opportunity to build a bond . . . or perhaps distract him while the police caught up.

Still, she chose her words carefully. "My father was an auto mechanic. He died of congestive heart failure after ignoring chest pains he thought were indigestion. I was only two."

"You were an only child?"

"No. I have an older sister and brother."

"It must have been difficult for your mother, being left to raise three kids by herself."

"She told me she got through it because she simply didn't have time to grieve. She juggled three jobs and three children."

"That had to be tough, too."

Tough? Renata remembered living in their car after they lost their Chicago home. From there they moved to a one-room apartment in a neighborhood so bad she wasn't allowed outside.

"So was it your father's untimely death that prompted you to become a doctor?" he asked.

"My best friend died from an asthma attack when we were in junior high. By the time they got her to a hospital it was too late." While she didn't remember her father, she did recall the pain of losing her friend and the helpless feeling of not knowing what to do.

She glanced at Adam, wanting to change the subject. "What about you?"

"Me?" He checked the road behind them. "As in, what did my father do? Or why did I decide to pursue a life in crime?"

"Both."

"My father was a world-class bastard. He ran my mother off when I was eight. I never forgave her for leaving me behind."

Renata detected a chilling change in his voice. "Your father was abusive?"

"And alcoholic. I grew up in the slums. A perfect childhood for a prospective criminal, wouldn't you say?"

"Perhaps. It's also an overused cop-out for not taking responsibility as an adult, for your actions. Few people are truly unable to distinguish wrong from right, regardless of their upbringing. And nothing negates the ability to choose a better life."

"You are right."

Once again he surprised her. "It's not too late for you," she rushed on. "You could change. It's apparent you're well educated, if not formally, then self-taught—"

"None of which matters if I go back to prison." He pointed to a road sign. "And we'll have to continue the pop psychology quiz later. Highway 96 is two miles ahead. Tell me again where we go from there."

* * *

They didn't talk anymore as the weather grew worse, the rain blinding. Twice they were forced to find new routes because of flooded roads. Lyle remained asleep.

The sky was starting to lighten in the east when Adam finally stopped at a gated road leading onto private property. The road was muddy, barely passable, and it ended abruptly at the crest of a hill amid a stand of pine trees.

He grabbed the flashlight. "There's supposed to be a cabin here. I'll be right back." Tugging his collar up, he climbed out.

From the back seat, Lyle stirred. "Is he gone?"

She turned, cautiously watching over her shoulder. "He'll be right back."

Lyle groaned, coughed. "Christ! Don't tell me you're feeling sorry for him because he had a rough childhood. Well, I did too, you know. How about some pity for me?"

Renata didn't respond, uncertain of his mood. The last time he'd grabbed her, he'd been too weak to do more than pull her hair. This time though, she knew to stay out of his reach.

"I kept waiting for him to tell you what happened to his last girlfriend," Lyle continued. "She disappeared, you know. They're calling her number seven. Want to know why? Huh? Do you?"

"No. I don't."

"Aww, come on. Surely you've wondered about those six scars on his chest?"

"I haven't seen his chest or his scars!"

"Yeah, right," Lyle sneered. "Actually, they're notches. One for each person he's killed."

Killed? She thought back to the newscast she'd

watched at the clinic. "I thought he was serving time for stolen property."

"I know. Ain't it cool? He's good."

Bile burned the back of her throat as she thought of the times she'd been alone with Adam. Times he could have . . .

Lyle gave a weak laugh. "So if a seventh notch appears, that means they found his girlfriend's body. Hell, you may end up as number eight."

Outside, Adam was having trouble locating the cabin. The downpour didn't help. He swept the flashlight around several times before spotting a structure. He approached it cautiously. In the darkness and with all the rain, they might have taken a wrong turn.

When he got a better look at the place, he hoped that was the case. More shed than cabin, the structure was maybe twelve feet square with a door that hung by one hinge. He swept the light inside.

One wall had a broken window, letting water blow in. Part of the dirt floor had already turned to mud. This couldn't be right.

He started to turn, then spied a box covered with a blue plastic tarp. Swearing, he uncovered it. The box held bottled water and more peanut butter crackers, along with canned sardines, three apples, and a lone blanket folded at the bottom. A cryptic note indicated they should leave the Buick at the gate before five-thirty. That was barely twenty minutes from now. A different car would be left later, with more instructions.

How much later? Adam wanted to crumple the paper. Instead he lit the kerosene lantern hanging on a nail. The additional light made the interior look worse.

This place could barely be classified as shelter. By comparison, the barn they had stayed in looked like a palace. They'd be more comfortable inside the car than here.

He reread the note, not liking any of it. Especially the idea of being without wheels, without a means for escape. With Lyle injured, they were sitting ducks. And what if Lyle took a turn for the worse, became sicker? How would Adam get him to a hospital?

To his surprise, Lyle was awake when he returned to the car.

"I heard we had a close call," Lyle said. "What happened?"

Adam told him about outrunning the cop. "And now we're supposed to leave this car back at the front gate. Which doesn't seem too smart since they probably have an APB out for it."

"If Nevin said leave it, it'll be fine. Trust me, no one will bother us here."

"I wouldn't bother us here. This place is a dump."

"Then I'm sure we won't be here long, but I'll try reaching my brother anyway."

Adam helped Lyle, then carried their supplies in before returning for Renata. While the distance from car to shed was minimal, they both got soaked.

The wind picked up, rattling the shed.

Looking around, she shook her head in disgust. "Lyle shouldn't stay here."

"None of us should. But we need a different car."

She lifted her wrists for him to unfasten her handcuffs.

Adam pointed to the tarp he'd spread on the ground. "Sit first."

When she complied, he knelt down, but instead of

freeing her hands he bound her ankles with a piece of rope.

She tried to wrestle away but couldn't. "Damn you! Don't!"

"I'll untie you when I return."

"When will that be?"

"Soon."

"Don't worry. I'll watch her," Lyle said.

"No! Take me with you," Renata pleaded.

Her distress bothered Adam. He ran a hand under her jaw. She recoiled as if he'd struck her, repugnance etched in her features. He noticed Lyle paying close attention. Too close. Had the little prick been terrorizing her? Probably. And who knew what he'd said. Or done.

Adam shot Lyle a warning look. "I'll be right back."

As soon as he returned to the car, he pulled Renata's cell phone from his pocket. Unfortunately, Stan still didn't have it reprogrammed. He turned it off. In a true emergency, he could use the other cell phone.

He wondered briefly how close Ethan's men were, and whether they were the only two following. While exact details of the bust had yet to be finalized, once Adam connected with the McEdwins, Ethan would lead a team to make the arrests. Which might get hairy considering the McEdwins had sworn not to be taken alive. Ethan would definitely need more than two men.

Adam reached the gate and climbed out of the car. Just in time. Headlights appeared on the road. He dropped back behind some brush to watch the approach of a boxy SUV. The vehicle stopped at the gate.

Adam's hopes rose. If they left the SUV, he'd drive it back to the cabin. Sleeping in a car beat the hell out of the tumbledown shack.

But the SUV's stop was temporary. A man jumped out of the passenger side and ran to the Buick. Not even bothering to look over his shoulder, the man cranked the engine and pulled forward, disappearing down the road behind the SUV.

Disappointed, Adam memorized the tag number. He'd been unable to get a clear look at the men, wondered if they'd return soon with another car.

By the time he jogged back to the cabin, his clothes were waterlogged, his shoes muddy. Inside he found Lyle curled on the tarp. He was pale, his clothes and hair soaked. A dark stain spotted his pants where blood seeped through.

"What happened?" Adam asked.

"I needed to take a leak . . . got dizzy," Lyle said.

"He almost passed out," Renata said. "Uncuff me."

Adam quickly released her then watched as she checked Lyle. While he wasn't running a fever, he was shivering. They all were, but Lyle's reserves had to be dangerously low.

"Those wet clothes will leach his body heat. Get him undressed and wrap him in that blanket while I get another IV started and change his bandage." She looked sharply at Lyle before continuing. "It's important that these dressings stay dry and—"

Lyle cut her off. "Yeah, well, your advice would be easier to follow if we weren't on the run, in the rain."

As soon as she finished, Adam helped her to her feet. "The storm's getting worse, so I suggest we go outside now if you need to."

Renata was almost too tired to care about basic body functions. She'd had little sleep in the last forty-eight hours, with maximum stress. The combination left her exhausted. And punchy.

She couldn't stop thinking about what Lyle told her earlier. She prided herself on being a good judge of people, and she honestly couldn't see Adam as a cold-blooded murderer. Had he truly killed six people and gotten away with it? Or was Lyle simply tormenting her? And why did it matter?

Outside, Adam once again gave her rudimentary privacy, but there was no place to run. The rain fell in torrents, soaking her anew. When she finished, she followed him back, nearly colliding with him when he stopped short of the door.

"Watch." He stood close to the eaves where the rain fell in sheets. Cupping his hands, he caught the water then scrubbed his face.

"Try it," he encouraged. "It's the closest thing to a shower we're going to get. And we can't get any wetter standing here."

Tentative, Renata cupped the cold rainwater and sluiced it over her face. It felt surprisingly refreshing. She repeated the motion, combing water through her hair, then wringing out the excess. She couldn't imagine what she looked like at this point—she'd been in and out of rain, living in the same clothes for two days. And she'd long ago lost the elastic holding her hair back.

She shivered as the wind gusted. The temperatures were cooler and when combined with the wind and rain, it felt downright icy. Even in July.

"Cold?" he asked.

"No."

"Guess that means you wouldn't be honest enough to tell me if Lyle's been bothering you, either." He turned toward her, his voice low. "If he's done something that's upset you, I want to know."

Her jaw tightened. "Upset me? He said you killed some men. And your girlfriend. And that you have scars to prove it."

Adam turned his face up to the rain, scrubbed it yet

again, buying time before answering. He should have known Lyle would tell her that. To the kid's hoodlum mentality, killing someone was the ultimate badge of criminal high achievement.

He could imagine how she felt hearing that. So how could he dispel her fears without destroying the myth he purposely created in prison?

"Don't believe everything you hear. Some rumors are baseless, but it's advantageous to let them stand."

"What about your girlfriend?"

"I make it a point to never discuss past affairs. But— just between us—last time I saw her, she was alive."

"Just between us? It sounds like you want Lyle to believe something different. How do I know you're not lying to both of us?"

"You don't. So trust your instincts. And if it's any comfort, I'll try not to leave you alone with him again." He drew close and caught her chin in his hand. "I will not let anyone harm you, Renata. You have my word. Now, come on. You're shivering." He held the broken door open.

Inside, the lantern light cast flickering shadows around the small enclosure. Lyle snored unnaturally loud, a clue that he'd helped himself to painkillers again. She checked his IV.

When she looked up, Adam held out a bottle of water, then pointed to the box of supplies. "Sardines or crackers?"

She wrinkled her nose but took the water. "I see the menu's no better than the accommodations."

"You expected a chocolate on your pillow?"

"Right. And French-milled soap in the bathroom." She struggled to remove the cap on her bottle. The cheap plastic threads had stripped, leaving it to spin uselessly.

Adam offered the bottle he'd just uncapped. Shrugging, she traded with him.

He gave her the crackers while he ate a tin of sardines. "We'll save the apples for later."

When they finished eating, Adam lowered himself to the tarp-covered ground close to where Lyle slept. Sitting with his back against the wall, he pointed, indicating she should do the same.

Renata tried to step away to the opposite side, wanting to be closer to the door but Adam caught her hand and tugged. Balance lost, she pitched forward.

He caught her, pulling her onto his lap. His hands closed over her hips and forced her back against his chest. No part of her touched the ground.

"Get some sleep."

"I . . . I can't sleep like this." She tried to rise.

Adam locked an arm across her abdomen, holding her in place. "You can. And you will. I won't hurt you, Renata. Just relax."

"Let me sit beside you. Then I'll relax."

"If I'm not holding you, I have to handcuff you."

"Fine," she extended her wrists. "Do it."

He sighed. "You've been bound too long. And short of shoving Lyle off the tarp, I've got the only available dry spot, though there's no guarantee how long it will stay that way."

As if to emphasize his point, thunder echoed, low and heavy.

"Seeing as we're both soaked, that's a moot point," she snapped.

"Regardless. For now I'm your makeshift mattress. I'm also the best chance you have at getting warm."

"I'd rather freeze."

Adam ignored her remark. "If you prefer we can lie down, side by side."

"No!" She bucked her body, trying to get away.

He wrapped his other arm across her chest and tightened his grip. "If you don't quit wiggling we're going to do exactly that."

Immediately she stilled. The last thing she wanted was to lie next to this man. One second passed. Then two.

She heard his slight snore and wanted to scream. How could he do that? Fall asleep so deeply, so completely? So totally unbothered by the fact someone sat in his lap?

She waited for him to relax his hold. He didn't. His heavy arms remained wrapped across her breasts and stomach in an impersonal manner, his thighs solid beneath her buttocks. Some mattress.

To her chagrin, her shivering subsided. Whether she wanted to admit it or not, the man did radiate welcome heat. Waves of it.

Rain pounded the metal roof, the sound hypnotic. She leaned her head back. Drowsiness overwhelmed her so completely she felt sick with the need to close her eyes.

I'll just close them for a second, she thought, shifting slightly. Just a second . . .

Adam had started to wonder whether Renata would ever let herself fall asleep. When struggling against him proved futile, she had tried to hold her body rigidly away from his, as if he'd contaminate her. That hadn't lasted long either. After two nights of no sleep, she simply gave in.

He had known the minute she'd succumbed; her body slumped against his in a boneless unconsciousness. He shifted her slightly, studying her. Wet, her hair looked black as ebony. His eyes dropped. He noticed the way her nipples pearled beneath her wet shirt and bra.

In sleep she squirmed, snuggling deeper into his arms, her mouth open slightly. Damn if he didn't want to kiss her again. Which she'd never allow.

Hell, she hadn't liked the fact he'd insisted on holding her. He also knew she'd have preferred the mud to his arms, so he hadn't bothered allowing her a choice. Besides, he'd been looking for any excuse to touch her again.

In prison, touch was associated with punishment. Or a demeaning act. It brought a sense of fear. Dread. In some small way, holding Renata healed that.

Relaxing slightly, he drifted in and out of consciousness, not sleeping, continually monitoring his environment. It was a habit he developed in the army. He'd enlisted the day he turned eighteen, spending ten years working covert ops with Special Forces before joining the FBI.

The army, while tough, ultimately provided the only stability Adam had ever known. He recalled what he'd told Renata earlier about his childhood. It had been basically the truth. Except for changing the names and places, that part of his background had been real.

His parents' roller coaster marriage dissolved when he was eight. And while his father was brutally abusive when he drank—which was always—his mother had been no better. A drug addict, she had split, taking Adam's younger brother, Zachary, with her.

If Adam's childhood had been hell, Zach's had been no better. Zach had been only six when they left. Up till that point Adam had virtually raised his younger brother, protected him as best he could from their father's abuses and their mother's neglect.

His mother had resurfaced once, looking for money. She told them Zach had died in a car accident. Adam didn't see or hear from her again until three years ago, when he was notified that she'd been institutionalized. When he finally went to visit, she didn't recognize him. Worse, she thought he was Zachary.

And she apologized for selling him.

She had lied about Zach's death. From her ramblings, Adam pieced together the truth: that his mother had sold his, by then, eleven-year-old brother to a drug dealer.

Adam had searched without avail, until last year when he'd found Zach's flowers at their mother's grave and traced him through the floral service. It had been an awkward reunion.

Adam was on leave, recovering from the shooting. When he returned to active duty, he learned Zach's background was as shady as some of the outlaws he'd chased through Central America.

Zach offered little explanation for the years after his mother sold him, but from what Adam had gathered, he'd survived a situation that few could. Compared to the drug dealer, their mother looked like a saint.

The haunting guilt over what his brother had endured never left Adam. Hell, it was part of the tangled reasons he'd taken this assignment. To clear his brother's name. As if it could make up for Adam's failure to protect him all those years ago. But what if Ethan Falco was lying about the information he had? Like he'd lied about the length of Adam's prison stay?

Uneasy, Adam slept.

When he next flicked his eyes open to check the cabin, he sensed something wrong. Taking care not to move or change his breathing pattern, he looked around and immediately discovered the problem.

His hand was under Renata's shirt.

He didn't question how it got there. And in spite of the fact that it was wrong . . . damn it, it felt divine. In sleep, she had curled into him, pinning his hand in place with her arm. The weight of her breast pressed against his wrist. Pure torture for a man too long without. He needed to do something, fast.

Wind buffeted the small building, the rain drumming harder on the metal roof, warning of the approaching storm front. The deteriorating weather would wake her if he did not.

A movement caught his eye. Lyle? Careful not to wake her, he turned his head . . . just as something black and shiny slithered into the shack.

Chapter Nine

The large black snake was either searching for dry ground or a spare mouse. Perhaps both. Its effortless glide across the muddy ground halted as it sensed Adam.

The creature froze, but instead of retreating, it spit out its forked tongue a few times and copped an attitude. It considered them trespassers.

Thunder exploded, shaking the ground and releasing an onslaught of hail. The ice chunks hitting the roof sounded like a barrage of gunfire. Renata jerked awake, frightened and disoriented.

"Shhh." He sought to calm her.

While it was actually the middle of the afternoon, the storm had darkened the sky, making it appear like night outside. The unsteady light from the lantern did little more than shroud the room in shadow.

"We have a problem here." Adam kept his eyes on the snake. Detecting movement, the creature had stalled, its head raised, alert.

"Problem?" Renata had just become aware of his hand beneath her shirt. She scrambled to get to her feet, but in her haste, she cracked him squarely in the chin with the crown of her head. The force of impact tumbled her back down in his lap.

Adam swore, seeing stars. He knew by the way she winced that she had suffered from the blow as well.

"Are you okay?"

"No, I'm not okay!" she snapped. "What the hell did you think you were doing?"

"You had my hand pinned."

She tried to rise again. "That is the lamest—"

He tightened his arms to keep her from head-butting him again, then quickly located the snake. It had moved away, toward the corner.

"Are you afraid of snakes?"

"If you're trying to throw me off, it won't work." She twisted to glare at him, saw him staring over her head. "Oh, God. You're not kidding, are you? Where?"

"There. It's not poisonous," Adam assured. "And it's as scared as you are."

"He doesn't look scared."

Her choice of pronoun amused Adam. "Look at his head, then, and—"

"I hate snakes. Especially their heads." Shuddering, she buried her face in his neck as she drew her legs onto his lap. "Get rid of him."

That she had Adam virtually pinned in place didn't seem to register. He hugged her close, surprised by his own reluctance to let her go. But to get rid of the snake he had to stand.

"You'll be safe right here." He tucked her behind him and moved toward the snake, which had slithered to the opposite wall.

Cornering it, he forced the snake to retreat the same way it had entered: the gap beneath the door. When the snake's tail disappeared, he placed a rock in front of the door in hopes of discouraging its return.

He moved back to where Renata stood, her arms crossed tightly over her chest. But before he could say anything, thunder burst, this time with a fierce show of lightning.

Lyle moaned, drawing their attention. He shoved away the blanket, his frame wracked with tremors. "Water," he rasped.

Renata saw the saturated bandages and scrambled to his side. "He's bleeding again. Get the supplies."

Adam watched as she took his temperature. "Fever?"

"One-oh-three-point-one. Something's cooking." She pulled away the bandages. "He's not responding to the antibiotic I've been administering, which isn't too shocking, given the circumstances."

Lyle roused. "Just . . . gimme a shot of penicillin."

"What I've been giving you is penicillin." She looked at Adam. "I need better light."

He grabbed the lantern and moved it closer. She frowned, not liking what she saw. "Infection is setting in. If I don't irrigate the wound and keep it clean, pretty soon it will become necrotic and I'll have to debride it."

Lyle coughed, wincing in pain. "De-what?"

"Debride; scrape away the dead tissue to help it heal."

"Shit. Hit it with alcohol and stick a bandage on it. It'll be fine."

"Until your leg falls off from gangrene," she began.

"If you're going to tell me to go to the hospital— don't." Lyle closed his eyes, seemed to almost pass out.

"She's right," Adam said. "You won't get better under these conditions."

"Where's the phone?" Lyle dialed a number and waited. "Fucking answering machines." He paused before leaving a message. "Hey, asshole! I'm dying thanks to this pigsty we're staying in. Call me."

The phone slid out of his hand. Adam caught it before it landed in the mud.

"He better call back soon," Lyle muttered.

Outside the storm hit its peak. The wind raged, buffeting the walls. Adam worried that the shed would collapse. They had to leave. He picked up the phone to make his own call just as it rang.

He answered with a curt, "Hello."

The caller breathed into the phone, but said nothing. Adam's temper flared. "Damn it, this is no time to play games."

Lyle roused. "Is it Nevin?"

A gruff voice came across the phone. "That my boy?"

Adam gripped the phone tightly. It wasn't Nevin. It was Willy McEdwin.

"Yeah, that's your boy. But he's not doing too well."

Willy swore. "Thought you had a doctor. Can't she fix him?"

"Not when he's sleeping in the dirt." Adam described their location. "The barn we stayed in yesterday was better than this. And I don't even have wheels to get him anywhere."

"Those goddamned idiots! Nevin set this up, didn't he? No matter. I'll get it straightened out. Then you can bring me my son."

"Good, because I'm tired of playing nursemaid. I'd have been better off alone."

"Don't blow a gasket," Willy said. "I know you haven't been treated right, but I aim to fix all that. But first let me talk to that doctor."

Reluctantly, Adam passed the phone to Renata. "Take it."

Confused, she pressed the phone to her ear. "This is Dr. Curtis."

"And this is Lyle's father. Don't mince words. How's he's doing?"

"Terrible. He's running a fever and needs stronger antibiotics than I've got. Perhaps you can convince him to go to the closest emergency room."

"That's not an option. They'll pack him off to the nearest prison ward and I know what kind of medical care he'll get there."

"You don't understand," she began again. "Anything short of going to a hospital could ultimately mean a death sentence."

"Yeah. *Yours*. You better make damn certain he survives."

The man's threat was clear: if Lyle died, so did she. She glanced at Adam. Did his promise to keep her safe include protecting her from Lyle's father? She doubted it. After finding his hand up her shirt, she doubted all of Adam's intentions.

Two things were clear: She didn't want to die. And as much as she despised Lyle, she didn't want to see him dead either. Her job was to save lives. All lives.

"Just tell me what you need medicine-wise," Willy continued. "And I'll get it."

"The drugs I need are controlled substances."

"Not a problem. I can get anything."

His cavalier attitude maddened her. Still she rattled off supplies and spelled the names of several stronger antibiotics. "I may need to try more than one before he responds."

Willy repeated the list. "If that's it, let me talk to my son."

She knelt beside Lyle and pressed the phone to his ear. "It's your father."

"Pa!" Lyle groped for the phone, a near smile hovering on his face. It faded as he grew quiet, listening.

Then his face reddened. "How was I supposed to know that? Nevin should have told me."

Adam moved closer, not caring if anyone knew he eavesdropped. He heard nothing as Lyle abruptly ended the call, then flipped his middle finger at the phone.

"Problems?" Adam asked.

"Timing." Lyle took a deep breath, clearly agitated. "He said I've complicated things."

"What things?"

"His almighty plan." Lyle tried to lift his head. "He's . . . he's pissed because the FBI has agents crawling out of the goddamned woodwork looking for us. Guess they're causing headaches for him. Like I can control what the FBI does!"

Adam could guess Willy's *almighty plan:* to blow something up. The question was what. And how much did Lyle know about it? Up till now the kid had maintained a poker face when it came to Willy. He'd fooled them all with his laments of missing his family. Hell, he'd even withstood the guards' abuse without talking.

But Adam knew if he pressured Lyle in front of Renata, he'd clam up. Better to let the subject drop. For now. "We'll discuss it later. I'll get you some food."

Lyle shook his head. "I'm not hungry. I need water though." He fumbled beneath the blanket and withdrew the bottle of painkillers.

Adam discreetly counted how many tablets the kid took. There were unwritten rules about a prisoner's drug usage. First and foremost, you never questioned anyone's habit. The choice to abuse drugs was considered as sacred as the choice not to.

When the phone rang again, Renata jumped.

Adam answered. "Yeah?"

It was Willy. "There's a vehicle heading to you as we speak. You don't even have to drive this time."

Adam glanced at Renata. "Not so fast. Where are we going?"

"To a better place. Trust me. It has everything you could possibly need including medical supplies. You'll be safe there for a couple days. Until the heat dies down."

"So it's temporary?"

"Yep, but I'm working on a permanent fix. Be patient. We'll talk tomorrow."

The phone went dead just as a vehicle pulled up outside.

Placing himself between Renata and the door, Adam drew his gun and peered out the window.

"Tell me it ain't the cops," Lyle hissed.

"It's not."

Parked outside was an ancient Winnebago. How the motor home made it up the muddy drive without getting stuck baffled Adam. Until he saw the heavy-duty suspension, the oversized tires. Someone had outfitted the Winnie with four-wheel drive.

The driver, a burly man dressed in paint-spattered work pants and a faded T-shirt, swung out of the motor home and into the pouring rain. He dashed toward the cabin and yanked open the door. Once inside, he shook himself like a big hairy dog.

In his mid-sixties, the man had a weather-beaten exterior that hinted at years of farming. The lackluster glint in his eyes spoke of mistrust, suspicion. And a latent hostility. Adam wondered which antigovernment group this man belonged to. There were at least a dozen he could serve as poster child for.

The man eyed his gun. "You can put that away. Willy sent me. I'm Calvin. Where's the boy?"

From behind them, Lyle grunted. "Who you calling 'boy,' old man?"

Calvin peered around Adam. "Shit, son. You do look bad."

"Nice to see you, too, Calvin." Lyle raised his hand, then quickly dropped it, groaning.

Calvin turned, pinning Renata with an icy glare. "Judging by the way your patient looks, you must not be much of a doctor. Hell, my vet treats animals better than this."

"Then by all means, take him to your vet. See if—"

Adam grasped her arm and shook her, cutting her words off. "She's done the best with what she's had to work with. But staying in rat holes like this will kill anybody."

Calvin looked around as if noticing their accommodations for the first time. He knelt beside Lyle. "If your daddy had known you were this bad off, he'd have called me before now."

"This bad off? I was shot, damn it!" Lyle shook his head. "Don't tell me: He thought I was crying wolf, right?"

"Now, now, you know how your pa is." Calvin launched into a lecture on Willy McEdwin's virtues.

Adam resisted the urge to roll his eyes. Calvin plainly idolized Willy McEdwin. One of the reasons he'd been so hard to catch was the scores of men like Calvin who'd do favors like this at a moment's notice and feel honored to be called. To be trusted. Men who could keep secrets while privately thumbing their noses at the federal government.

He listened, hoping to discern Calvin's connection to the McEdwins. It was clear he was a close family friend, someone Willy could trust to give him an honest assessment of Lyle's condition.

"I got dry clothes in the RV." Calvin helped Lyle to his feet. "Let's get you out of here."

"Hold up. I want to know where we're headed," Adam said.

"Reckon you'll find out soon enough," Calvin replied.

"Now. Or I split. With the doctor."

"Go ahead and tell him," Lyle interrupted. "We're in this together. I'd be dead if it weren't for him. Make sure my pa gets that message, too."

Calvin sighed. "I'm taking you across the state line. To Kentucky. I understand the place you'll be staying is right decent. And it's out-of-the-way. Quiet. But I suggest we get going. Cops are all over the place."

The inside of the Winnebago, while tidy, looked as prehistoric as the outside. Decades of cigarette smoke permeated the walls. One of the couch cushions was completely covered in dull gray duct tape, a worn remote control tucked in a TV Guide beside it. A skillet, a fork, and a plate had been left to dry in a small rack in the sink, making Adam wonder if the man lived in the motor home.

Lyle let Calvin help him change clothes, but refused to stretch out in the rear of the trailer, opting instead to recline in the captain's chair on the passenger side. Both men lit up cigarettes, though Lyle started coughing so hard he tossed his out the window.

"There's more clothes in the overhead," Calvin called over his shoulder to Adam. "You and the woman can change back there, too."

Adam opened the cabinet and found a shirt and pair of jeans that looked small enough for Renata. He dug out a flannel shirt for himself.

"Is it okay if she uses the bathroom?" he asked. At Calvin's nod, Adam quickly checked the small compartment for potential weapons, finding only soap and toilet paper.

"I'd prefer to stay in my own clothes," she whispered when he moved to let her pass.

"They're soaked."

"But—"

He reached for the buttons of her blouse. "I'll help."

She smacked his hands away. "You've done enough."

While she changed, Adam listened to Calvin fill Lyle in on the news reports of their escape.

"First they had you in Georgia. Then you showed up in Pennsylvania. Now they think you're headed north. Get this: the FBI scared some old lady half to death in New Jersey when her license tag was given out on an APB. You got the cops so rattled they don't know which way's up."

When Renata stepped out of the bathroom she clutched her wet clothes in her hands. Adam noticed she'd put her soggy sneakers back on, which would keep her feet cold. He eyed the matted carpet, unable to discern its original color. He didn't blame her for not wanting to be barefoot.

Once again he found himself wanting to touch her—offer physical comfort. He couldn't. She sat beside him at the table in the kitchen galley. Adam made no attempt to restrain her. With Calvin driving, there was no need.

When Lyle fell asleep, Calvin grabbed an eight-track tape and jammed it in the player, turning the volume up. The bluegrass harmonies sounded tinny.

"What happens next?" Renata asked softly.

"Getting Lyle stabilized is our first priority."

Adam wasn't sure beyond that. He needed to formulate a plan and coordinate with Ethan and Stan. Now that he'd made contact with Willy, Adam felt certain they'd unite soon. Which meant he needed to arrange to drop off Renata. The sooner she was out of the picture, the better he'd feel.

They drove most of the night, once again staying on back roads, winding through the countryside. Adam noticed Calvin doubled back frequently, pulling off here and there to check for a tail, weaving a convoluted trail that would be impossible to follow. He wondered how Ethan's men were keeping up, or if they were simply tracking them electronically.

Calvin remained uncommunicative until they reached their destination. "This is it."

Adam peered out the window. "You sure?"

Illuminated in the headlights was a spacious log cabin. A very expensive log cabin, he amended as he took in the soaring roofline.

"Guess it's quite an improvement over your last place," Calvin said.

"Our last two places."

Calvin carried Lyle inside, taking him directly into one of the bedrooms. While the older man settled Lyle, Adam tugged Renata into the living room and turned on a lamp. Tight-fitting blinds sealed the windows from prying eyes.

He looked around, missing nothing. The place had the impersonal air of a vacation rental. Or it had been sanitized. No pictures, no personal touches. There were two bedrooms, the large living room, plus a kitchen and bathrooms. Cardboard boxes covered the kitchen table.

Calvin joined them. "The supplies you asked for should be here. And more. I'll be taking off, but Lyle knows how to reach me if he needs anything else." The blatant emphasis on *he* left no doubt where the old man's allegiance rested.

Adam locked the door behind Calvin, then steered her toward the kitchen. He pointed out two cardboard boxes marked MEDICINE. "See if everything you need is here. I'll see if there's anything to eat besides crackers."

She looked in the first box, saw it held a range of generic supplies: Bandages. Gauze. Latex gloves. Splints. Ointments. Aspirin. Ibuprofen. Two cases of saline sat on the table, too.

While Adam had his back to her, Renata furtively checked out her surroundings. According to the digital clock on the microwave it was only 10 P.M. Usually they arrived at dawn. Their pattern of traveling at night, hiding during the day had scrambled her sense of time and direction.

She had heard Calvin say they were headed to Kentucky, knew they had to be in the eastern part of the state since they were in the mountains. She'd also heard the men discuss staying here for a couple days. Remaining in one spot could increase her chances for escape.

She studied the rear door, noting it had a deadbolt lock, the key missing. The curtains were drawn tightly at the single window over the sink.

She turned back to the table. Flipping the lid off the second box, she found it held the medicine she'd requested. She checked labels, examined the expiration dates. The antibiotics were the exact suspensions she'd requested. But there were also vials of morphine, along with a box of disposable syringes and another bottle of tablet painkillers. These narcotics shouldn't have been easy to come by. Judging by the packaging, the supplies had been stolen from a hospital.

"I hope some patients aren't suffering because all these supplies are missing."

Adam did a cursory check of the box. "Is there anything there that can't be readily replaced? Anything a hospital would only have one of?"

She shook her head. "That doesn't make it right."

"Granted. Just remember: You didn't steal it or cause it to be taken. So don't feel guilty for using it."

Adam had already gone through the remaining boxes. There were clothes, towels and toiletries, plus canned goods and soda.

He saw her eye the two boxes of ammunition that sat on the counter beside a fresh loaf of bread.

"Do you anticipate a need for all that?" she asked.

He grabbed the ammo, stuck it in a cabinet beyond her reach. He'd move them again later, when she wasn't watching. "I hope not."

"I wonder how many innocent people I could save by getting rid of those?"

Not enough, he thought. "Don't even think about it."

He picked up the bread. "Grab the lunchmeat and cheese from the refrigerator. I'm heating a couple cans of stew before we take care of Lyle. I'm sure a little decent food will help the kid."

A knock sounded at the front door. A bold rapping.

That fast Adam clamped a hand over her mouth. He forced her into the living room as the knocking repeated. Had Calvin returned for some reason?

Moving to the door, Adam lowered his voice, disguising it. "Who's there?"

"Nevin."

Nevin McEdwin. Dropping his hand to Renata's waist, keeping her close, Adam opened the door. "Got any ID?"

The other man grinned. "My baby brother will vouch for me. Where is he?"

"In the bedroom." Adam backed up, allowing Nevin to enter. "He's not doing real swift."

A frown flitted across Nevin's face. He started to say something else when he spotted Renata. The grin returned. He whistled, his eyes sliding over her more thoroughly than Adam liked.

"Lyle said she was hot but I figured a mama hog would look good after nine months in prison." Nevin's smile widened. "How about the doctor and I go in the bedroom? To, uh, check him out."

"She stays with me." Adam shifted closer to Renata, drawing her to his side with a possessive arm before pressing his lips to her temple. She stiffened, drew a sharp breath. He knew she didn't like it, but staking a claim was the best way to protect her right now.

"We were just getting ready to eat." Adam turned her out of the other man's line of vision. "But I wasn't expecting company."

"It works better that way. Besides, I wanted to see for myself how Lyle was doing."

"You? Or your old man?"

Nevin's jaw tensed. "Me. I'm sure Calvin's already given Willy a full report."

From the bedroom, Lyle called out, his voice weak. "Adam? I need some water."

"I'll get it." Nevin moved to retrieve a glass.

Adam nodded to the tray of food on the counter. "Perhaps you can convince him to eat, too."

Lyle's exclamation of surprise echoed through the cabin, confirming that he hadn't expected to see his brother either.

"Grab your supplies." Adam rushed Renata, wanting to hear as much of the brothers' conversation as possible. Did Nevin's appearance mean they were even closer to being united with Willy?

Lyle was in the master bedroom, a large, well-appointed room. A love seat and chair sat in front of a big screen television equipped with a satellite receiver. A handful of remotes were scattered on the mattress next to Lyle.

Nevin sat sprawled in the love seat, his leg hooked over the arm as he entertained Lyle with stories about their escape. It was similar to what they'd heard from Calvin: more false sightings in New England. Except Nevin gave it a swashbuckling twist.

Lyle started to hand the tray to Renata, his food untouched. "Here. Take this."

"Uh-uh. You gotta eat, bro," Nevin said. "Trust me, you won't get better on that piss-water." He pointed to the bag of saline Renata set on the nightstand.

"Let me take these first." Lyle swallowed two painkillers then picked up the spoon and stirred the stew. "You talked to Pa, lately? He's pretty hot."

Nevin watched his younger brother, nodding in approval when he finally took a bite of food. "Yeah, but it's me he's ticked at, not you. I left Burt and Tristin to deal with him and both of them are ready to kick my ass, too."

Ignoring them as best she could, Renata set out her supplies. She had to change the IV, as the site showed signs of infection. She was acutely aware of Nevin watching her. He gave her the creeps. While she hadn't liked Adam's little show of propriety earlier, she wouldn't hesitate to exploit it if it kept the McEdwins at bay.

"I'm done." Lyle shoved his food away and almost immediately fell asleep as the painkillers kicked in.

When Renata removed the bandages, Nevin stood, leaned closer to the bed.

"Gross! It's worse than I thought. He'll survive, right?"

She started cleaning the wound. "I don't know."

"'Course he will. He's a McEdwin." Dismissing her, and grabbing the remote, Nevin turned to Adam. "You caught any news lately?"

Adam shook his head. "Just what we could tune in on the car radio."

"Me, too." Nevin flipped channels, pausing frequently. "Here's something." He punched up the volume.

Renata glanced sideways at the television, recognizing the logo for one of the twenty-four hour news stations. The bold graphic read: MANHUNT.

"The nationwide hunt for two North Carolina escapees intensified today," the reporter said. "The men are believed to be in the Elmira, New York, area after a car they were driving was found abandoned at a shopping mall."

A photograph of the white Buick surrounded by yellow crime scene tape flashed on the screen.

"Sources close to the case said the fugitives are most likely headed toward Canada. Still no word on the missing prison guard or the Durham doctor authorities believe were abducted by the men."

Renata's heart sank. The news that police had indeed tied her disappearance to the men was eclipsed by reports they were headed to Canada. They weren't even warm. She started to turn away when a photograph of Jim Acton appeared on the screen. She hadn't heard anything about her friend since they left the clinic two days ago.

"Also today, formal charges of murder were filed

against the fugitives in the shooting of Sheriff's Deputy Jim Acton. Police have vowed to step up efforts to bring these alleged cop killers to justice. Funeral arrangements—"

The roll of tape dropped from Renata's hands. She drew a sharp breath. Murder? "He's . . . dead?"

Nevin glanced at her. "They said his funeral is tomorrow. That usually means they're dead."

Renata felt a hand cup her elbow. She looked up, surprised to find Adam right in front of her. For a moment she'd lost attentiveness.

"I'm sorry about your friend."

His words burst the bubble of grief welling inside her, leaving her feeling bitter. Angry. She balled her fist against the urge to strike out.

Very early in medical school, she had learned that illness and injury had no sense of fairness, no sense of right or wrong. Same with death. She accepted that, dealt with it daily. This yearning for revenge, however, was foreign. And she did not like the way it made her feel: fallible. Vulnerable. Guilty.

She narrowed her eyes at the man on the bed. It hurt to see Lyle sleeping peacefully, knowing that back in Durham, the family and friends of Jim Acton mourned. An eye for an eye had never been her credo, but all of a sudden she understood it.

There was now another reason to make sure Lyle lived: to see him brought to justice. She couldn't bring Jim back, but she'd do everything in her power to make sure these men were tried.

"Let me help you finish up," Adam said.

"That's not necessary." Shaking off his hand, she knelt down to search for the tape she dropped.

It had rolled under the bed beyond her reach. She went to stand and caught a glimpse of the adjoining bathroom. Was it her imagination or had the edge of the curtain fluttered slightly? The pale yellow chiffon moved again. *An open window.*

"Did you find it?" Adam asked.

Brushing off her hands, she climbed to her feet. "I can't reach it. And I'll need a new roll since it's been on the dusty floor."

"Stay here. Nevin and I will get more." Adam reached behind her, collecting the scissors she'd used earlier. "Do you need us to bring back anything else?"

Renata's pulse accelerated as she realized both men were leaving the room. She bent over Lyle and began fastening a bandage using the strips of tape she'd cut before dropping the roll.

"Yes. I need a box of large square pads and a bottle of Betadine solution."

"We'll be right back."

Nevin followed Adam out of the room. As soon as they disappeared, she hurried to the bathroom, knowing she didn't have much time. There was no Betadine in the boxes, but she hoped his searching for it gained her a few minutes

The window was slightly ajar. She eyed the opening. It would be tight, but she could squeeze through.

She pushed against the sash, found it raised easily, without the slightest noise. Heartened, she poked her head out and looked down.

"Blast it!" Dismay slapped her as she realized why Adam had not worried about leaving her alone. The cabin was built on a steep slope, which placed the windows at the back of the house nearly two stories up.

She peered out again, tried to see what was below but the shadows were too deep.

Would she let that stop her?

She recalled Adam's warning from when she'd pulled the scalpel on him. *Don't hesitate.*

She had to chance it.

Without pausing, she boosted herself up and swung out the window.

Chapter Ten

Renata clawed the air uselessly, hitting the ground harder than expected.

Pain exploded in her left ankle. She tumbled backwards, smashing into the woodpile and touching off an avalanche of split oak.

When she finally skidded to a stop, she gulped in air. Each breath fanned a fire in her body. She wanted to scream; knew she couldn't.

Her shirt was shredded, torn; the skin beneath raw and scraped. She pressed her fingertips gingerly along her ribs. They were sore but none were cracked.

Her ankle, though, worried her. It throbbed and was already swelling. She quickly checked for broken bones, moved the joint experimentally. Not broken, but definitely sprained.

Woozy, she climbed to her feet, struggling to remain upright, determined to get away. But when she placed weight on her ankle, pain shot up her left leg. She closed her eyes, fighting a sharp need to cry out.

She hobbled a step or two and had to stop. Damn it! At this rate Adam would catch her before she'd gone ten feet. He wouldn't even need Nevin's help.

Time was running out. Biting her lip, she just went for it. "Remember Jim," she murmured.

A three-quarter moon illuminated the small swath of

yard that had been carved from the surrounding dense woods. With her ankle slowing her, she wouldn't make it far in the dark forest. In fact, her only chance of getting help lay in making it to the main highway where she could flag down a car.

She circled toward the front, heading for the road. The cabin remained eerily quiet, making her wonder if they'd even realized she was gone.

The wet ground and thatched undergrowth were hard to navigate but finally she reached the road. She increased her speed, grateful for the mud that muffled the crunch of gravel.

When she looked back seconds later, the cabin was no longer visible. Yes! She was going to make it! She had escaped . . . alive and relatively unharmed.

Encouraged, she started to turn away. A movement caught her attention.

Adam!

Still twenty yards back, he ran toward her. Panicked, Renata tried to jog, but nearly toppled. She switched to an uneven hop.

At home, she ran four miles daily. In an even match she could probably outmaneuver him. But right now he had the advantage. He wasn't injured and he had Nevin helping. Both men were armed.

Her only chance lay in concealment. She turned toward the woods. A rain-filled ditch paralleled the roadbed. Undaunted, she slogged through it, shocked to find the water nearly waist deep. She struggled to the opposite incline. Grabbing at tangled weeds, she pulled herself up the slippery bank, ignoring the pain.

Clouds scudded over the moon. She welcomed the small break, knew the enhanced darkness would help hide her in the woods. She was almost there.

A strong hand grabbed the back of her shirt.

"Renata, stop!"

"No!" She surged forward. "Let me go!"

Adam tightened his grip, yanking her backwards. The wet fabric of her shirt ripped, costing him his hold.

The unexpected momentum of being released made Renata lose her balance. She pitched forward awkwardly, grasping her ruined shirt with one hand as she struggled to regain her footing. Staggering, she leaped away.

He tackled her, hugging her close as they hit the ground and rolled down the embankment toward the ditch. They stopped just short of the water, Adam on top, Renata trapped beneath his large frame.

She sank into the wet ground, her scraped side burning. The disappointment over not getting away cut to the bone, crushing her tenuous hold on her temper.

She drew back and punched him. "Let me go, damn you!"

He caught her wrists, yanking them over her head and pinning them.

"Give it up," he shouted hoarsely. "You don't stand a chance against me. You never did."

"And what about my friend? Did Jim have a chance before Lyle shot him?" She looked away, not wanting him to see how close she was to breaking down.

"Nothing I can do will bring your friend back," he said finally. "I'm sorry."

His sincere tone—regret? remorse?—clashed with her image of him as a ruthless criminal. *But Adam hadn't pulled the trigger.* Lyle had.

"You can do what's right now," she pleaded. "Release me."

"I can't."

Tears of mourning, of frustration, rolled down her cheeks. Once started, the sobs were hard to stop.

Adam bent closer, whispering sounds of comfort. No words because he didn't have any. Just soothing noises. He let her cry, using the time to rein in his own emotions. If she had gotten away, alerted police . . . his case would have been blown. And he was so damn close to success.

"We have to go back," he said. "Come on."

"No!" With a renewed vigor, she tried one more time to wrestle free.

"Have it your way." He countered by simply letting his full weight ease against her.

Renata yelped as if in pain. Adam eyed her suspiciously. He had underestimated this woman once. He wouldn't do it again. Wary, he rolled to his feet, tugging her with him. He kept his hands vised around her wrists, expecting a trick.

The moon broke free, offering the palest light. Only then did he notice where her shirt was ripped. The front gaped open, revealing a torn lace bra, a bare breast. Blood trickled along her cleavage.

"You're hurt." Loosening his grip, he flicked the torn edge of her shirt up, covering her.

"Leave me alone!" She tried to put weight on her ankle, but swayed, nearly fell.

He steadied her. "Correction: You're hurt bad."

"Good thing I'm a doctor."

"Is it your knee?"

She grimaced. "My ankle."

"Is it broken?"

"Sprained."

Without another word, he scooped her up. "What the—" He shifted his hand lower. "It feels like your side is bleeding, too. I assume you checked for broken ribs?"

"Yes."

"You're lucky you didn't kill yourself."

"And deny you the privilege?"

The remark stung. Adam glanced at the cabin, saw Nevin waiting for them on the front porch. He recalled their prior conversation. Nevin had made it clear that his father wanted Renata dead as soon as she was no longer useful. In fact, Adam suspected that was the reason for Nevin's visit. Until he saw how sick Lyle was. And how attractive Renata was.

When Nevin had expressed interest, Adam had declared her off limits, making it clear that her usefulness included serving him. *"She's mine to do with as I please. We have a score to settle—she tried to stab me. So I'll get rid of her when I'm ready."*

"I've told you, you'll come out of this okay. You have to follow my orders, though." Adam glanced down, saw part of her breast again. "And fix your shirt, damn it! Unless you want him to see."

"Could he be any worse?" She struggled to pull the edges of her shirt and ripped bra together.

"You don't want to know."

They reached the porch. Nevin held the cabin door open. "Hurt yourself, princess?"

His leering grin gave Renata creep bumps, reminded her the worst was yet to come. She fought the tears of self-pity and defeat that prickled her eyes. It was bad enough she'd wept earlier with Adam, but she refused to let Nevin see her cry.

Adam set her on the couch. After removing her shoe, he examined her ankle. It was swollen and bruised.

"Sore?"

"No."

He ran his fingers along the bottom of her foot. She nearly shot off the couch.

"Liar."

"I'll get ice," Nevin volunteered.

"What are you going to do to me?" she asked when they were alone.

"Take care of your injuries."

"That's not what I meant."

"Are you worried I plan to punish you?"

"Yes."

"Looks like you did enough of that already."

"What about him?" Her gaze darted toward the kitchen, where Nevin banged ice cube trays in the sink.

"Keep your guard up around him." Adam looked her directly in the eyes. "He won't touch you as long as you're with me."

"What does that mean—*with you?*"

"Literally? I've told him you're mine. Let me check your side." He reached toward her.

Renata hugged her torn clothes to her chest. "It's nothing."

"You're bleeding."

"It's just a scratch."

"Now you sound like him." Adam hooked a thumb toward Lyle's room. Loud snores echoed, confirming that, thanks to the painkillers, Lyle had slept through the entire episode. "He says he's fine, yet he's running a fever and keeps tearing his wound open."

"But—"

"No buts." Adam lifted the side of her shirt and shook his head. "You're current on tetanus?"

"Of course."

"These cuts are packed with grass and dirt. We need to get them clean before they get infected."

He stood and toed off his shoes. She noticed for the first time that his jeans were as ripped and muddy as hers. Her eyes drifted, taking in the wet T-shirt plastered against his chest.

He bent and scooped her into his arms once again just as Nevin walked back in, a plastic bag of ice in one hand.

"Hey! Where are you taking her?"

"The bathroom," Adam said.

"Put me down!" Renata demanded. "I can get there on my own!"

He did not set her down until they were both inside the bathroom down the hall. Then he shut the door and crossed his arms, looking mean and fierce as he towered over her.

"We need to get something straight. I'm the captor. You're the hostage. I give the orders. You follow."

"Or what? You'll shoot me? Beat me up?"

Her response, while not what he wanted, didn't surprise him. She wasn't easily intimidated. She viewed her botched escape as a setback, not a defeat.

He eyed the window. They were in a different bathroom, but this window was the same size as the other. And she'd make another break first chance she got.

It was time Adam enforced his point: that they would do things his way from here on out. Stepping back, he pulled his shirt over his head and tossed it to the floor, heard her muffled gasp as she spied his bare chest.

He'd expected it.

It had been a long time since he'd undressed in front of a stranger. A long time since a woman had seen his scars. Knives, acid, did horrible things to human flesh. Most women overlooked them, especially after he dropped his pants.

But this wasn't about seduction. To her, his chest probably looked gruesome. Of course in comparison to what Lyle had told her, the truth was a fairy tale.

"They're not what you think," he said. Six kills.

Transfixed, Renata extended her hand and traced light fingertips over the six precise notches carved above his left nipple. Then her fingers skimmed lower, brushing the scarred patches of mottled flesh that covered his stomach and sides. Her hands were gentle, thorough, as they examined him. Healing hands.

"This doesn't look self-inflicted," she murmured. "Prison?"

"Childhood."

The flash of pity in her eyes was unbearable. That was the last thing he wanted.

Eager to shatter the moment, he unfastened his jeans and lowered the zipper.

Her face flushed as she twisted away. "What are you doing?"

He turned on the water in the tub. "We're taking a shower and going to bed."

"You're crazy! I'm doing no such thing."

She tried to shove past him but he stopped her by putting his hands on her shoulders. With a flick of his wrists, he ripped the remnants of her tattered shirt and bra apart, let them fall to the floor.

She ceased struggling and covered her bare breasts with her arms. "You bastard!"

Paying no heed, Adam pressed on. He tugged at the snap on her jeans, slid them down. Unwilling to expose her breasts, she couldn't stop him.

He straightened, leaving her underwear in place, her jeans bunched at her feet. "You can take them off yourself. Or I'll do it."

"This is my punishment, isn't it?"

"For escaping? Hardly. So undress. Now."

When she didn't obey, he stepped closer. "Your choice."

"Please don't." She lowered her head.

Catching her chin, Adam forced it up. He ran a hand through the wet hair at her nape, then held his fingers in front of her face. Thick muck caked them.

"Believe me, we're both this filthy. I need a shower just as much as you. And while I don't trust you alone, I won't hurt you, Renata. I promise. Get in."

There was no mistaking the finality in his tone. *Get in or be put in.*

Renata's options were excruciatingly limited. Fighting him was ludicrous. Even without her injuries she'd lose a physical confrontation with this man. And if Nevin came in to help . . .

Avoiding his eyes, she awkwardly stepped out of her jeans and underwear, keenly aware of her nudity. And his. To his credit, he didn't gawk.

Without warning, he tucked his hands under her arms and lifted her into the tub. "You first."

His touch scalded her flesh. He set her beneath the spray, cupping her elbow until she found her balance. Then he released her.

For a moment she thought he was leaving her alone to shower. Then he stepped in behind her and closed the curtain. She panicked. The area was too small for two adults, especially one as large as Adam. And as naked . . .

She slipped.

His hands shot forward, steadying her. "Breathe."

He whispered the word so softly she thought she'd imagined it. She struggled to draw in air. Couldn't.

"Exhale." His breath brushed her ear. "Blow."

She forced air out, inhaling again on reflex.

"One more time," he ordered.

Her trembling subsided.

"Here." He pressed a washcloth into her hand,

pointed to the bar of soap on the ledge. "Trade places with me."

Renata twisted sideways as he slid past. Moving mechanically, she lathered her body, in a hurry to finish. Each sweep of the washcloth confirmed new hurts. The abrasions on her side stung. Biting her lip, she worked loose the bits of debris.

She glanced over her shoulder. Adam had his back to her as he scrubbed vigorously at his own skin. Unlike his chest, the skin on his back was smooth. Except for a small round scar on his left shoulder. A bullet. *In the back.* What all had this man suffered?

She turned away. Reaching for the shampoo, she soaped her hair, working free the clods of mud and small twigs. Brown water pooled in the bottom of the tub. She'd been even dirtier than she'd imagined.

When Adam touched her shoulder, she jumped, nearly fell.

Once again, his hand was there. "You can rinse your hair."

Turning sideways, Renata inched toward the front, grasping the molded ledge for support. But in the close confines their bodies brushed. She recoiled, trying not to think about what part of him had brushed her buttocks.

Shampoo dripped into her eyes, stinging. Closing them, she turned her face up to the spray. When her hair was rinsed, she glanced back, wary.

Adam stood, unmoving, watching her. His arms were folded casually across his scarred chest and one shoulder leaned against the wall, in a stance that said he was uninterested. Bored.

Then her eyes dipped lower, grew wide.

With a strangled sound, she turned away. Mortified. She hadn't meant to look at his groin, but once she had, she couldn't stop. It was impossible not to notice his penis. Semierect, it seemed overlarge. Too long. Too thick.

And that fast it had swelled, rising away from the dark whorls of pubic hair. Perilous. Threatening.

She sucked in air, recognized the signs of hysteria. *Calm down,* she ordered. *Think.* His wasn't the first penis she'd ever seen. She was a doctor, damn it! She knew the biophysical mechanics of erections.

But she was also a female. In a vulnerable position.

She heard the shower curtain move, the wet plastic making a slashing noise. Open. Close. She looked, found Adam had stepped out, left her alone. But not for long. The curtain parted slightly right behind her.

He set a disposable razor on the edge of the tub. "If you want to shave, be quick."

Without another word he jerked the curtain closed. She knew he remained in the bathroom, could hear water running in the sink.

She stared at the cheap razor, dumbfounded. The man makes her shower with him . . . then this? His show of thoughtfulness unnerved her. He was a bad guy. Her expectations of him were dirt low.

Yet he hadn't misbehaved in the shower. Which was probably a ploy to throw her off. His true colors would show through soon enough.

She examined the single-blade razor, satisfied it was new and dismissing its value as a weapon. It was useless. Even if she wanted to save it for later, where would she hide it?

Grabbing the soap, she lathered her leg. It was awkward shaving with her injured ankle and she nicked her skin twice. She gave up just as the water turned cold. When Adam stuck his head in the shower again, she automatically turned away.

"Give me the razor." He shut off the water.

She handed it to him, then watched over her shoulder as he checked that the blade was intact. "Satisfied?"

"Yes. Here's a towel." He thrust his arm forward.

Her fingers brushed his, the sensation as startling as grasping a live electrical wire. The towel dropped.

Adam bent to pick it up and when he straightened, their eyes met.

She lurched as his transformation registered. The three-day stubble that had enhanced his thuggish appearance was gone, leaving those high, perfect cheekbones that she'd admired that first night when she'd thought he was a doctor. She'd been struck then by his good looks. Now that fist-in-the-stomach returned.

He had his hair combed straight back, the wet coal-colored ends brushing his shoulder. But it was his eyes that held her. They were too blue, too deep. Too hypnotic. They haunted. Seduced.

She felt her nipples tighten almost painfully. Alarmed, she dropped her eyes to break the spell.

Immediately she raised them, blushing. He was still fully erect. And, damn it, she was still naked. How could she just stand here like this? Zoned out . . .

She wrapped the towel around her, nearly losing her balance when she put too much weight on her ankle.

Adam caught her, lifted her out of the shower and set her next to the sink so she could balance against the counter. "Dry off." Then he handed her a packaged toothbrush.

"Can I have a little privacy?" she asked.

"To use the toilet? Yes. For everything else, no." He stuck out his hand, pointing to the towel. "In fact, I'll take that with me. I doubt you'll climb out the window naked. The person you flag down for help might not be such a gentleman."

"My expectations of gentlemen were left in Durham." She stuck out her ankle. "Besides, I've had enough climbing out windows for one night."

He shrugged, unapologetic. "Me, too. So hand over the towel. Or I'll take it."

His unspoken I-don't-trust-you angered her. "I hope you burn in hell for this."

"I have a seat reserved."

Turning away, Renata tossed the towel. When the door closed, she looked longingly at the window. He was right. She'd try again first chance she got.

When Adam returned, she once more turned her bare back to him. He set a pair of jeans and a T-shirt on the counter beside her. She recognized them from the boxes that had been left on the kitchen table earlier.

"Where are my clothes?" she asked, momentarily forgetting her nudity.

"They were ruined. I threw them out."

The clothes had been Calvin's, so she didn't care about them, but she did want her underwear, had hoped to repair her bra.

"I meant the clothes I had on originally."

"I left them in the RV."

"What?" Incensed, she looked up and caught his reflection behind her, in the mirror. He wore jeans, his chest bare.

And he could see every inch of her in the mirror.

Embarrassed, she snagged the shirt and slid it over her head, relieved it at least fell to her hips. She whirled to face him. "You had no right getting rid of my things."

"Give it a rest. These are dry and clean."

"But they're not mine!"

Adam reached for the jeans and withdrew. "Fine. Stay naked."

"Damn you!" She held out her hands for the jeans.

But instead of giving them to her, he dropped to one knee and held them open.

"I need underwear."

"I'll write Santa. Until then, we all go commando."

Her cheeks burned at the thought of him naked beneath his jeans. She thrust her injured foot forward wanting to get dressed as quickly as possible.

He leaned in, carefully tugging the pant leg over her ankle. The move put his mouth at the same level as her groin. She jerked, nearly falling and had to brace a hand against his shoulder. With one smooth move he caught her, supporting her weight.

"Let me," he whispered.

He pulled the jeans up easily, his fingers inside the waistband, trailing lightly along her leg. Sparks of awareness danced along her skin. Memories of him in the shower flitted across her mind. His wet, gleaming, muscles. His erection.

Alarmed, Renata drew her knees together and shoved his hands away, acutely aware she wore nothing beneath the shirt. His fingers would have touched her . . .

She cut off the thought, zipping the jeans. They were snug across the hips, had obviously been included for Lyle.

Adam picked her up.

She protested. "I can walk." That he took extra care not to hurt her only made her madder. She didn't want his thoughtfulness.

"Keeping weight on that ankle is only going to aggravate it."

He carried her into the smaller bedroom and shut the

door avoiding the living room and Nevin altogether. He sat her down in the middle of the double bed that was pushed against the wall. Propping her ankle on a pillow, he laid a plastic bag filled with ice across it.

"Rest. Ice. Compression. Elevation," he said. "Just not in the right order."

She frowned, not wanting to give him credit for correctly identifying the treatment for a sprain. "Your medical training is showing again. You were a medic, right?"

He shrugged away her question. "I still need your help with Lyle, so don't get any more ideas about leaving. Not until I'm sure he's out of the woods."

This last gave her hope. "And once he's out of the woods—then what?"

"We'll discuss it later." He nodded toward the door, reminding her of Nevin's presence. He picked up a tube of antibiotic ointment from the nightstand. "Raise your shirt."

She crossed her hands over her abdomen. "I can take care of myself."

"It's quicker if I do it."

"Why the big hurry?"

Out of patience, Adam shoved her hands away and raised the shirt to expose her abraded side. "The only reason you got away tonight is because I'm sleep deprived. And as much as you may think otherwise, the only thing I'm interested in right now is getting some sleep."

It was only a partial lie. Adam was exhausted. But that did little to abate his interest.

He eyed the white cotton T-shirt she wore. He could just make out the dark shading of her aureoles. The soft fabric outlined the thrust of her breasts perfectly, called attention to the fact her nipples were on high alert.

He wasn't a eunuch. He'd seen her fully naked, had enjoyed memorizing every sweet detail. Hell, he'd have to be dead not to be interested—but that didn't matter. *She wasn't interested.*

Oh, she was curious. They all were, making him feel like a circus freak some days. He was used to that. But he required more than curiosity from a woman. End of story.

He grabbed a square of gauze and covered her side. "That cut on your breast needs salve."

She snatched the tube of ointment so fast he almost laughed out loud. Instead, he gently picked up her ankle and began wrapping it with an elastic bandage.

"It needs more ice," she said.

"In the morning." Finished, Adam looked down at her. "Scoot over."

"I am not sleeping in the same bed with you."

"Don't fight me on this, Renata. You'll lose." He put a knee on the bed, hovering.

She backed away, eyes darting toward the door.

That fast Adam pinned her flat. His hand cradled the side of her neck, his face just inches from hers. "You won't get away again," he whispered. "I promise."

"And I promise: I will! You'll see!"

Shaking his head, he rolled away, freeing her. But not for long.

Punching his pillow, he stretched out and caught her waist. Drawing her close, he threw one leg over hers, effectively shackling her to his side.

"You're right. We'll see."

Chapter Eleven

Willy McEdwin shuffled through the last of the paperwork Tristin had given him.

While his eldest son, Nevin, shared Willy's military and ordnance genius, Tristin and his twin, Burt, were computer experts. Whoever said that spending too much time on the Internet was bad for kids didn't have a clue how hackers were groomed.

He closed the file. Tristin had accessed every record that existed on Adam Duval. Duval had been a delinquent since high school, but had avoided serious trouble with the law until his senior year. Then he'd been accused of selling test results he'd stolen from the school's mainframe. Accused but never charged.

Duval's penchant for getting away with murder started early. A guidance counselor had suggested a deal in which Duval enlisted in the army in lieu of expulsion. He'd spent six years in the military, earning an honorable discharge. Two years later his name popped up in a federal investigation of stolen military arms. But without proof, he remained merely a suspect.

The man was good, with one exception: his poor judgment when it came to women. Duval had been sent to prison after he and his girlfriend were busted with stolen property. It was obvious to Willy that the man had been set up. The FBI had cut his girlfriend a generous deal. Too generous. The sneaky little bitch had sold him out. They weren't called the weaker sex for nothing.

"Still no word on the girlfriend's whereabouts?"

Tristin nodded. "They're calling her Number Seven."

Seven. Willy knew the story behind the notches Duval had carved on his chest. One for each person who'd betrayed him. Once more: There was no proof Duval had murdered anyone. But whether it was truth or legend, it made him a fearsome enemy. Willy admired that.

"What did you get on his partner, Daniel Montague? Anything?"

"From what I gather, Montague's a brainiac. He hacked the prison computer, moved Lyle and Duval onto the same road gang, then scheduled the bus for a trip to BF, Egypt." Tristin leaned forward. "There seems to be a link between Duval, Montague, and a military project called the Jade Labyrinth."

"What the hell is that?"

"Near as I can figure, Uncle Sam has caches of weapons scattered about that could be accessed by small, specialized military units in the event of a widespread terrorist attack. Top, top secret. We're checking on it now."

Willy narrowed his eyes. Had Duval and Montague raided these stockpiles? "Where's this Montague at now?"

"The FBI thinks he fled to Canada, but they have no real leads. The man's a master at disguises, too. You can bet your ass that Duval knows exactly where he's at."

"Get me more on Montague, then. A man with those

kinds of talents has real value. Now what did you find on those prison guards?"

Burt, who'd been quiet up till now, cleared his throat. "They both have a long history of shaking down inmates, but it looks like Irv Wallace—the guard who's missing—was working for the Feds. Lyle swears they left him behind. Uninjured. So I'm guessing the reports attributing his disappearance to the prison break are part of the FBI's propaganda campaign. I bet Wallace is sitting in a safe house somewhere."

"Probably. The FBI wants Lyle and Adam to look dirty as hell." Willy steepled his fingers. "Don't worry about the guard for now. There's too much heat and I don't want to jeopardize this job. It's bad enough Nevin almost blew it."

"But Pa—"

"Don't start. I've got enough problems. Once Lyle's better and that doctor's taken care of, I'm reeling Nevin in."

Chapter Twelve

As Adam expected, once Renata quit struggling, her body collapsed from sheer exhaustion. She hadn't slept more than a scattered handful of hours in the past three days. That lack combined with high stress had taken a toll.

Once more he marveled at her strength. She'd been abducted, threatened. Add to that her short-lived escape and subsequent injuries. Most people would have crumbled long before now.

They were lying side-by-side, his arm anchored loosely at her waist. She felt soft. Perfectly feminine. And that worried him.

He'd been aware of her as a woman from the beginning—since kissing her—but he'd controlled it. Hell, he'd had three months of prison to perfect his control.

But seeing her naked tonight had nearly killed him. He'd only gotten a couple of too-short glimpses of her breasts. They were high, firm. Large. With the prettiest nipples he'd ever seen. Little flashes of copper. He'd also caught a peek of the dark triangle of her pubic hair, a thick, coal-black pelt that his fingers ached to explore.

She'd kept her back to him, which he hadn't minded. The view had been lush. He'd admired every inch.

From her sweet ass, round and curved like a peach, to her trim waist and those distinctly female-flared hips.

He'd been fine with looking . . . until she'd turned. Until she'd looked at him. All of him. His face. His scars. His cock. And for one infinitesimal moment—damn it—she had wanted *him*.

He'd never had a woman look at him like that. With pure, sweet desire. Not lust. Not greed. Not excitement. Want . . . He'd nearly lost it.

In her sleep, she pressed her spine more fully into his belly, wriggling her butt even more snugly against his erection. He gritted his teeth. Damn thing would probably never go flaccid now.

Her snuggling was more proof of just how deeply she slept. If she were even semi-conscious, he was certain his cock would not be cradled so thoroughly.

He checked the time. While he desperately needed sleep himself, he had to try reaching Stan again. And Ethan. Nevin's unexpected appearance was a positive sign. It meant they had to be close to Willy. Which underscored the urgency for releasing Renata.

Before Nevin showed up, Adam had debated telling her the truth. A sanitized version, at least. Now it was out of the question. If his cover were blown, they'd both be in danger. And Willy and sons would escape yet again.

The news of the deputy's death had solidified Adam's resolve to make certain the McEdwins were captured and brought to trial. For all their victims' sake: the thirteen people who died in an explosion outside a federal office in Chicago two years ago. The nine people in Omaha the year before that. Des Moines . . .

The list of victims was long. Too long. Adam's sacrifices, Renata's hardships, were piddling compared to

the lives cut short. And now he had the chance to make
sure no one else died.

Climbing from bed, Adam tracked noiselessly across
the room, avoiding the two boards that squeaked. With
no windows in their bedroom he wasn't worried about
leaving Renata alone for a few minutes.

He listened at the door, caught the heavy snoring.
Nevin was asleep on the sofa, but like Adam he'd
probably trained himself to awaken at the slightest
noise.

Slipping into the bathroom, he turned on her cell
phone. The LED indicated a strong signal, confirming
that Stan had successfully reactivated the phone. He
turned on the shower to muffle his conversation.

He tried Ethan first, hanging up when he got voice
mail. Was he out at a fund-raiser? He dialed Stan, who
answered on the first ring. Both men knew there was
no time for chatting.

"About time," Stan said.

"What have you got?"

"Someone's checking you out. The Labyrinth files
were hacked."

The Jade Labyrinth was part of Adam's fabricated
past, designed solely to whet Willy's interest. "Think
they bought it?"

"Of course! That was some of my best work."

"Any news on that C-4 you were tracking?"

"Nada. Except I'm not the only one sniffing around.
Customs has put out feelers, too."

"Trouble?"

"Possibly."

"Keep on it," Adam said. "Have you talked to
Ethan?"

"He sent a generic keep-up-the-good-work e-mail.
Guess he's too busy buffing his political image to

worry about you and me." Stan lowered his voice. "I've been doing some checking on him. The deeper I dig, the less I like the idea of him as VP."

"I'm afraid to ask what files you've been hacking."

"Enough to know lots of people share my opinion."

Adam grunted. Ethan Falco was the type of behind-the-scenes power most politicians feared. He had influence with the CIA, FBI, NSA, and most important, the White House. He'd been around too long—he knew everything on everybody. He was the enemy no one wanted, so while most politicians privately reviled him, publicly they lauded him.

"Look, I need you to arrange for Ethan's men to pick up Renata."

"Why involve me?"

"Because once she's tucked away, I want you to keep track of where she is and how she's doing." Until the job wrapped up, Renata would have to be hidden.

Stan was silent, then, "Has the dame gotten under your skin?"

"I don't have skin." Adam refused to examine his feelings. "She's been through a lot. I want to make sure Ethan doesn't push too hard with the debriefing."

Stan laughed. "Let me rephrase my original question: Does she mean something to you?"

With a growl, Adam switched off the phone and made his way back to the bedroom. He climbed into bed, beside Renata, and pulled her close.

The thought that she'd soon be safe made it easier to fall asleep.

Renata awoke from a nightmare.

She'd been trapped in a tall building, running up flight after flight of stairs to escape Lyle. But when she reached the top floor, he was there, a gun trained on her. She retreated, seeking the door and found herself trapped against a window. Lyle fired. She fell backwards, through the glass, screaming as she plummeted to the ground.

Then Adam caught her, breaking her fall before drawing her tightly to his chest. He soothed her fears and kissed her again. That had been the most shocking aspect of the dream. Adam's benevolence.

She closed her eyes, tried to calm her breathing as she threw off the murky remnants of the nightmare. Her pulse was elevated from fear. The sensation of falling had been so real, she'd felt her stomach roll. Being shot had been terrifying.

But worst was the act of kissing Adam. The thought that she enjoyed the kiss—even in a dream—disturbed her. So did the niggling suspicion that her still-racing pulse was an after effect of that kiss.

The man had an unsettling effect on her. She had a physical . . . sexual . . . awareness of him. A feeling of being drawn to him. Turned on by him. Seeing him naked hadn't helped. Bad guys shouldn't be so alluring. Not that she was falling for it.

Opening her eyes, she remained still. Adam was asleep behind her, his breathing deep and even. He was curled on his side, his arm still anchored around her waist. Under different circumstances his closeness would have been comforting. Personal. Sensual. Used thus, it was merely a means of bondage.

So why wasn't that upsetting to her right now? She'd been furious last night when he'd climbed in bed with her. What had changed while they slept?

Nothing. She was still a prisoner. She was still being held against her wishes.

But she didn't fear him as much this morning *be-*

cause he'd passed an important test. He hadn't taken advantage of her in the shower. Nor had he tried to force himself on her during the night.

Which didn't make him a hero. Or even a decent person. She expected the worst of Lyle, and he fit the mold. Adam didn't.

Oh, she believed he was dangerous. If it came down to saving his own neck, she had no doubt he'd sacrifice her. But . . . What? Something didn't add up.

He hadn't physically harmed her. Even when she'd cut him. Likewise there had been no retaliation for her attempted escape.

It was a small comfort. The bottom line remained unchanged: two fugitives held her. One of those men was a murderer. *Lyle.* And while she could imagine Adam doing a lot of things, killing wasn't one of them. Which didn't absolve him of guilt.

Behind her, he shifted, drawing her close as his chin nuzzled her hair. His hand clutched her hip.

"Mmmmm," he whispered. "Sleep good?"

"No."

"Could have fooled me the way you were snoring earlier."

"I don't snore."

He laughed, and she realized he had been teasing. Which infuriated her. Bad guys shouldn't tease, either.

"I need to use the bathroom." She struggled to sit up and found more sore muscles. Her ankle throbbed.

Adam swung his legs over the edge of the bed. "Stay here. I'll be right back."

"Like hell I'll stay here," Renata whispered to herself. She scooted to the edge and stood, testing her ankle. It wouldn't take her full weight, but she could hop.

Adam's voice startled her. "Planning to make another run for it?"

She turned. The rebuttal on her lips died. He wasn't wearing a shirt, which gave her a nice view of firm abs as he walked. His hair was still disheveled from sleep, his cheeks dark with overnight stubble. Under different circumstances, she could imagine her jaw dropping to see him striding toward her.

He lifted a hand to cover his scars. "Sorry." Snagging his T-shirt off the floor, he tugged it over his head.

Too late, Renata realized he assumed she stared at his scars. She hadn't noticed them.

He picked her up and carried her out of the bedroom.

"I can walk."

"Limping doesn't count. Besides, this keeps the pressure off your ankle."

He set her down beside the half bath off the kitchen. "Your toothbrush and clean clothes are already in there. I'll be out here if you need anything."

The bathroom had all the necessities but one—a window. She leaned against the vanity, finding her balance before trying to change clothes and examine her injuries.

Her ankle looked more swollen this morning, the bruising and soreness worse, too. She touched her side gingerly. It hurt. So did her arm. She stripped off her shirt. Quite a few bruises had risen on her arms and legs, nothing serious. But the scrape on her side looked nasty, red. She'd need to clean it with peroxide.

She finished dressing and raked her fingers through her hair. Her appearance was her last concern. Except for her lack of underwear. Particularly, a bra. She looked down at her nipples poking out beneath the T-shirt. She pulled the fabric away, which only seemed to make it worse. She grabbed the shirt she'd slept in and put it on, too. The extra layer helped.

Adam was in the kitchen making coffee when she opened the door.

"Have you checked Lyle yet?"

Adam nodded. "He's still sleeping. Nevin said he took more painkillers during the night."

She put a hand on her hip, displeased. "He shouldn't have free access to them. They're not candy."

"It's hard for me to say much without getting in his business."

"Oh, right! I forgot the prisoner's code of ethics. Tell me this much then: Has he abused drugs in the past? Had any addiction issues?"

Adam gave her a wry look. The police files he'd seen mentioned under-age drinking at parties, but not drug abuse. Of course that could be one of the things his family had swept under the rug. Before landing in prison, Lyle had been arrested several times, but charges were always dropped when witnesses refused to testify or evidence disappeared.

"I don't believe he's an addict. But he's not above recreational use. I'll mention it to Nevin, though." He pointed to a chair. "Now let me wrap your ankle and we'll go outside."

"I can do it myself."

He ignored her, taking her foot gently in hand. "It looks sore as hell. I'll get you some ibuprofen."

When he finished, they went out the back door onto a large, elevated deck. Renata shielded her eyes against the glare of sun.

"Wasn't sure I'd recognize it after all the rain." Adam turned his face up and drew in a deep breath.

His pensive tone made her wonder what it must be like to be locked away. Had he not considered the punishment before committing the crime? Or had he thought he'd get off?

She stared at his handsome profile. With his eyes closed, his dark lashes seemed even longer; the hollows beneath his cheekbones more profound.

His eyes opened and he turned, smiling faintly when he caught her staring.

Flustered, Renata raised her chin and scowled. "How much longer will you keep me?"

"I'm not sure."

"Would you let me contact my mother? Or sister? Let at least one of them know I'm alive."

"That won't make them feel any better," he said. "The minute you hang up, they'll begin wondering whether you're still alive."

She hated that he was right. Which didn't lessen her desire to contact them. Wanting distance from him, she limped to the far side of the deck and looked over the rail. The ground was fifteen feet straight down. She saw the scattered woodpile.

Adam followed her. He shook his head. "That explains your skinned up side. You're lucky you didn't break your neck."

Renata nodded absently, her eyes skimming the woods beyond the yard. If she got another shot at escape, she needed to know the lay of the land.

From what she could see, it was good she had opted to avoid the woods last night. The uneven terrain was pocked with gullies. Downed trees crisscrossed one another, broken branches sticking up like spikes.

She started to turn away when a flicker caught her eye. She narrowed her gaze, trying to see what had moved. A squirrel? Bird?

A person. Had Adam noticed?

She glanced sideways, debating what to do next. If

she screamed, she could put the other person at risk as well as blow her chance at rescue.

Adam's hand closed over her mouth as his arm snaked around her waist, restraining and lifting her at the same time. She struggled, but in seconds they were back inside the kitchen.

She bolted for the front door, ungraceful but determined.

"Stay down, damn it!" Handling her roughly, he pulled her to the floor then snapped the deadbolt in place.

"Is it the police? Will you let me go?"

"Be quiet or I'll have to gag you." Adam had only managed a brief look at the man. He'd been dressed in camouflage and was pressed into a small ditch, his assault rifle pointed right at them.

Easing up, Adam peered around the edge of the window blind, but saw nothing. Shit! The man had either moved or was too well hidden. One thing was certain: The man was careless to let himself be spotted. Which meant it might be someone acting alone. A bounty hunter? A kamikaze jackass?

He'd take a bounty hunter any day over the police. Adam could easily take out a single man, even a couple of men, whereas a confrontation with the law would blow everything. A screwup now would send Willy and his other two sons deeper underground.

He wondered how they'd been found. Had one of the McEdwins' contacts been careless? Or dropped a dime for the reward?

What now? They had no car. They couldn't make a run for it. With Lyle injured and doped up, they'd never make it on foot. And the last thing Adam wanted was a shootout. He couldn't afford bullets flying with Renata inside.

"Follow me." He dragged her toward the hall. He needed to alert Nevin about the intruder.

Lyle was awake and talking on the phone. If he was talking to Willy, they needed to get help. Now.

Bursting in, Adam pointed to the phone. "Who's that?"

Nevin, who'd been reclining on the couch, pulled his own pistol when he saw Adam's gun. "What the hell's going on?"

Lyle's face grew red. "Look, sugar, I need to go. Me too. Can't wait."

Adam felt his jaw tense. Was that how they'd been found? "You called your girlfriend? Don't you know the FBI has tapped the phone of your every known associate?"

"Give me a little credit. She's safe. Her father is—"

Nevin interrupted. "Her father's no dummy. He knows what to watch for."

"Well, somebody's slipped up." Adam motioned toward the window. "I just spotted someone behind the house, in the woods. He's in camo."

Nevin lowered his gun and put his hand over his chest. A grin spread across his face. "Jesus Christ! You almost gave me a heart attack. That's one of my men. Keeping watch."

"Keeping watch? For what?"

Nevin nodded at Renata. "After your girlfriend's little disappearing act last night, I figured we could use backup."

Adam didn't bother to hide his fury. "When did you plan on telling me? I don't like being kept in the dark. And I damn sure don't like someone creeping through the woods with a gun leveled at me."

"It wasn't leveled at you." Nevin glanced at her again. "Just think of it as an early-warning system. You and my little brother were a hot commodity before that deputy died. Now you're cop-killers. Every law enforcement person in the nation just made you their personal enemy."

"An early-warning system doesn't mean jack if we don't have a means to get away. I want a car. If that had been the cops, we'd have been shit out of luck." Adam pointed to Lyle. "And he wouldn't make it fifty feet without collapsing."

"Wait a minute," Nevin frowned, confused. "You mean there's not a car out in the garage?"

"Not yet," Lyle confirmed. "Pa's making arrangements."

Nevin swore. "I'll have one here by nightfall."

That Nevin didn't know who was providing a car surprised Adam. Willy had usurped Nevin by bringing in Calvin to move them, then Nevin had shown up unannounced and kept his own man posted outside. What was going on? Obviously the McEdwins weren't working in unison.

Adam tugged Renata back into the kitchen. He knew she was disappointed, but he hoped she'd remember to be more circumspect in the future. With someone watching they both had to.

And when the time came to free her, Adam would have to be even more careful to ensure she got away safely.

They remained inside the rest of the day, watching television in the living room until late.

Renata knew Adam felt as restless as she did, his eyes drifting frequently toward the bedroom where Nevin and Lyle stayed.

She was grateful the McEdwins remained in the other room. Both brothers made her uncomfortable.

She read through the stack of newspapers that had been left with the supplies, hoping to catch a hint of what the police were doing to apprehend them. She also hoped to read some news about her family's reaction to her abduction.

While the papers shed little light on her family, she did learn a more complete history of the McEdwins.

Willy, the patriarch, had been a decorated Vietnam veteran who worked with explosives during two tours in Southeast Asia. After his discharge, he returned to his Missouri hometown, married his high-school sweetheart, and settled down on the family farm.

Within four years, he filed for bankruptcy and lost everything to repossession and foreclosure. One article blamed Willy's failure on economics. A lot of Midwesterners lost farms at the same time and felt stung by a government that had urged them into debt but did nothing to protect crop and livestock prices.

In retaliation, some displaced farmers joined antigovernment groups. Willy fell in with a paramilitary outfit whose leader touted a plan to take control away from the federal government and return it to the individual states. With his prior combat experience, Willy rapidly rose through the organization's ranks, simultaneously increasing his visibility within federal law enforcement circles.

Renata closed her eyes after reading about Willy's wife, who had died when two crooked policemen rigged a bomb at the McEdwin home—a bomb that had been meant for Willy. Their reason for targeting him was widely speculated but remained unclear as both officers died on a subsequent assignment.

Lyle, who had only been a few months old at the

time, had nearly been killed along with his mother. The report said she had literally tossed him out of harm's way seconds before the blast went off. A maternal aunt raised Lyle while Willy was wrongly imprisoned for his wife's murder.

The newspapers also covered each of the bombings attributed to the McEdwins. At first the explosions at various federal facilities appeared to be strikes against government in general: FBI, Department of Justice, U.S. Marshal. Until they noticed that many of the key people involved in Willy's trial had died. The judge, the federal prosecutors, the Marshal who arrested him. Even the warden. While they were the primary targets, a lot of innocent bystanders were killed as well.

Jim Acton had been one of the McEdwins' many victims.

She heard the cell phone ring in Lyle's room. Adam lowered the volume of the television and moved to sit beside her on the couch, shoving the papers to the floor to make room.

She knew he'd moved closer to eavesdrop, but still her pulse jumped. Then he threw an arm around her shoulder. Renata's first instinct was to move away. Then she recalled her resolve to soften Adam and forced herself to relax.

A few minutes later, Nevin walked out of the bedroom and dropped into the chair Adam had vacated.

"That was the old man. He's working on the transportation issue." He looked at Renata. "He also wants to know if you need any other supplies to care for my brother, princess."

She kept her features neutral, not wanting to give him the satisfaction of knowing the endearment irritated her. That everything about him irritated her.

Adam hugged her, his arm uncomfortably close to

her breast. Once again she struggled with the desire to shove him away, settled for shooting him a dirty look. His embrace was nothing more than a statement of ownership. *Play along,* she reminded herself.

"The supplies I have are adequate," she said. "If he doesn't respond to these antibiotics soon, he'll need to go to a hospital—"

Nevin's easy-going demeanor vanished, his voice cold and harsh. "Yeah, well, if he doesn't respond soon, he won't be the only one needing a hospital."

Chapter Thirteen

Adam stood, cutting Nevin off by tugging Renata to her feet. "We're going to bed."

But instead of going to the bedroom, he steered her toward the bathroom. "Do you need a minute before we take a shower?"

Her face grew warm at the word *we*. A vision of him naked flashed through her mind.

"Let me shower alone," she began.

"No way."

Before she could protest, he leaned close, snaking his arm behind her. Opening the door, he forced her inside.

She put her hands on her hips. "Look, you—"

"No, you look." He lowered his voice. "Don't push Nevin."

"How can telling him the truth about his brother be construed as pushing?"

"They've made it clear they have no intention of taking Lyle to a hospital. Repeatedly bringing the subject up just pisses them off."

"And you think that bothers me? Maybe I like pissing them off."

He edged closer. "It bothers me. But I suppose you like pissing me off, too."

She opened her mouth to say more, then closed it.

Which annoyed Adam even more. He preferred to know her thoughts. He understood her frustration at the McEdwins' refusal to heed her medical advice. It went against every tenet she held.

"Let me check your ankle." He indicated she should sit on the edge of the tub.

Instead of moving to the tub, Renata leaned against the counter.

Choose your battles. Adam dropped to one knee and picked up her foot. Removing the bandage, he examined it, cupping her heel in his hand before gently massaging the ball of her injured foot. "The swelling's gone down. How's it feel?"

"Better. But you don't have to do that."

"I know." He rubbed her foot a few more seconds then set it down and straightened. "After we shower, I'll wrap it again."

She crossed her arms over her chest. "I . . . can't do this."

"You already did once. And you're still safe, Renata. Trust me."

He grasped the bottom edge of her T-shirt. He could guess why she wore two shirts, and with the McEdwin brothers around, he didn't blame her.

But they were alone now and Adam had been looking forward to this moment all day: their shower . . . where he'd get a glimpse of her naked. And once they were in bed, fully clothed, he could hold her, under the guise of keeping her captive.

He didn't try to gloss it over. Forcing her to shower and sleep with him were guilty, wicked, pleasures. Like recalling what it had been like to kiss her. Or remembering the feel of her body when he'd searched her for weapons. Or held her in his arms as she slept. *And dreamed about making love to her.*

"Then just let me check your side. Make sure it's not getting infected," he whispered.

"It's not. It's fine."

"If that's true, then it won't hurt for me to look." He lifted her shirt a few inches. "Can you raise your arm a bit more so I can loosen the bandage?"

She let out a noisy sigh as she gave him freer access.

His fingers lightly pressed on her skin as he examined her scraped side. "Uh-oh. You better take a look."

Concerned, she straightened and turned toward the mirror. "Is it showing signs of infection?"

The second she moved, Adam tugged the shirts up and off her head.

She crisscrossed her arms over her breasts. "Trust you? Right! That was a dirty trick."

"But effective. We're going to take a shower. The only question is: Do I take your clothes off or do you?"

She raised her chin. "That's not a choice."

Adam nodded toward the living room. "I've already explained that it's important to keep up certain appearances in front of them. So let's get on with it."

Stepping back, he ignored her and stripped off his shirt, tossed it to the floor. He unfastened the top button of his jeans, then paused. "Do you need help?"

"No!" Renata squared her shoulders, told herself that showering with him would be easier since they'd already done it once. And he hadn't gawked or made any wrong advances the last time. Which made the process no easier to contemplate. Still, if she were going to end up naked regardless, she'd prefer it was by her own hand.

He turned away and adjusted the water, then finished removing his jeans. She stared at his buttocks for a long time before realizing he was trying to shield his groin from her. Her face flamed as she realized she had been trying hard to see *it*. What was wrong with her? Why was she so . . . eager to see him again?

He half-turned, lifting her into the tub before climbing in right behind her and promptly turning his back.

She grabbed the bottle of shampoo, squeezed it hard. She'd seen lots of naked men, viewed their bodies with clinical detachment. A detachment that was wholly absent right now.

She scrubbed her hair and rinsed before looking behind her. Adam patiently waited for a turn beneath the spray. Keeping her back to him, she traded places.

Twice, she peeked over her shoulder. The first time was quick. He had his back to her as he soaped his arms. The second time he was shampooing his hair.

She stared as his long fingers worked through his thick, dark mane. Rivulets of soap ran from his nape, down the indentation of his spine to swirl near the two dimples just above his buttocks. The soapy line curled along the crevice between his cheeks before disappearing.

She blinked, mesmerized.

Then Adam turned toward her. Fully. She gasped. But he didn't move.

Neither did she.

She let her eyes drift over him. Over his chest. His abs. And lower . . . His erection was enormous, sticking straight out from his body, the head gleaming with water droplets. It was frightening and fascinating at the same time.

The man was pure temptation. A dark invitation to sin. Unable to resist, she brought her hand up, toward his penis and let two fingers glide over the tip. The heat surprised her. So too the hardness, the shimmering strength. The beauty.

His reaction was immediate.

With a groan, he captured both her wrists and pulled them up above her head, pinning her ungently against the tiled wall. She panicked, expecting to feel him thrust roughly into her. Instead he lowered his head and took her mouth.

Sanity fled as his tongue swept forward. She opened her mouth, accepting him eagerly. His kiss was all heat, all passion. It tempted, promised, soothed, and teased, driving her mad for more. Thought and reason fled beneath the divine onslaught.

She struggled to free her hands, to draw him closer. For he not only controlled the kiss, he controlled the contact of their bodies. And right now only their mouths touched. It wasn't enough. She wanted to stroke, grasp, scratch. To take all he would give.

Her hips strained forward, seeking to rub against his groin, seeking ease. But he denied her, continuing to hold her so that only her mouth was ravaged. She fought, whimpered. Begged.

And when she finally grew weak and surrendered totally, he broke the kiss. Her breath came out in long ragged gulps. Like she'd been held underwater, too long without oxygen.

His face was inches from hers. His eyes were dilated, fierce and dark with a stark hunger that scared her even as she recognized it. He found her desirable. *And didn't want to.*

"Don't start something you have no intention of finishing." He released her wrists so abruptly she nearly fell as he stepped out of the shower.

God, what had she done?

The water was cold now. Trembling, she leaned into it welcoming the coolness, desperately needing time alone. But Adam flung the curtain open and shut off the water. Then he thrust a towel at her. He already had one wrapped low around his hips, the towel dipped V-like toward his groin.

There was no disguising the bulge that tented the front. He was still fully erect.

"If you're that interested, I can drop this." His hand moved to where the edge of the towel was tucked.

"Don't flatter yourself."

"Hurry up and get dressed. I'll be right outside."

She noticed that he left the door ajar about four inches, enough for privacy, but not enough to block sound. If she tried to open the window, he'd hear.

She caught sight of herself in the mirror. Her lips were red and puffy, her nipples erect and elongated. Her breasts felt tight, swollen. Needy.

This couldn't be happening. She wouldn't allow it.

She scrambled into the clean clothes he'd left, then looked up to find him leaning casually against the doorframe. He wore no shirt, no shoes, only jeans. A dark line of fine hair arrowed down from his navel drawing her eyes to the bulge at his crotch. He moved closer.

Feeling claustrophobic, she tried to push past him. He stopped her, swinging her into his arms as he carried her to the bedroom. She caught a glimpse of Nevin, watching them. Probably enjoying the show, the bastard!

When Adam closed the bedroom door, she cleared her throat. "I am not sleeping with you again!"

"Did I give you the impression you had a choice?" He strode to the bed and dumped her on the mattress. She scooted toward the end, but he blocked her. "Don't push your luck, Renata."

She could see by the glitter of banked emotion in his eyes that he was a hair's breadth from losing his temper. She backed away. "Can I sleep on the floor? Tie my hands and legs if you must."

Adam shook his head. "Move over."

With a groan that was part indignation, part resignation, Renata rolled onto her side and scooted to the far side of the bed.

For long moments Adam stared at the curving silhouette she presented. Her ribs tapered down to a dip at her waist. Her hips flared up in come-on curves. Did he dare climb into the same bed with her?

His thoughts flew back to their shower. When she'd touched him, he had nearly come on the spot. Her fingers brushing his cock had felt almost painful. He hadn't wanted to stop her. No, he'd wanted to take her hand and encourage her to touch more. To touch harder. To caress, squeeze, explore. And he had wanted to touch her in return.

Kissing her had been a huge mistake. When he thought it would quench his desire, it had fanned it. Had threatened to erode what precious little control remained. He closed his eyes.

He knew he couldn't have her. But that didn't stop him from wanting her. Nor would it stop him from imagining the deed in his dreams.

And if thinking about making love to her was a sin, he'd gladly pay his dues because he knew better than to think he'd stop.

It took Renata hours to fall asleep. Adam lay awake, content with her keeping a slight physical distance between them. But in sleep she had snuggled closer. He abandoned the bed, prowled the room. The woman had to go.

A car door slammed outside. Alert, he moved

silently to the living room, found it empty. Nevin
wasn't on the couch. Adam lifted a blind on the front
window, watched taillights speed away from the cabin.
Who had left? Or was it simply a changing of the
guard?

A dim light shone from Lyle's room where the television set was still on. He found the younger man
agitated as he sat up in bed watching the news. When
he saw Adam, he motioned him closer and boosted the
volume.

> *"Customs confirmed that one hundred pounds
> of plastic explosives were seized today at a Texas
> seaport."*

Adam's attention perked as he listened. This had to
be the same shipment of C-4 that Stan had mentioned
earlier.

The report had clearly hit a nerve with Lyle. "Fucking bastards."

"Who? Customs? Or the fool trying to smuggle it
in?"

"Hey! Watch who you call fool."

Lyle's reaction confirmed the shipment had been for
his father. And Adam would bet his pension that the
kid knew exactly what the McEdwins had had planned
for the C-4.

Adam pointed to the television. "It's damn near impossible to bring that stuff in through a port anymore."

"Versus what? Bringing it in on land?"

"That. Or getting it from a domestic source and
avoiding borders all together."

"Right. The way they watch that stuff these days?"
Lyle snorted. "And who, besides the military, has it in
those quantities?"

"Does it matter where it comes from?"

"Are you serious?" Lyle shut off the TV. "Damn, now I wish Nevin hadn't taken off so fast."

"He's gone?"

"Yeah. But they left a car for us. Keys are in the kitchen."

"Where to now?"

"Nowhere. We're supposed to wait here. Lay low." Lyle eyed the IV needle in his arm with distaste. "They're treating me like an invalid, you know. But I think I just figured out a way to get the old man's attention."

"How?"

"What you said about acquiring C-4 domestically. Can it really be done?"

Adam feigned indifference. "With the right connections, yes."

"And you still have these connections?"

"That depends. Let's cut the crap. It was obviously your father's stuff they seized. Now I know your family's got grudges, but a hundred pounds? That's a lot of damage."

"Only if used all at once."

Lyle was trying too hard to downplay the potential. Which made Adam wonder what the hell they had planned. He recalled Lyle's prior contention that his father hadn't wanted him out of prison yet—because something was going on. Obviously that *something* required a hundred pounds of explosives. And if the McEdwins were searching for a new source of C-4, Adam damn sure wanted to be involved.

"It won't come cheap. Not in that quantity," Adam said.

"Money's not the problem. Time is. We need it within two weeks."

Adam shook his head. "You know what it would take to pull that off?"

"Name it. And before you say no, just put out a feeler. Check with your partner."

"Who says my partner would have anything to do with it?"

Lyle popped a couple of painkillers in his mouth and swallowed. "My pa's had your background checked. He knows you and your partner were brokering military arms."

"Knows? There was no proof, kid. No formal charges." Adam watched Lyle's gaze drop to his chest. The six notches. "No proof; no charges there either."

"Look, I saw that high-tech radio jammer. You can't tell me that wasn't military. To be honest, I think my old man's pretty impressed with you. I figure if I can locate another shipment of C-4, he'll be just as impressed with me."

And Lyle's reputation as the family fuck-up could be permanently retired. Adam realized now why the guards hadn't been able to break Lyle. Above all else, the kid wanted his father's approval.

"Let me do a little checking," Adam promised. But Lyle was already drifting off. "We'll talk in the morning."

He checked on Renata before slipping into the bathroom to call Stan. If Willy thought Adam could supply more plastic explosives, their rendezvous would undoubtedly be moved up. Especially if the old man needed it on such short notice.

"You were right," he said when Stan answered. "That C-4 was for Willy."

Stan whistled. "Any idea what they had planned for it?"

"Had? They're searching for a source to replace it,

so whatever they planned, it's still a go." Adam repeated his conversation with Lyle.

"Wow. I bet that's why Nevin took off. To line up a new supply."

"Maybe. But after today's bust, you know it will be even harder to find. All the usual suspects will close shop until the heat dies down. I don't know what kind of background you concocted for my supposed partner, but the McEdwins are salivating."

Stan coughed. "Yeah, well I can't take credit for that one. That's something else we need to discuss one of these days. Long story."

"All that matters is it worked. Lyle's completely convinced that my partner, Montague, and I were dealing military arms. He wants us to help him locate another stash of C-4."

"Sounds like a perfect opportunity to learn what their target is, too. And hook up more quickly with Willy," Stan said.

"I need to go; give Ethan an update and tell him I expect to free the doctor within the next day or two."

"Can McEdwin survive without her?"

"Not yet. He's still running a fever, but I hope the new medicine will start working soon. Then it's just a matter of finding a place to leave Renata for Ethan's men."

"Roger that," Stan said. "Just be careful. I have a feeling things are getting ready to heat up."

They ended up staying at the cabin another two nights. Nevin and Willy both remained incommunicado, though the guards outside were doubled.

Adam burned to take action but couldn't seem too eager to deal and raise suspicion. He also worried that

Nevin would find a replacement source for the explosives.

Adam knew the time weighed heavy for Renata, too. Being forced to care for one of her captors didn't help. While Lyle's fever lowered, it didn't completely go away which frustrated her.

Adam's admiration for her inner strength increased each day, just as his desire for her body increased each night. They continued to shower together, but rushed through it. His erection was perpetual. A curse. He dreamed about past lovers, the women who'd used his body without inhibition. But all of them looked like Renata.

To pass time, he spent part of each day doing calisthenics; sit-ups, push-ups, crunches.

By the third day the swelling in Renata's foot had gone down and she even worked out with him, though he refused her request to go jogging.

"Do you jog daily?" he asked.

"When I'm not being held against my will? Yes."

Lyle called out, breaking into their conversation. Leaving her handcuffed, Adam walked into the bedroom and found him sitting up.

"Get ready. We're finally leaving here."

"Now?" It was barely dusk. "Going where?"

"Kansas. It's a temporary stop."

"Not again."

"My old man's spooked because of that shipment getting seized, so he'll stay on the move himself for a little while."

Adam frowned. "This is getting old, kid. I expected to be a thousand miles away by now."

"It won't be much longer. The fact we're heading west is a good sign. And I mentioned that we're working on the C-4. He nearly shit." Lyle's grin stretched from ear to ear. "If we can pull this off, I'll be a hero."

Once again they traveled at night. The directions were tedious, and took them through the darkest stretches of landscape Adam had ever seen—the unending cornfields of southern Illinois.

The brakes of the vehicle ahead of them suddenly flashed on, the bright red lights careening crazily before spinning into the air.

Adam stopped short, his headlights sweeping the scene. A minivan had flipped, coming to rest upside down in the middle of the road. The mangled body of a deer lay in the van's headlights.

Renata sat forward. "My God! Someone's lying in the road! We have to help!"

Lyle roused in the back. "Why are we stopping?"

"An accident." Adam pulled over, turning on his flashers as he threw the car into PARK. "I'll be right back."

Renata lunged for his shoulder, held out her cuffed hands. "Take me with you. They may need a doctor."

"Don't do it man," Lyle warned. "She'll run."

"If I run, shoot me," she said.

"Agreed." Adam unlocked her cuffs and grabbed a flashlight, before turning to Lyle. "We'll be right back. I'll leave the car running."

Tugging her from the car, Adam kept her close as they hurried toward the body in the road. An eerie death-like chant of cicadas filled the night. He saw only the one victim, a man, who he'd guess had been thrown from the car.

Adam had expected to find a dead body, but the man

stirred when they approached, in pain. "My legs are broken . . . Please . . . get my son!"

A child's sobs broke the night.

"Stay with him," Adam said to Renata. But she was already on her knees, checking the man's pulse as she asked questions.

Adam hurried toward the van. The front seats had been completely demolished, the engine shoved forward. Oddly, the radio still blared, sound popping and crackling from a shattered speaker. *"The search continues for the escaped convicts . . ."*

He flicked on the flashlight and peered inside at the back seat, afraid of what he'd find. A small boy, still strapped in the car seat that had saved his life, hung upside down, red-faced and screaming.

Relief hammered in his chest. "Easy, buddy. I'll get you."

Adam tried to open the doors but found the frames jammed too tightly. Dropping to the ground and lying on his back, he wedged his shoulders through the busted-out window, praying he didn't get stuck. Broken glass bit into his flesh as he forced his upper body farther into the vehicle.

The smell of fear and urine hit him as the kid continued to scream. Adam reached up, realized his hand was covered in blood. His? The kid's? Then he caught the scent of ketchup, saw the long forgotten french fry still clutched in the child's hand.

The little boy cried even harder when Adam freed him from the seat and slowly backed out of the wrecked vehicle.

Cradling the boy carefully, he hurried to Renata. As they drew near, the injured man held out his arm. "Tanner!"

Adam lowered the little boy to the pavement beside

his father. Tanner promptly buried his face in his father's neck and howled even louder. Renata moved closer, soothing the child with low sounds as she ran a tentative hand down his back, checking for injuries.

She nodded at Adam's shirt. "Is that your blood or his?"

"Mine. I don't think he's hurt. He was still in his car seat."

A new set of headlights flashed on the horizon. Another vehicle approached and pulled over in front of Adam's car.

A woman came running up, a cell phone pressed to her ear as she shouted the location of the accident into the phone. Adam moved closer to Renata.

"I'm an RN," the woman said to Adam. "Is anyone hurt?"

"Thank God! This man needs help." He yanked Renata to her feet, pinned her to his side. "You've called the police? Our cell phone's dead."

"They're on the way." The woman dropped beside the injured man and began asking questions and checking his vital signs.

Behind them Lyle honked the horn, flashed the headlights.

Adam turned to the nurse. "That's our kids. We left them in the car and they're probably fighting. My wife and I will be right back."

The nurse, who had looked up at the honking, nodded absently and refocused on the injured man and child.

They had almost reached the car when a siren echoed in the distance. Adam clapped a hand over Renata's mouth and pulled her into a run. At the car, he shoved her inside and quickly handcuffed her.

"Don't—" Renata struggled in vain.

"Jesus Christ! The cops are almost here and they ain't stopping!" Lyle yelled. "We're fucked!"

"They're coming for the accident, not us." Adam dropped the car in DRIVE and took off.

Behind them a patrol car approached, lights blazing. From the corner of his eye, he saw Renata look over her shoulder just as Lyle leaned forward and wrapped an arm around her neck. Yanking her backwards, he pressed a pistol to her temple.

Her scream was cut off as Lyle tightened his arm.

"They get too close, I'll shoot her," he slurred. "And when I toss her body in the road, I guarantee they'll stop!"

Chapter Fourteen

"Whoa there!" Adam kept his voice steady, to calm Lyle. "Look, the cop already pulled over at the accident. Once we clear this curve, I'll floor it and they'll never find us."

Undoubtedly, Nevin had provided yet another handgun—a problem he'd deal with later. His only concern right now was Renata's safety. And his choices were brutally simple. Stopping to disarm Lyle while lights were still visible behind them would only agitate the kid further. Adam had his own gun drawn, but out of sight. If he couldn't talk Lyle down . . .

"Yeah? Well, they can still come after us," Lyle persisted. "That's why I say we dump her. So what if we get rid of her a day or two earlier?"

"You're still running a fever."

"Big deal. Once we hook up with my father—"

"And when will that be? Your old man's pushed us off several times already." Adam glanced over his shoulder. "Besides, we may need her as a hostage."

Lyle swore, then suddenly withdrew the gun and released her. "You got a point. But let's get the hell out of Dodge."

His own fury barely under control, Adam hit the gas, eager to get away from the accident scene to disarm Lyle.

* * *

Lyle snored like a warthog in the back seat, having taken yet more painkillers.

The incident left Renata feeling as if she sat three feet from a rabid dog, wondering if the leash was about to break. Could Adam truly protect her from Lyle's escalating volatility?

She thought back to the accident, wished she had tried to tell the injured man who she was. But he'd been barely conscious, worried only about his child. And it had been so dark, so chaotic, that neither the man nor the woman who stopped had seen them clearly.

Adam stopped at a riverside park just across the state line. He pressed a finger to his lips then climbed out of the car. She watched, not understanding, until he opened the back door and snatched the gun from Lyle's waistband.

Lyle stirred, disoriented. "What's up?"

"Pit stop," Adam said.

With a groan, Lyle sat up. "Hey! Where's my gun?"

"In a safe spot."

"Give it back."

"Not while you're popping pills."

"Who died and left you in charge?"

"I've always been in charge. Remember?" Adam moved closer. "Don't ever pull a stunt like that again, kid. You were waving the pistol all over the place, and I was this far from shooting you myself."

Lyle swallowed, clearly unable to recall the incident. "I'm sorry, man. I—"

Behind them, headlights swept the gravel lot. But as quickly as the car arrived, it sped away with a loud burst of music and laughter.

"A bunch of kids." Adam straightened. "This is

probably one of their drinking spots, which means the local cops patrol it. We've got to go."

Renata's knees complained when she finally climbed out of the car. They'd crossed the Kansas line shortly after sunup, having lost even more time with an unexpected detour caused by road construction. She knew their chances of being recognized in daylight were far greater, which was why Adam had ordered her to crouch down.

Lyle was once again unconscious-via-pills and Adam made no attempt to rouse him.

She squinted against the sun, taking in her surroundings. They were parked in front of a fairly new doublewide trailer set off alone near a creek. Wheat fields stretched as far as she could see in every direction.

"Welcome to the Middle of Nowhere." Adam unlocked the handcuffs and offered her a bottle of water.

She drank greedily, more dehydrated than she'd realized.

"Easy," he said. "Don't get sick guzzling it all at once."

His reminder irritated her. She was the doctor, damn it. She took another sip and capped the bottle.

He pulled her away from the car. "Did Lyle hurt you earlier?"

She bit back the urge to snap at him. Lyle pointing the gun at her head had frightened her terribly. "Physical hurt? No. But I know what he's capable of now, and that scares me. Especially since he mentioned getting rid of me *early.*"

For a long moment Adam didn't answer. Then, "I

promised in the beginning that you wouldn't be harmed. It's a promise I intend to keep."

He kept his voice low, nearly unintelligible, but sincere. Did she believe him? Oddly, she did. After watching him help the accident victims, she had concluded once and for all that he and Lyle were as different as sun and ice.

To her surprise, Adam moved behind her and started rubbing her shoulders at the exact spot that hurt.

"I know it wasn't comfortable riding on the floor like that."

She started to jerk away, then stopped, recalling her plan to soften him. Exactly what would it take to convince Adam to free her? Bribery? With what? Seduction?

The idea wasn't nearly as repugnant as it had been a few days ago. Was it because she'd do anything to gain her freedom? Yes . . .

I can do this, she thought. *Just take baby steps. Fake it.*

She shifted closer to him. "Lower, please."

His fingers found the knot of tension at the base of her spine. As he rubbed, she pressed backwards, felt his body against hers.

A twig snapped, the sound distinct.

Adam stepped away. "Get inside."

She scanned the horizon, sensed someone watching. She should have known the McEdwins would have sentries posted here too.

Adam brought Lyle in right behind her.

"Bed," Lyle said, his voice slurred. "And before you ask, no, I don't need her to check me and I ain't sleeping with an IV."

The younger man had barely climbed into the bed before passing out again. Adam did a quick search of the room. He didn't expect to find another firearm hidden, but he wasn't taking any chances.

Renata watched, but didn't speak until they were alone in the living room. "He still needs the antibiotics."

"I'll press the issue later, after we've all had some sleep. Right now, he'll just fight us over it."

He unfastened her handcuffs and led her down a short hall to the other bedroom. Adam eyed the king-size bed. It looked like heaven. For what little sleeping he'd be able to do.

Guilt over Renata's predicament weighed heavy. Her well-being was his responsibility. He needed to get her out before Lyle's behavior grew more erratic.

He rifled through the stack of clothes that had been left. Both he and Renata had blood on their clothes from the accident. He probably had glass embedded in his shoulder. He tugged out a clean shirt and found several new articles of women's underwear. He eyed the bras, found himself wishing his request had been ignored. He'd enjoyed seeing her braless. And at night, when they slept, his hands had sought the silky expanse of her back, unfettered by straps.

"Come on." He tugged her toward the bathroom. Having the master bedroom meant they had a private bath. With a window. A ready excuse for not letting her shower alone.

Renata pointed to the window. "Do you really think I'd risk running away knowing there are people skulking around outside?"

His hand came up, cupped her cheek as his thumb stroked the soft skin beneath her chin. "I didn't think you'd take the risk you did before. And I'm not in the mood to argue, so please get undressed."

He turned, ignoring her as he peeled off his clothes before reaching in to turn on the water.

She caught a glimpse of broad shoulders, tight buttocks and looked away. Their last two showers had been fast, sterile affairs which were no less embarrassing.

She took a deep breath and tugged off her jeans. It was less awkward undressing while his back was turned and the sooner she got it over with, the better. She peeled off one shirt, then the other, reminding herself that she had a plan: seduction.

The moment she let the shirt drop from her fingers, Adam turned. His eyes flared as they swept over her. She caught the fire in his gaze, saw his erection move, swell.

He quickly turned away. "You first."

Confused by his actions, she stepped into the shower. He'd been affected, but sought to hide it. As if he didn't want to be aroused by her. Why? And how could she possibly seduce her way to freedom if the man wasn't interested?

When she looked over her shoulder, she found him staring with undisguised heat. *He did want her.* She did have some power. Thank goodness. After days of feeling weak, the knowledge made her daring. Reckless.

She turned, faced him fully, and watched his eyes skim from her throat to her breasts. Her nipples drew tight.

Then his gaze dropped to her groin. The warmth that had been building inside her flared. Burned. She had never experienced a white-hot sexual craving. The sensation was heady. Intoxicating. And she shook with a desire that threatened to devour her as she waited for Adam to make a move.

He didn't. He simply stared.

Until she touched him.

She hadn't had a conscious thought to do so, but once her hand moved forward, she couldn't stop. He trembled, fiercely, and bucked as her fingers closed over the head of his penis, clasping it.

She looked down. He was rigid, fully erect. Her hand was tiny against his swollen flesh. Fascinated, she slid her fingers lower, grasping the thick shaft. He was rock hard, and grew longer at her touch.

Wet from the shower's spray, her hand slipped easily up. She glided her hand back down, shivering at the sensation of silk over steel, felt him harden even more. That he made no move to touch her in return puzzled her.

"God . . . damn."

At his strangled curse, she looked up.

"You have to ask me to touch you," he whispered. "But if you're not going all the way, don't start."

His words shocked her. Titillated her. She closed her eyes, breathing with difficulty. *What the hell am I doing?* This was supposed to be about him getting excited. Not her.

If you're not going all the way . . .

She couldn't say yes. She didn't want to say no. Yet her hand remained around his erection, unable to release him.

Adam felt as if hot daggers were being traced over his skin, the edge touching but not slicing his flesh. Drawing blood one moment, ecstasy the next. The line between pain and pleasure contracted then expanded. *The dance.*

He sensed her hesitation, knew she was torn. Yes, she was turned on. Yes, she wanted him. The proof was written all over her body. Her nipples were hardened into pearls. Beneath his stare, they grew tighter. Made him wonder what they'd taste like in his mouth.

He knew that if he touched her as intimately as she touched him, he'd find her wet. Eager. One finger would prove it, just one finger slid up between those dark curls. She would be hot. Tight.

And the regret would destroy her. She thought of him as a criminal. A low life.

Christ! What if there were no lies between them? Just desire. The thought was too painful to contemplate.

For the first time in his life, Adam knew the feeling of wanting someone so bad it physically hurt. He had to back away. End it.

As much as he wanted her, he couldn't lose sight of the fact that she was not there of her own free will and didn't know the truth about him or what he was doing.

When they made love, *if* they made love, it would only be after she knew the truth and made her choice accordingly.

This, though, had to stop. He was only human, and she was still teasing his cock with those elegant little hands of her. It was killing him.

Grasping her wrist, he went to yank her hand away, to end it.

But she resisted, tightening her hand around him so that when he pulled, her fingers hugged his shaft, tugging against him. He felt the head of his cock pop.

Adam's world shifted. He swore violently. After days of torment, that one simple move pushed him over the edge. There was no turning back. No sucking it up. No holding on till later. *Damn her.*

With a growl, he pulled away and grasped his own flesh. He hadn't jacked off since he was a kid. Hadn't had the need. Women had thrown themselves at him since he was a sophomore. He was jaded when it came to sex.

Except when it came to her.

Closing his eyes, he squeezed his shaft, running his hand up and down, finding the right rhythm. His swollen testicles tightened as hot flames licked them, his flesh demanding relief. He pumped his fist and heard her shocked intake of breath, felt a perverse satisfaction knowing that she watched—knowing his cock grew harder and longer with each stroke.

He opened his eyes, expecting to see shock, disgust. Wanting it, even.

But instead she seemed . . . fascinated, her eyes wide, unblinking as she stared down at the movement of his hand. Her pelvis thrust forward slightly as she rocked onto her toes, her body unconsciously answering his.

She had her mouth open, making him wonder what those full, luscious lips would feel like on his flesh. A vision of her on her knees weakened him.

Then her tongue, tiny and pink, darted out to lick her lips. The gesture undid him.

With a shout he clenched his fist tighter, pumping furiously. Harder. Faster. Ejaculate ripped up his shaft, building, swelling, ready to explode.

And as it did—Renata reached forward and caught it in her hand.

It felt like time stopped. And stayed suspended . . .

Then restarted with a jolt as the orgasm Adam thought would never end, did.

Spent, and barely able to stand, he turned back into the spray. He sucked in air, desperate for oxygen. Shutting the water off, he grabbed a towel and thrust it at her, never once meeting her eyes.

Renata knew he was angry, didn't blame him. *What*

had possessed her to touch him was no longer the question. *Why hadn't she finished what she started?* was.

An unrelenting tension coiled in her stomach. And lower. The moment Adam had touched himself she'd felt a stab of searing excitement. And as he masturbated—relieving himself in an act she could only call beautiful—her ache had grown. He had spilled into her hand, semen shimmering with heat and energy.

Over and over she visualized his granting himself relief. The memory burned. So did her body. With excruciating detail, she recalled the feel of his penis. The heat, the hardness. While touching him, holding him, she'd been so turned on she couldn't think straight.

Too late she realized what she had wanted: to feel him burn inside her. To know just once what an honest-to-God, blazing, erotic experience did to one's soul, the consequences be damned.

She knew it was crazy. Wrong. But still she wanted him. Desperately.

He thrust clothes at her. She looked at them, still foggy, and realized he was fully dressed. Then he walked out, leaving the door open.

He hadn't said a word.

She watched the doorway, hoping Adam would return and try to take advantage of her. She'd let him. Encourage him. Help him. But that wasn't his style. He wouldn't touch her without permission.

In fact, he'd never once touched her inappropriately—even when they'd been naked in a shower. Or asleep in each other's arms. Yet she'd touched—stroked—his penis. More than once. *Without asking.*

If he had done the same to her, would it have not been interpreted as harassment? Guilt warmed her skin. She owed him an apology.

It was also high time she examined a few more truths. Like the fact that she didn't fear Adam. Yes, he acted rough and tough in front of Lyle—and in front of her sometimes. But he wasn't like Lyle. He wasn't a cold-blooded murderer. He wasn't beyond redemption. And she wanted to save him. For herself . . .

She dressed quickly and when she looked up again, Adam's bulk filled the door. His hair dripped, his shirt damp from being pulled onto wet skin. And he was hard again. She stared, not trusting herself to speak. Not yet. Not when her body still ached with an unmet need.

She heard the clink of handcuffs. "No," she protested.

"It's not what you think." He grasped her wrists. "I'm staying up for a while. You're going to sleep."

"We need to talk."

He snapped the cuffs closed. "No. Right now I need to be alone!"

Adam paced the living room, fists balled at his sides. What the hell had come over him?

Her hand.

It was that friggin' simple.

He had been fine until she reached out and touched him. In fact, if she had left it at a touch, he'd still be okay. She'd touched him before—the memory of those two delicate fingers resting lightly on his flesh was burned permanently in his mind—and he'd survived. Kept control.

But this? This had been deliberate. Calculated. She'd clutched him. Stroked him. Then she watched him. And when she should have turned away, she'd stepped closer, brought her hand forward just as he came.

Leaving him with yet another memory he'd never forget.

And in that instant she had wanted release. She'd been on the brink of climax, her body screaming for relief. Adam could have touched her and given her immediate satisfaction. One hard stroke of his thumb across her clitoris would have pushed her into deep orgasm.

Or he could have prolonged it. Given her a series of shorter orgasms, one after another, making them build in intensity until he was damn good and ready to let her off the hook. Yeah, she had been ready. Her nipples had been hard, begging. Her hips thrusting lightly. But anyone—even a damned vibrator—could have fulfilled her need just then.

And he wanted her to want only him. He wanted to see her burn with a flame only he could extinguish.

The thought was sobering. He'd never felt that way about a woman in his life, had never known the feeling of wanting one person at the expense of all others. Of wanting that one person to know everything about his life, every pain, every hurt. Every laugh.

He didn't like the implication. Especially now. He had a job to do. She was part of his job.

That fast his fury died, leaving guilt in its wake. His behavior tonight had been unacceptable. And while part of him felt he owed her an apology, he knew he wouldn't.

Hell, what was one more sin on his scorecard? He'd already kidnapped her, made her shower with him, exposed her to danger. Jacking off in front of her was the least of his crimes.

Besides, she wasn't exactly without guilt herself. Little Miss Prim and Proper had touched him first. He closed his eyes, remembering.

She needed to leave. Today.

Adam checked that the door to Lyle's bedroom was still shut tightly. Then he withdrew Renata's cell phone and stepped outside.

He tried Stan first, puzzled when he couldn't reach him. Then he dialed Ethan, surprised when his boss answered instead of the answering machine.

"What's going on down there?" Ethan demanded.

Adam gave him an update, including Lyle pulling a gun on Renata. "She's got to go now. How close are your men?"

"They're about four hours behind you. Guess you lost them in a detour, but they're still getting a signal on the homing device. Once they're close, they can pick the woman up and get her to a safe house. Here's their number."

"Let them know to expect a call."

"Any word on when you'll meet up with Willy?"

"No. But as soon as Renata's gone, I'll tell Lyle that I've confirmed delivery on the C-4. That should speed things up."

"Just keep me posted. I want to be there for the bust and I need a little advance notice."

"To get a TV crew in?"

"Don't get smart. I want to bring in a tactical unit."

They discussed the pending arrest in brief terms. Until they knew specifics, it was hard to plan. Both men agreed Adam should play bad guy until all the arrests were made.

He hung up and went back inside. To brood.

In order to get Renata out, he needed to get away from Lyle for a short time. It would be easy to concoct a story that he had to meet someone regarding the explosives. And when he returned without her, he'd insinuate that he'd killed her.

He also had to find the right time to tell Renata who
he was. Yeah, Ethan or his men would explain, but
damn it, Adam wanted her to hear the truth from him.
He wanted to look her in the eyes and tell her he wasn't
a convict, a felon. More, he wanted her to look at him
without that underlying fear.

He rubbed his face, tired. He'd grab a few hours
sleep, then take off.

Renata wafted up from sleep and found herself
curled atop Adam's chest, not one part of her touching
the bed.

Half in a haze, she realized her shirt had ridden up,
baring her stomach and half her breasts. And since
Adam was shirtless, she—her cheek, one hand, her exposed midriff—rested on his bare skin. Her other hand
was cast up along his neck, her fingers tangled in the
warm strands of his hair.

Strong arms cradled her; one hand low and cupped
possessively against her hip, the other tucked beneath
her shirt, resting on her back. More bare skin on bare
skin.

The sensation was not unpleasant. Neither were the
vague wisps of her dreams. In sleep, she'd seduced him
in order to win her freedom. But then she had stayed.
Why?

Beneath her, Adam moved, tightening his grip
slightly, drawing her closer. Against her thigh, she felt
the unmistakable rub of his erection. Now she remembered why she hadn't left. In her dream, they had made
love and it had been so wondrous she had begged to
stay.

She gasped, rejecting the dream.

Her sound of anguish woke Adam.

That fast, he rolled her to one side, thrusting her behind him as he grabbed the gun he had stuck beneath the mattress.

He swept the room with his weapon. "What was it?"

"Nothing." Renata tried to shove free, but he had her arm pinned. "You're hurting me!"

Shoving the gun away, Adam raised up enough to free her arm. But when she tried to scramble off the bed, he caught her, forcing her to lie back down. He leaned in beside her, braced up on one elbow.

His fingers grazed the wildly beating pulse at her neck before brushing the hair from her face. "Tell me what scared you."

The genuine concern in his voice muddled her image of him even further. Not wanting to meet his eyes, she glanced down, her gaze following the firm muscles of his chest and abdomen.

She had expected the bulge in his jeans, had already felt the taut ridge of his erection. She hadn't expected to find him partially exposed.

With the top snap left undone, his swollen flesh had refused to be restrained. Couldn't be restrained. The head and first few inches of his shaft pressed out the denim V of his open fly.

With a cry, she closed her eyes.

Adam could guess the cause of her distress. Part of him wanted to remind her that she had started it by touching him. Except that wasn't totally true. He'd fought one erection after another for days now.

And as tortuous as it had been at the time, he'd enjoyed her touch. Hell, he'd gladly endure the anguish again. But not if it caused her distress. Not if it frightened her.

Very gently, he nudged her chin. "Look at me, Renata."

Her eyes fluttered. Wary. Woefully humiliated.

He kept his voice low and soft. "I'm sorry if it frightens you. I can't stop it from happening. Take it as a compliment, but know that you are safe. Can you believe that?"

She wanted to look away, to deny his words . . . but she couldn't. The truth was she did feel secure with him, for reasons that made no sense. Reasons that made her uncomfortable. Reasons she'd never give voice to.

She desired the man and that was wrong. If it had simply been the desire for sex, she could understand it. Write it off as combat fatigue. This yearning for only *him* though, was upsetting.

She felt Adam's fingertips press just beneath her earlobe, his thumb stroking the underside of her jaw. She gulped in air. Once, twice. Then exhaled. So did he.

She became aware that the palm of his other hand rested lightly against her stomach, against her diaphragm. Barely touching. Her breathing calmed. She inhaled, her next breath softer, more even.

He was doing it again: that thing where he seemed to control her breathing. He'd matched his breath to hers, then changed the pattern. Slowed things down. Her awareness narrowed. They were the only two people on earth.

He moved fractionally closer, his fingers stroking down her neck. He was going to kiss her again and she felt incapable of stopping him. She recalled the power of this man's kiss, knew that if he touched her lips again, she'd surrender fully —

From the doorway came a sound. Lyle cleared his throat.

Renata wanted to disappear. Even though Adam's frame completely blocked her from the other man's view, she could imagine what it looked like. She bit her lip, felt her skin flush as Adam turned and glared over his shoulder.

"We need to talk," Lyle said. "I just heard from my father."

Chapter Fifteen

Adam found Lyle in the living room, the television blaring. The younger man was somber and more coherent than he'd been the night before.

Lyle pointed at the set with the remote. "The old man just told me about this."

Adam braced for bad news, expecting to hear that he and Renata had been identified after stopping at the car accident. While they were now miles away, in Kansas, their being spotted in Illinois would divert police away from their erroneous search in the Northeast.

"They found that prison guard—Irv Wallace. Dead," Lyle continued. "They claim he was killed with his own shotgun, which they recovered with both our fingerprints."

The news stunned Adam. He watched the television report, which was half over. Apparently the guard's body had been found less than three miles from where they'd escaped. The exact time of death was pending autopsy results, but anonymous sources speculated the guard had been dead for several days.

Adam's thoughts flew back to their escape. It seemed like eons ago. That his and Lyle's fingerprints were on the guard's shotgun wasn't surprising. They'd both handled the weapons.

"How much you wanna bet Franklin Potter did it?"

Lyle sneered. "It would be just like that bastard to shoot Wallace and leave the gun with my fingerprints on it, next to the body."

"I don't know." Yeah, the other two inmates could have followed and retrieved the shotguns. But where would they have gotten ammo? Adam had unloaded the guns and taken the shells with him. And then there was the lack of additional fingerprints. Where would a con get gloves on the spur of the moment? "Are you saying your family wasn't involved?"

"Exactly. So it had to be Potter," Lyle said. "At any rate, Pa's bringing us in. And he also wants a confirmation on the C-4."

"I'm expecting that shortly."

"See if you can speed things up. And one last thing." Lyle nodded toward the bedroom. "We need to unload the luggage, man. We're almost home free. And I don't care how good a lay she is, she's a liability."

Adam felt the muscles in his chest contract. "I'll take off with her now, then. It'll give me a chance to check with my partner."

Renata was sitting on the edge of the bed when Adam walked back in. She knew by his grim expression that something was wrong. She had tried to eavesdrop, but hadn't been able to hear anything above the noise of the television.

When she went to speak, he touched a finger to his lips, signaling silence.

He quickly removed the handcuffs. "Get your shoes. Quick."

"We're leaving now?" She looked at the bedside alarm clock. It was four in the afternoon. They never traveled during daylight hours.

"Now," he confirmed. "Just the two of us."

The two of them. Her heart rate accelerated, thudding dully behind her eardrums. Lyle wasn't going? Why? Were the two men parting ways?

She opened her mouth again, but he cut her off. "We'll talk in the car."

Ten minutes later, they pulled onto the highway and sped away from the mobile home. She had not seen Lyle before they took off, yet Adam assured her the younger man was fine. It was that assurance that bothered her. If Lyle were indeed fine, she was no longer needed. She closed her eyes, knew she should feel frightened. She didn't.

"Get the map from the glove box," Adam said. "And tell me where the closest park or recreation area is."

Renata studied the map. "There's a county park about ten miles from here. On a river."

"That'll do."

Adam pulled a cell phone out of his pocket. She recognized it as hers, was surprised he still had it.

He dialed a number, swearing when no one answered. He dialed again, and this time left a terse message. "We need to talk. I'll contact Ethan's man to have the woman picked up."

Renata listened, confused. Then suddenly it fell into place. All the reasons she'd sensed he was different.

"You're working with the cops," she whispered when he disconnected.

"I *am* a cop. FBI."

It felt as if the seat had just been pulled out from under her. Reality shifted.

"FBI. You . . . you're not one of them?"

"I'm undercover."

Outrage filled her. "Why didn't you tell me?"

"I didn't think we'd be together more than a day or

two." He glanced at her. "Until I knew exactly when I could free you, I didn't want to worry you'd inadvertently give me away. Both our lives could have been at risk."

"At risk?" She recalled the close calls they had. "And when exactly were we not at risk?"

"Your safety has been a top priority."

"My safety? Or your mission?" Renata turned to the window. Her mind whirled as she re-examined every moment of her captivity in new light. And every time she found herself thinking *he didn't have to do that,* she realized that everything he did was consistent with what she would have expected from a criminal.

Yes, she'd suspected all along he was different. But in retrospect she realized she'd fostered some of the suspicion because she was looking for a reason to justify her growing sexual attraction to Adam. She couldn't have allowed herself to fall for an escaped convict.

And yet she'd done exactly that.

She cut off her train of thought. "Where are you taking me?"

"To that park. From there you'll be taken to an FBI safe house and kept under wraps. The McEdwins will be told you're dead."

"What about my family?"

"They will still think you're missing. You won't be able to contact anyone until the McEdwins have been arrested."

She started to protest until she remembered Adam would still be in danger. "If they hear I'm alive, you could be killed."

The cell phone rang, preventing Adam from responding. It was Ethan Falco, which surprised him. He had left the earlier message for Stan.

"I'm taking the woman to a drop-off point now." He gave Ethan the location.

"My men will be there in fifteen minutes," Ethan said. "Tell the woman whatever you need to get her co-operation, then get back to Lyle, fast. I don't like him being left alone. If we lose him now, we'll never find them."

When Adam hung up, Renata looked at him. "How long have you been working on this?"

"Months. And there's something else you should know. The missing guard has been found murdered. They're saying Lyle and I are behind it. I assure you, that guard was alive and well when we left him."

"Then who?"

"I don't know, but I'll find out."

They were at the park entrance now. Adam reached over and took her hand, squeezed it. "We don't have much time. I know I owe you an apology for . . . a lot of things. I'd like to contact you when this is over, but I'll respect a 'no.' Or even a 'drop dead.' And I don't expect an answer now."

She nodded. "It's hard to realize that it's finally ending. For me, anyway. How much longer will you be involved?"

He knew that an answer like "till it's over" wasn't what she wanted. But he couldn't give her an exact date. In a perfect world, he hoped to join up with Lyle's family by the next day. The rest would depend on how quickly Adam could draw a bead on all the McEdwins and relay their location to Ethan.

"It should wrap within a few days."

He circled the park, was relieved to find few cars. He parked close to a picnic shelter by the boat ramp. A bathroom and phone booth were close by. He debated staying with her until Ethan's men arrived, but he had to get back. If Adam was spotted, he was screwed.

He handed her some cash. "Just in case. I can't emphasize how important it is you don't use that phone. Someone will pick you up within ten minutes or so. They'll approach you and say I sent them. If they don't show or you start to feel uncomfortable, call this number." He scribbled Stan's cell phone number on a scrap of paper.

"And you just told me not to use the phone."

"I have to go."

"Be careful." They both said it.

She reached for the door handle. He stopped her.

"Hell." He pulled her back into his arms and pressed his mouth to hers in a possessive kiss. Now that there wasn't time, he could think of a million things to say. Things that would sound soft and sappy.

He broke off the kiss. He saw uncertainty, knew she struggled with some of the same feelings. Or at least that's what he told himself. Once she was debriefed, however, she might hate him.

"Now go."

She climbed out of the car and hurried away.

He watched her in the rearview mirror as he headed out of the park. More than ever, he wanted to get this job wrapped up.

He forced his thoughts to the story he'd tell Lyle. He'd give as few details as possible. Just confirm she was dead, her body dumped where it wouldn't be found anytime soon.

He would also tell Lyle that his partner had firmed up a plan to obtain the C-4. It was one of the things he wanted to discuss with Stan—whenever he reached him, that is. He might need someone to pose as Daniel Montague and Stan knew the character inside out.

Adam had purposely not mentioned the possibility to Ethan, for fear Ethan would insist one of his own men pose as Montague.

He tried Stan's home phone this time, instead of his cell.

"It's about goddamn time," Adam began when he answered.

"You're alive."

It wasn't Stan who picked up the phone, but it was a voice he recognized. *His brother, Zachary.*

Completely bewildered, Adam checked the display to make sure he'd dialed the correct number. "Of course I'm alive. Why wouldn't I be?"

"I received an e-mail stating you were dead and that I was executor of your estate."

Adam pulled off the road. Before going undercover, he'd given Stan a copy of his will and his brother's e-mail address. In the event Adam was killed on this assignment, Stan had promised to notify Zach. He had no other family, and with Zach's problems with the law, Adam didn't want the Bureau to handle it.

A bad feeling settled over him. Only one person could have sent the e-mail to Zach. "Where are you? And where the hell is Stan?"

"Since we're skipping the social formalities, I'll tell you point blank: Stan's en route to the hospital."

"Hospital? Is he okay?"

"I'm not sure. Last I saw, he was breathing, but unconscious."

"What happened?"

"I think he was poisoned. There's a small bruise and puncture on his neck. He started having convulsions right after I found him. I called 911, but scrammed when paramedics showed up."

"I'm obviously missing something here. What were you doing at Stan's apartment to begin with?"

"The e-mail said I was supposed to make sure a Chris Tashley in Washington got an attached data file with evidence that would lead to your killer."

Chris Tashley was a former FBI deputy director and Adam's mentor. Known as a straight shooter, he'd recently been elected to his third congressional term.

"What was in the file?"

"Nothing except your last will and testament. There was also a cryptic postscript from Stan that you died trying to clear my name. What the hell kind of case are you working on?"

"I'll explain later," Adam said. "But how did you manage to track Stan down?" Stan prided himself on his ability to be invisible online.

"Through his e-mail account. He left a clear trail of who sent it. When I couldn't reach him by phone, I decided to visit. I must have arrived right after his attacker did. When I rang the doorbell, Stan yelled. I broke in, but his attacker ran out the back."

"Did Stan give you any clue who did it?"

"He was babbling about his laptop, but I couldn't make out much more. He was fairly agitated. Kept saying your name. And that you were being framed."

"What about the perpetrator? Was there more than one?"

"I only saw one, but he wasn't much more than a shadow. It looks like there was a struggle. A lamp's knocked over and the papers on his desk are scattered. Whoever was here tried to take Stan's laptop, but dropped it on the way out. The case is cracked. I haven't turned it on."

"You have it?"

"I practically tripped over it running out the back.

Whoever attacked Stan tried to jump the back fence and had a run-in with the neighbor's Doberman."

"That means the file Stan was sending you is probably still on the hard drive."

Zach snorted. "Must be something big for them to murder over. Who else knew what you and Stan were working on?"

Renata. And Ethan Falco. Shit! Ethan had double-crossed him again.

"I've got to go. I'll call back." Dropping the phone, Adam did a one-eighty and hit the gas hard, praying he could get to Renata before Ethan's men did.

The picnic shelter where Adam had left Renata was deserted.

He checked his watch. It had been barely ten minutes.

Swearing, he raced toward the park exit. Ahead of him was a green Ford. He sped up, disappointed to see only one person in the car.

Until he saw the person. It was one of Ethan's men, the same one he'd met back in Durham. And he'd already spotted Adam in his rearview mirror.

Forcing a neutral look, Adam signaled for the man to pull over. For a moment, he thought the man would keep going. Then he eased onto the road's right shoulder.

Parking behind him, Adam climbed out and walked calmly toward the driver's door. When he drew close, he yanked out his gun and stuck it to the man's head.

"Where is she?"

"Are you nuts?"

Adam leaned in. "I'm asking the questions. Where?"

The man didn't respond. Adam pressed his gun forward, thinking back to the spot where he'd left Renata. Had the man already killed her and dumped her body in the woods? Or in the river?

"Easy!" The man's lip trembled. "She's in the trunk."

"Hand me your weapon. Then remove the keys and get out."

The man kept his hands raised. "I'm just following orders, you know."

"Yeah, I know. Now unlock the trunk."

The sight of Renata lying on her side, bound and gagged, tore through Adam. She hadn't moved or responded to the trunk being open. Was he too late?

He pressed a finger to her neck, felt the weak pulse. "What did you do to her?"

"Chloroform," the man said. "Just enough to get her in the trunk. She'll be waking up soon."

"Untie her and help her out."

Renata roused uneasily. Disoriented, she blinked against the sunlight. Frightened, she looked from Adam to the other man.

Adam grasped her arm, supporting her. "Are you okay?"

She nodded. Turning back to the trunk, Adam pointed to a long object wrapped in a tarp. He had a strong suspicion what it was. "Open it."

Inside the tarp was the other shotgun Adam had taken from the prison guard. Renata would have been killed with it, the shotgun left behind with Adam and Lyle's fingerprints. Just like Irv Wallace.

Adam turned on the man. Only one person could have told him where the shotguns had been left: Ethan Falco. Ethan had advised Adam to leave them behind in the first place.

"Did Ethan order you to kill the guard? Or was it your own idea?"

"I don't know what you're talking about."

"Maybe this will help jar your memory." He nodded toward the trunk. "Get in."

"You can't do this," the man sputtered. "Ethan won't stand for it."

"Ethan's crossed the line. Now get in. And I may call and tell him where you're at." It would do little good to question the man. Ethan wouldn't be stupid enough to let this fool know too much. "If I were you, I'd be more worried that Ethan might decide to leave you in there for a few days."

Once the man climbed into the trunk, Adam closed it, and pressed the key into the dirt beneath the right rear tire.

"You can't leave him like that—" Renata began.

Adam tugged her toward the driver's door. "He won't be in there long. I'll call someone and tell them where the key is."

He grabbed the man's briefcase off the front seat, glanced briefly at the contents. Gun, a cell phone, and the tracking device. Adam took the entire case. He'd have to destroy it before returning to Lyle, but at least Ethan wouldn't be able to trail them. Which gave Adam a little time to figure things out.

"We need to clear out before we get company."

Renata pulled back. "Where are we going this time?"

"Back to the trailer before Lyle gets suspicious. Later I'll make new arrangements to have you picked up."

"I don't trust your arrangements anymore. Couldn't you just leave me at a motel somewhere?"

"Can't risk it. There's a chance this guy's partner

may be close by. And you'll be able to trust my next arrangement. You'll be with my brother."

"Your brother's an FBI agent, too?"

Adam helped her in his car. "Hardly. But he's the only person I can trust right now." Speeding off, he quickly explained the full story, including Zach's finding Stan.

She was confused. "If you suspect Ethan Falco is behind Stan's attack, doesn't that end your investigation?"

"It depends. As long as my cover remains intact, I still have a shot at bringing the McEdwins down."

"Alone?"

"No." Adam needed to think through that part. He had to be cautious of who he contacted until they knew who the moles helping the McEdwins were. He also wanted to find out what Ethan was up to.

He turned to her. "Until I can get you hooked up with my brother, it's critical that we both act as if nothing's changed. You're still a hostage; you need to do everything I say without question. And I can't treat you any differently in front of Lyle. Think you can manage it?"

"I have to. Both our lives depend on it."

"I know it's a lot to absorb. And I'll try to keep you informed of what's going on, but don't speak of it, even when we're alone unless I tell you it's okay. You never know who is watching or listening."

Taking the cell phone again, he quickly dialed Ethan's number. The call was routed directly to voice mail. Was Ethan on the phone or did he know Adam was onto him already?

He left a detailed message about the man locked in the trunk. Then he hung up. There was a lot more he wanted to say to Ethan, but for now he'd keep his cards close. They had almost reached the trailer's driveway now. It would be dark soon. And they needed to get far away.

"I need to handcuff you," Adam said. "To keep up the act."

She nodded, but he didn't miss the slight flinch when the metal snapped into place.

Lyle's surprise at seeing her was obvious. "What the hell's going on?"

"Give me one sec."

Adam pulled her into the bedroom, kissed her cheek, and pointed to the bed. "Get some sleep if you can."

"What's she doing back?" Lyle demanded when he returned to the kitchen.

"The roads were crawling with cops. I didn't want to risk it. As it was, one followed me for a few miles. I circled north just to lose him."

"Fuck."

"Don't sweat it. We've got bigger fish to fry. My partner called."

Lyle leaned closer. "With good news, I hope?"

Adam nodded. "He confirmed availability on a hundred pounds. The price is $200,000, cash on delivery. But I have to confirm fast, so he can start making arrangements on his end."

"Then I'll go call my pa." Lyle grinned. "And the price just became $250,000, *partner.*"

Within an hour, they were ready to hit the road. A different car had been left, an older four-door Pontiac. Lyle let Renata check him and change his bandage.

"Looks to me like it's starting to heal," Lyle said.

She shook her head. "It's stopped bleeding since

you've been resting. But it continues to show signs of infection and you're still running a fever—"

"Fever, schmever. I always run hot." Lyle popped two painkillers into his mouth. "And don't say a word about the pills. The way I look at it, I deserve them."

Adam transferred their supplies to the car's trunk then sat at the kitchen table to study the road map.

Lyle scanned their newest set of directions. He pointed to a small town in Utah. "Finally!"

"Is that home sweet home?" If they were headed to the McEdwins' headquarters, Adam needed to drop Renata off before they got there.

"Not yet. But I know these folks, which means the old man will be close by."

"Then let's get going. That's a lot of miles to cover in one night." And Adam wanted to make sure they weren't being tailed.

Whoever drew up the route must have felt confident the cops were searching strictly in New York, because they traveled on the interstate, making good time until they reached Denver.

He glanced at Renata. She sat beside him, her hands cuffed in front, her eyes unfocused as she stared out the window. Was she thinking of her mother who lived close by? Or was she pondering the same unanswered questions he was?

Adam's ears popped as they changed altitude. Bypassing Denver, they switched to smaller highways, and headed deeper into the Rockies. Driving became more tedious, the road an unending series of S-curves and steep grades. He turned on the heat as the temperature grew cooler.

A muffled bang echoed as the car suddenly jerked and swerved. Cursing, Adam struggled to keep the wheel under control.

Lyle stirred from a drugged sleep, confused. "Was that gunfire?"

"We blew a tire. Right, rear."

Adam slowed, but didn't stop. He couldn't. There was a wall of rock on one side of the road and a steep drop-off on the other. No shoulder. They had to make it to one of the turnouts scattered about every quarter mile.

When they reached the next pull-over, Adam parked as close to the tree line as he could. "There better be a decent spare."

He grabbed the flashlight and climbed out. In the trunk he found a spare tire and a crowbar. But no jack. Of all the goddamned luck.

"Now what?" Lyle asked when he returned.

"We passed a car at the last overlook. I'll see if it has a jack." Adam had considered taking Renata along. Except he could get there and back quicker, alone. "You two get out and hide behind those trees. If someone does come along they'll see the flat tire and think the owner will be back in the morning. I shouldn't be gone more than a few minutes."

As soon as Adam disappeared, Lyle climbed out of the back. She waited for him to open her door, so they could move to the trees, but instead he moved in behind the wheel and started the car.

"What are you doing?" she demanded.

At first Lyle didn't answer, too busy lighting a cigarette. Lowering the windows, he put the car in gear, his movements sluggish.

"I'm going to move the car up just a little, under that pine." He blew a stream of smoke in her direction. "Were you afraid I'd take off? That you wouldn't see lover boy again?"

Renata felt her face flame. Of course Lyle assumed

they were intimate. She and Adam slept together, showered together. Still, she opened her mouth to deny it.

"Hey, I got my own piece of ass waiting at the next stop so it's nothing to me." Lyle eased his foot off the brake.

The car jerked, but didn't move because of the flat tire. Swearing, he hit the gas.

This time the car shot forward. It skidded along the guardrail before pulling sharply to the right with a bump. Lyle had driven off the edge of the pavement.

"Stop," she yelled. It was too late. The right front wheel had already lost traction.

The car tilted and slid in slow motion. Metal scraped on metal as the guardrail loosened. Without warning it gave way. Renata braced her feet and held her breath as the car crept forward an inch at a time, gaining momentum as it started down the ravine.

Suddenly they stopped. She peered out the passenger window, seeing little in the odd-angled headlights. She could see trees, make out their shapes.

She struggled to right herself, hampered by the handcuffs. The car wobbled, rocking back and forth, like a seesaw. Sweat broke out on her brow as she realized they were hovering on the edge of another precipice.

"Shit! I dropped my cigarette," Lyle said.

"Don't worry about that now! We need to get out of the car."

Lyle shoved his door open. The car teetered.

"Easy," she hissed. "We have to move slowly, in unison."

But as soon as the car stopped pitching, he bolted. "Fuck slowly. I'm outta here."

Renata lunged, but the door slammed shut before she reached it. "Wait!" she screamed.

The impact of the swinging door, combined with Lyle's hasty exit, shifted the car's delicate balance. It swayed, dangled . . . and with a horrible rending of metal, slid into the dark abyss.

Renata hit the dashboard then slumped to the floor as the car rammed against something solid. Then it creaked and moved before stopping again. She held her breath, worried that even the slightest motion would trigger another slide.

All sound ceased. She moved an inch at a time, climbing back in the seat. The car seemed to be resting solidly, at least for the moment. Good news.

Until she smelled smoke.

Chapter Sixteen

It took Adam less than two minutes to sprint the quarter-mile downhill. They were fortunate to have hit an area with pull-overs this close.

And if that hadn't been good enough, he found the abandoned car already jacked up, its front left tire missing. The hapless owner had had the opposite problem: a jack but no spare.

Adam quickly lowered the car. But before heading back, he called his brother. Zach answered on the first ring.

"How's Stan?"

"It's touch and go. He hasn't regained consciousness."

The news troubled Adam. Like him, Stan had only one relative, a distant uncle. He'd mentioned it at the beginning of the assignment when Adam gave him a copy of his will.

"I don't even bother to keep life insurance. Nobody I care about enough to leave it to," Stan had joked.

Of course, Stan hadn't considered his behind-the-scenes work to be high-risk. Which made Adam wonder again why Ethan wanted Stan dead: What was in the file Stan had tried to send to Zach?

"Were you able to retrieve anything off Stan's computer?"

"Yeah. Probably more than I should have," Zach said. "The attachment he tried to send me outlined your entire investigation. How much do you know about this Ethan Falco?"

"Evidently, not enough. I suspect he set me up from the beginning."

Adam knew Ethan had targeted him for the job. Since Adam had worked overseas, he wasn't a familiar face. He was also a seasoned undercover agent—even if his last assignment had turned sour. Thanks to his tainted promotability, Ethan had no doubt considered him expendable.

And Adam's desperation to get his career back on track had blinded him. He'd have agreed to anything.

"You weren't the only one. It looks like Stan suspected he was being set up as well. Guess Ethan had something incriminating on him," Zach said. "So Stan started compiling some interesting data of his own. Seems Ethan had some ties to Willy McEdwin years ago. Back when Ethan was still with the FBI himself."

"What kind of ties?"

"Financial ones. Ethan used covert government funds to finance several antigovernment groups, including the one McEdwin belonged to."

Adam pressed the phone closer to his ear. "Are you saying Ethan supported their doctrine?"

"Only to the extent it gave him job security. Ethan anonymously created a formidable enemy that he then controlled via the purse strings. It made him look damn good in Washington. Nobody had his knack for getting the inside track on these groups. I haven't read through all of it yet, but it looks like Stan has connected all the bodies and bank accounts, and traced them back to Ethan."

"Jesus Christ."

"It gets better. Apparently Willy has spent the last several years tracing the origins of that money. I guess he got real close once, which has made Ethan nervous."

"Because it could end his political aspirations," Adam finished.

"Ethan knew you and Stan were planning to bring Willy the rest of the C-4," Zach said. "You two would have died in the bust, and been eulogized as heroes."

"Wait. Did you say 'the rest of the C-4?'"

"Yeah. Only one shipment was seized. Half of it got through."

Adam closed his eyes. Willy already had a hundred pounds of C-4 and wanted more. What exactly did he have planned?

"I still have a shot at stopping the McEdwins. But I need to get Renata out before our next stop."

"You can't take them down alone."

"But I'm not sure who I can trust at the Bureau. On paper, it looks like I resigned to join Ethan's Task Force." Adam checked the time. He'd been gone nearly fifteen minutes. "I need to go. You got a map handy? We need to find a rendezvous spot."

He told Zach where they were headed.

"You'll be close to Flaming Gorge National Park, just across the Utah state line. I can be there by late morning," Zach said.

"Do it. I'll be in touch."

Tire jack in hand, Adam started jogging back uphill. His mind whirled. All Ethan's inconsistencies made sense now. He'd played Adam like an old country fiddle, finding his weak spot—his career blights, his brother's checkered past—then dangling a carrot in front of him.

Adam's temper simmered. Taking Ethan down would be a pleasure.

He slowed, having reached the pull-over. But where was the car? He flipped on the flashlight, caught sight of the mangled section of guardrail. He sprinted forward. The gouged ground and flattened bushes told him the car had gone over the edge.

He shone the flashlight down, calling their names.

A voice answered. Weak. Male. "Adam! Help!"

He angled the light, saw Lyle clinging to a bent sapling about twenty feet to one side.

"Hold on." He made his way down to the other man. "Where's Renata?"

"Down . . . there." Lyle pressed a hand to his stomach and winced.

"What the hell happened?"

"The car slid over the edge and just kept going. I tried to get her out, but it happened too fast."

And he'd left her handcuffed. Turning, Adam scrambled downhill.

"Leave her!" Lyle called. "She's probably halfway to China by now. We were going to dump her anyway. I just saved you a bullet."

Lyle's last remark chilled Adam. While he didn't know what had happened—yet—he wondered if Lyle had caused the accident on purpose. Had the other man decided to get rid of Renata himself?

"I've got my own plans for her."

Adam kept going, grabbing a branch to slow his descent. He swept the area with his light. The ground was smooth, slippery, the vegetation scraped flat by the car.

How far down had it traveled? His gut tightened as he thought about what he would find at the bottom. His foot kicked metal. He bent and picked up a side mirror that had been ripped off.

As he straightened, he caught the heavy smell of gasoline.

Renata spotted the small orange glow near the driver's door. Lyle's cigarette was wedged against the frame, smoldering in the carpet. She stretched toward the driver's side, but couldn't reach it. And the movement caused the car to shift.

She held her breath until it stopped. But when she inhaled she caught the whiff of gas. Mother of God . . . fire!

She struggled to release her seatbelt, but the mechanism was jammed. The gas fumes grew more noxious, filling her with a choking panic. She'd worked the burn unit, heard victims' agonized screams as they were wheeled in, their frantic pleas for relief. For death.

She thought of her family. Her last words with her mother had been rushed, angry. Then she thought of her colleagues at the clinic. All those goddamned unfinished reports. And Adam.

Calm down. Think. She bit her lip hard, tasted blood. She welcomed the pain. The clarity made her choices chillingly simple: Get out or die.

She focused on freeing the seatbelt. Rocking the metal tab, she pressed the button over and over. "Come on."

With a jolt, it released. Whispering a prayer of gratitude, she moved clumsily to the driver's side. The handcuff chain clinked, the sound overly loud.

She pressed against the door. A low whine of metal from beneath warned that the car was going to slide again. Frantic, she shoved the door as hard as she could with her shoulder. The door gave way spilling her onto the ground. The car tipped, swayed, then skidded a few feet.

"Renata!" Adam's voice sounded far away.

"I'm here!" She waited but didn't hear a response. Had she imagined his voice? A burst of light broke through the dark. A flashlight.

Seconds later, Adam hurried to her side. "Take my hand."

Before she could react, a shredding noise filled the air. The car lurched, unbalanced, and shot further down the ravine. Sparks flew as metal scraped rock.

Without warning, Adam speared her, tucking her between his frame and the ground just as the car exploded.

Flames shot high into the air, torching the surrounding pines. A dozen small fires popped to life as embers sparked the forest's dry undergrowth.

Searing bits of fragmented metal rained down on Adam's back. He huddled his arms tightly around Renata, shielding her.

When it stopped, he rolled away. "Are you okay?"

"No, I'm not *okay*. I could have been killed." She thrust her hands forward. "Take these off. Now!"

He unlocked the handcuffs, tossed them in the dirt.

He pushed to his feet, helped her stand. "Can you walk?"

"Just let me catch my breath."

"No time. This area will be swarming with firefighters as soon as the observer in the closest fire tower reports the flames."

He stomped out a fire close to them, but with the trees in flames, he had no chance at extinguishing the blaze. And already it was spreading, growing.

"Let's get out of here."

When they reached the top, Lyle ducked out from the shadows. "I thought you were toast, man! I saw the fucking car blow and—"

Adam gave vent to his fury, grabbed the front of Lyle's shirt. "And what? Did you think beyond that? Like how will we get away without a car? Cops, firemen, will be here any minute."

"It wasn't my—"

"Save it. We need to find a hiding spot. Then you can call your brother."

Lyle shook his head. "The phone was in the car."

Adam reached into his pocket, only to find he'd lost Renata's phone as well.

"There was a forest service road, about a tenth of a mile back. We'll have to hide in the brush until I figure something out."

"I won't be able to keep up," Lyle said. "I hurt my knee."

Adam moved forward. "I'll carry you. Just hope to hell we make it before a car comes along."

They had only hiked a few minutes, when headlights flashed on the far horizon, disappearing and reappearing as the vehicle ascended the mountain. Another curve or two and the car would be right on top of them.

"Here!" Adam tugged Renata toward a shadowy notch in the woods where a steel post marked an unpaved road.

He ducked behind a large bush, helped Lyle sit up. Then he counted seconds until the vehicle, a forestry service fire truck, zoomed past. It would only be moments before others arrived.

Adam ran a hand through his hair. That they had

made it this far was a miracle. Lyle had groaned the entire time. What little strength the kid had built up in the last day or two had probably been shot climbing out of that ravine.

Yet when Renata offered to check him, Lyle snarled. "It's nothing. I'm fine."

The whine of a racing engine heralded the passing of another vehicle, this one a sheriff's car.

"We can't stay here," Adam announced. "I'll see where this road leads."

He pulled Renata to her feet. He wasn't about to leave her with Lyle again even for a few seconds.

As soon as they rounded the curve and were out of Lyle's line of vision, Adam hugged her. "You're a bigger person than I am, offering to help Lyle after his last fiasco."

"It's what I do. In some stupid way, I think I understand that even better now."

They came to a clearing. HIGHWAY MAINTENANCE—NO TRESPASSING, the sign read. Adam swept the area quickly with this flashlight. Dark pieces of equipment were stored behind a waist-high chain link fence. A backhoe. A tractor. Two flatbed trailers. *And a pickup truck with a snowplow.* A small barn was off in the corner.

Before she could protest, Adam picked Renata up and dropped her over the fence. Then he jumped it and headed toward the barn.

"What are we doing?" she asked.

Making a fist, he shattered a small pane of glass on the door. "We're breaking and entering."

He tugged her inside. The building was obviously a seasonal storage facility. Judging by the layer of dust on the floor, the place hadn't been used in months. He checked the interior with his flashlight. Hanging on the wall, beside a fire extinguisher, was a small locker marked KEYS.

He flipped it open and helped himself to the ones marked FORD and GATE. "Now we're going to steal a truck."

Renata held up a metal box. "We're stealing a first aid kit, too. All the medical supplies were lost with the car."

Outside, Adam helped her into the cab of the truck. The engine coughed and sputtered, then caught. A wrench lay in plain view on the floorboard. While the engine warmed up, Adam quickly unbolted the snowplow, then climbed in the truck and backed up, leaving the snowplow sitting in the lot.

"Did you get a sudden attack of conscience?" Renata asked.

He stroked her cheek. "A snowplow in July might attract attention."

After picking up Lyle, they drove six hours, stopping once for him to use a pay phone. They were instructed to stay on course, to get to their destination as quickly as possible. Lyle again rebuffed Renata's offer to examine him, so Adam stuck the first aid kit behind the seat.

Their destination turned out to be a small motel. The Howdy Lodge. The name was the only thing welcoming about the rundown motel. Only a few cars were pulled up to the twenty-odd units belying the NO VACANCY notice. The neon sign in one window marked the office.

Adam hoped the fact that they were staying in a town meant they were getting close to Willy. The noose was tightening, and they'd had their last close call. The police were overdue for a lucky break.

The window blinds at the office parted. As always, they were being watched. Adam pulled to the side of the motel.

"I need to get rid of this truck. It's a dead giveaway."

"You know the drill," Lyle said. "Leave the keys inside and it will disappear."

"And you know I don't like being without wheels."

"I'll call Pa. Just hurry."

They walked toward the front of the building.

"The doors will be unlocked," Lyle said. "You take unit seven. I'll take eight."

Adam started to speak when the door to room number eight opened. A woman with bright yellow hair slipped out the door and hurried toward them.

"She's cool," Lyle said. "Her uncle owns this place."

The woman sidled up to Lyle, hugging him as she pressed a noisy kiss to his mouth. Lyle made a pained noise, then swore.

The woman backed away. "What's wrong, sugar? I thought you were all better?"

Alarmed, Renata extended her hand. "You really should let me take a look."

Lyle nodded toward the woman. "Wanda works at a clinic. She'll be taking over my care now."

Renata eyed the woman skeptically. "I don't—"

"That's right," Lyle snapped. "You don't have a say in it. Not anymore. She does."

Wanda shrugged. "Whatever. But I put the supplies in their room, so I'll need to grab some stuff."

"Hurry back." Lyle disappeared into the room.

Wanda led Adam and Renata to room seven. "Your unit has a kitchenette. So I left all the food and supplies in there."

"Any chance we can get some clean clothes?" Adam asked.

"Check the closet and the chest." The woman went to the shelf in the kitchen area and grabbed tape and gauze.

Renata followed and eyed the supplies. It was basic first aid stuff. "There's no saline. Or antibiotics."

"He didn't mention those. In fact he said he was good to go." The girl grabbed a box, held it up. "He was more concerned that I have plenty of these. Got you some, too."

LATEX CONDOMS, the box read. *St. Luke's Crisis Center* was stamped on the box. Renata shoved them away. "You can take all of them."

Wanda lowered her voice and tipped her head toward Adam. "I wouldn't use 'em with him, either. Guess I just hear so much at work about safe sex."

"You're a nurse?" Renata quizzed.

"A receptionist. At the women's clinic."

"I think I should help you then."

The woman shook her head. "For now, he wants me. If we need assistance, I know where to find you."

Exasperated, Renata turned away. If Lyle didn't want her help, she wasn't about to force herself on him. *So why was she worried about him?*

She sighed. It was hard *not* to be a doctor.

As soon as Wanda left, Adam locked the door and finished checking the room. The unit, while dated, was clean enough. The small kitchen area had a table built against the wall. A bed, a mismatched dresser, a television, and two chairs filled out the rest of the room.

The dresser drawers were stocked with clothes of various sizes. They obviously weren't the first fugitives this place had housed. The only thing missing was a telephone. Not that he would trust using it.

Shoving the heavy drapes back slightly, Adam peered out. There was a pay phone near the office. He had little choice but to use it to call Zach. With the watchers, it would be tricky.

He turned on the television, bumped up the volume before turning back to Renata. "We can talk now."

"Is someone listening?"

"I doubt it, but just case, the TV will cover our voices."

Relief eased her brow. "What happens next?"

"The plan hasn't changed. You'll be freed. Hopefully by nightfall."

He moved closer, hovering. While he couldn't wait to secrete her away in his brother's care, to know she was safe, part of him didn't want to let her go. Stan had been right. She had gotten under his skin.

He brushed at the dirt smudged on her cheek. A woman like her should be adorned in precious jewels, wrapped in satin and silk. What had he given her? Misery. Grief. *Class act.*

He snagged the clean clothes he'd dug out and tugged her toward the bathroom. While sleep was the last thing on his mind, he knew she had to be exhausted. "Let's get you cleaned up. I'll see what I can find for food."

He turned on the water then knelt to untie her sneakers. A simple act, but one he'd done enough times it felt familiar. Adam's reaction was familiar, too. He immediately grew hard.

He didn't bother to fight it. But he did back away. With the pretense gone, there was no danger of her trying to escape, no reason to force her to shower with him. "I'll be right outside if you need anything."

"Don't go. I, I don't want to be alone right now."

The plaintive note in her voice reminded him that

this was the first time they'd had a moment to themselves since the car had gone over the ridge. Being on the run had forced them to push the incident from consciousness. Now the aftermath surfaced. She was shaking.

He tugged her into his arms. "You're a brave woman, Renata. You've been through hell."

"I didn't feel brave back there. Not when I thought the car was going to explode."

"It didn't." If it had . . . For long minutes he simply held her. Everything had gone crazy. He had questions without answers and all his plans were in tatters.

When she spoke again, her voice was husky. "Are you ever going to tell me your real name?"

"I'd rather wait till it's over."

She sighed, resigned. "The less I know the better, right?"

"Actually, no." He pulled away slightly, cupped her chin. "When this is over, I want to see you again, on a personal basis. I thought meeting under my real name would give us a fresh start. But now that I'm hearing myself say it, it sounds rather lame."

"No, it doesn't. And I'll look forward to that introduction." To his surprise, she reached up. Her fingers stilled over one of the buttons on his shirt. "May I?"

At his nod, she slipped the first one free. Adam caught his breath. There was something erotic about watching this woman undo his shirt. She pushed the edges of the shirt aside, raked her fingers across his torso, over the scars above his left nipple.

"Will you tell me about these someday?"

Someday. The word suggested a future. And offered an option. For him not to tell if it was too painful. She didn't push. She didn't demand. She asked. His chest tightened. For the first time in his life he understood how shared secrets, shared intimacies, built bonds. How they also made one vulnerable.

And as much as he didn't want to tell her the truth, he knew she deserved it.

"My old man was the worst kind of drunk. Beginning on my eleventh birthday, I had to take him on, try to whip his ass. Every time I lost, he'd make a notch." Adam ran his fingers over the six marks. "I was a slow learner."

"No one should suffer that."

"As warped as it sounds, I looked forward to it. It was my only opportunity to strike back. I could usually get in at least one good blow before he nailed me. And afterwards, I had a full year to plan. I finally kicked his ass two weeks before I turned seventeen. He never laid a hand on me after that."

Renata closed her eyes. She remembered his mentioning that his mother had abandoned him. What kind of woman left her child to such a fate?

Her hand dropped lower, to the mottled scars that etched his chest and sides. "And this?"

He hesitated. His father had decided one night that Adam looked too much like his mother. And while Adam had been able to keep the acid off his face, he obviously hadn't been able to completely disarm his drunken father.

"Another ugly tale," he whispered. "Best forgotten."

A million questions clamored in Renata's mind, but she quelled them for another time and let her natural instincts take over; her instinctive need to heal.

She eased his shirt off his shoulders, off his arms. Bending close, she pressed kisses across his chest, taking her time, making certain every scar was touched. She felt him shudder as her tongue darted forward, warm and moist, soothing the tense muscles, caressing his flesh with her lips.

When she finished, she straightened. One hand still stroked his chest, while the other strayed lower, stopping at the waistband of his jeans.

"May I touch you? Here?" Her hand hovered.

At his nod, her hand dipped lower, grasping his erection through the fabric, tracing the blatant outline with her fingers.

He groaned in pleasure, but didn't move to touch her. "Are you sure about this?"

Renata met his eyes. She wasn't sure about a lot of things. Who Adam was. Or when she'd be free. But one question haunted her: What if something happened to him? The thought of never seeing him again tore a hole in her heart.

She had feelings for this man. Whether they were right or wrong, or whether she'd regret them later remained to be seen. So much of this ordeal had been out of her control.

All the more reason that, for now, she wanted to take charge of the one situation she could.

"I'm sure of two things," she whispered. "I . . . want to touch you again. And I want you to make love to me."

Chapter Seventeen

Adam swore. Then apologized. "I'm sorry, but I've never wanted to hear those words so badly in my life."

"Then I'll ask again." She unfastened the top snap of his jeans and eased her fingers inside. "Will you make love to me? Please?"

With a groan he tugged off her clothes. One day, he'd slowly strip her clothing away, savor the sacred act of undressing her. Today, his sanity couldn't handle it.

He lowered his pants, eager to be naked. To feel, to touch. His erection brushed the soft skin of her abdomen, the drag of flesh on flesh so electrifying he nearly climaxed.

He slowed, gathering control. And giving her one last chance to back away—praying she wouldn't take it.

"Are you sure?"

She answered without words, pressing closer, rubbing slightly from side to side. He reveled in the delicious friction; wallowed in the sweetness of her welcome.

She pressed another kiss to his chest, her tongue swirling, devouring the mottled skin. He gritted his teeth against the unfamiliar sensation and emotion it evoked. No one had ever kissed his scars. Made him forget they were there.

He ran his fingers through her hair, marveling at its silky texture. She twisted her head and pressed her lips into the center of his palm. Another jolt shot through him as he caught her gaze. Her eyes were dark with desire. Longing. *She wanted him.*

And in that moment he was entranced. He was her captive.

He lifted her into the shower, closed the curtain around them. Then he put a hand on either side of her face and kissed her. It started gently, his lips moving lightly against hers. Her mouth parted. Eager. The kiss deepened and his tongue swept in, tasting her. Encouraging her. She responded, opening her mouth fully.

Adam's world spun. Dizzy, he ended the kiss, resting his forehead against hers. She gulped air, proof she'd been equally affected.

"I could do that forever," he whispered. "Kiss you."

"Me, too. But what about this?" Her hand slid down to his hips, then angled toward his erection.

"Easy, sweet." Adam stopped her. "It's my turn to go first. Remember?"

She blushed.

He chuckled and drew his hands up her sides. Knowing he could touch her freely, openly, was like mainlining an aphrodisiac laced with amphetamines. He felt a violent need to be inside her fully and completely, all at once; to press her against the wall and not stop until every inch of his aching cock was buried deep inside her.

Except it would be all over before it started. He needed to slow it down.

Grasping her shoulders, he turned her away from him, until she faced the wall. She drew a sharp breath, uncertain. But she didn't stop him. Her trust was humbling.

"Shhhh." He drew wet fingers down her arms, massaging lightly.

"Don't you want—"

"Oh, I *want*." He pulled her back, flat against him, bringing her backside in direct contact with his erection. He rubbed sinuously against her; pressed himself into her lower back. "And I'll *get*. Eventually. For now I just want to enjoy the journey."

"Did you think of this while you were locked up?" she asked. "I mean—"

"I learned not to." His hands were at her waist now, sliding over her smooth skin. "It was hell."

"I can't imagine. But it's over now." She arched backwards, intentionally thrusting against his groin. "So enjoy."

With a growl, Adam cupped her breasts. Being taller, he could see over her shoulders, could watch his fingers massage the twin mounds, kneading, tracing their shape. He circled her nipples, teasing before grasping them. He wanted to taste her. All of her.

He turned her around, letting his eyes explore fully before allowing his hands to curve over her breasts again. Beneath his palms, her nipples hardened. He stroked and fondled, before catching the tips between thumb and forefinger. He tugged lightly to test her reaction. She drew away ever so slightly, a wordless invitation to increase the pressure. He pinched softly.

She drew another sharp breath, encouraging him. Her eyes fluttered shut as her hips thrust forward slightly. Her responsiveness pleased him. She had sensitive breasts and probably enjoyed extended foreplay. Lucky him.

Adam kissed her again. She opened her mouth fully, welcoming.

He moved to touch her once more, but this time his hand dipped lower, his fingers seeking the dark tangle of curls between her legs. He stroked and petted, spreading her, his way eased by moisture.

"Open your legs," he urged. When she did, he pressed up and in, penetrating her with a single finger. She shuddered as he withdrew part way, stroked back in.

Continuing his play, he withdrew his finger—replaced it with two and gently coaxed them inside her body. Stretching her, preparing her. While she wasn't a virgin, he guessed it had been a while since she'd been with anyone. She was so damn tight—he'd die.

Her breath came in hurried, uneven pants. His thumb swept up, teasing her clitoris. She shifted against his hand, pressing. He responded, caressing her clit again and again, gradually increasing the pressure, the tempo. He watched the expressions play over her face, enthralled.

She stiffened, on the brink of an orgasm. "But we haven't—"

"It's okay," Adam whispered. "To do this."

He quickened the pace, inflaming her. When she tried to hold back, he changed the rhythm, but kept the pressure unrelenting. "Give it up, sweetheart."

With a cry, she came. Her eyes widened, then drifted shut as she pumped her hips against his hand. Lost. When the last tremor subsided, her head lolled to one side.

He waited for her to open her eyes. "I owed you that."

"For last night?" She looked disappointed. "You mean we're even?"

He grinned. "We're even. But we're not finished."

"*Ooooohhh.*"

His hand hadn't stopped stroking her. He could feel the tension building within her once more. "Feel good?" he teased.

"Good? You have an ungodly flair for understatement." She grasped his sides and pulled him closer to rub against his erection. "What about you? What about this?"

"*This* definitely needs attention, but let's move to the bed first. Making love in a shower is overrated."

He shut off the water and grabbed a towel, running it first over her, then himself, leaving them both more wet than dry. Carrying her to the bed, he yanked the covers back with one hand and gently laid her down, making no move to join her.

Renata felt reborn under his scorching gaze. That he liked what he saw made her feel powerful, vanquished her insecurities. Leaving her feeling deliciously feminine. She returned his stare, letting him know she found him every bit as desirable.

"I'll be right back." He straightened and crossed the room.

When he returned, he tossed a strip of foil packs on the nightstand. She hadn't even thought of that part, had even tried to get rid of them earlier.

Placing one knee on the bed, he bent and kissed her. She felt herself burn. For him. Only him. Not sex. Not satisfaction. *Him.*

She pressed a hand at his nape, her other hand trailing down to grasp at his hip, aching to get closer. Their coming together had a sense of inevitability. And their denying it had only made it grow stronger. With each touch, each stroke, she grew more frenzied; their uncontrolled passion threatened to consume her.

She drew back just enough to close her hand over his thick shaft, uncertain of what to do—yet doing it. Her fist stroked up, down, pumping his flesh as she'd watched him do all those nights ago.

"Harder. Like this." He closed his fingers over hers, showing her.

His words emboldened her. She tightened her grip, milking his flesh, determined to bring him pleasure.

He made a strangled noise. "That's it."

"You like a firm touch."

"We both do."

To emphasize, he bent, took her nipple in his mouth and sucked lightly. He drew his tongue lazily around her aureole, teasing. Then he sucked harder, grasping her with his teeth and tugging. She arched beneath him.

"More," she hissed.

He raised, trailing kisses down her stomach to her navel, as he shifted to the end of the bed. He grasped her ankles, easing her legs open, before bending low, to press a kiss to the inside of her knee. Then he inched upward, edging her legs further apart.

He nibbled at the soft skin inside her thigh, watched her jump. Continuing upward, he heard her draw a sharp breath as his cheek brushed her pubic curls. He inhaled, savoring her sweet scent.

He debated kissing her there, but didn't. There would be time in the future to explore everything. When she felt more comfortable. And when he didn't feel like he'd die if he wasn't soon inside her.

He shifted, trailing his mouth across her abdomen and slowly making his way back up to her breast. He latched onto her nipple in full and sucked. Hard. Her reaction was swift. Demanding. Her fingers speared through his damp hair holding him in place. Her hips arched, brushing against his knee. He moved closer, let her rock her pelvis back and forth against his leg as his mouth continued its play on her breasts.

At her whimper, he pulled away. Sitting up, he reached for a foil package. Opening the condom, he slid it on, pinched the end to form a reservoir.

Then he moved over her, his large frame dwarfing hers. He rested his arms on either side, to support his weight as he gave her a moment to get used to him. To his body. As he got used to hers. She was so goddamned tiny. And as delicate as a butterfly. He felt scared and excited him at the same time.

Renata felt his erection press against her as he slid his sheathed length against her center, not entering, just rubbing. He felt over-large, foreign. And she wanted him desperately.

He pressed kisses above her eyes, then moved lower to catch her mouth. His pelvis ground against hers in that maddening back and forth motion. She moaned.

"You okay?" he whispered.

Renata rocked her hips, trying to increase the pressure while loath to break the kiss. He was driving her mad, taking her to the brink, then leaving her suspended.

"I won't be okay until you're inside me. I beg you—"

Adam silenced her, thrusting the head of his penis inside her. He paused, barely possessing her as he ran his lips along the edge of her jaw. "I should be begging you. For this."

His sudden penetration made her dizzy. She'd expected it, craved it, yet still she wasn't prepared for his stark invasion.

As the sharp edge of sensation melted into pleasure, she realized he had stopped on purpose—to allow her body to adjust. She ran her hands down his back, urging him forward, seeking relief.

"Ready for more?"

"All," she demanded.

A wicked gleam lit his eyes. "My pleasure."

Grasping her hands, he eased them up, one at a time, over her head. The move brought his weight more fully against her lower body as he slid further into her, filling her.

Renata's world shifted. While part of her felt he couldn't—wouldn't—fit, another part knew he had to. She'd perish without this.

"Ease your leg up," he encouraged. "It will help."

She raised her knee. The move brought him fully into her. She felt her body resist, then melt. A raw, delicious ache followed by a slow, heated burn.

He pulled back, withdrawing. Then pushed back in. Deeper.

She groaned as each press of his body rubbed her clitoris, the back and forth motion tormenting her. Seeking release, she drew her leg up further, to his waist and pressed wholly against him. The pressure increased, the sensation sharpened.

Adam threw his head back, flexing fully into her. He'd tried to go slow and easy, but now he couldn't hold back. He had fantasized a hundred times about making love to her. But nothing came close to this. Being inside her.

He thrust deep and paused, savoring the luscious clutch of her sheath. "I can't take much more."

"Then don't." She raised and took his flat nipple into her mouth, kissing, sucking.

Adam hissed, control lost. Pumping his hips, he moved in and out of her, his strokes long and sure, gathering momentum. He watched as the first wave of her orgasm hit. Her eyes widened, her breath coming in rapid-fire pants. She cried out, a wild, satisfying keening.

It was over. Adam felt his testicles tighten. He stiffened as his own climax peaked and released, hot sperm exploding. He roared, plunging furiously into her as the fire washed over him, taking him crashing over the edge.

While she slept, Adam got up. As much as he wanted to stay in bed, he needed to contact his brother and make arrangements to get Renata out.

With the room's heavy drapes, it was difficult to tell that it was barely ten in the morning. He wondered briefly what Lyle was doing. Peeking out the window, he eyed the pay phone. It was close to the office but he had to risk it.

Shrugging into clothes, he whispered to Renata that he'd be right back. The bright sunlight nearly blinded him as he slipped outside.

Zach answered on the first ring.

"This isn't a good time." On the off chance the phone was bugged, Adam had to be careful what he said. "Where are you?"

"Colorado. Just across the Utah border, within a few miles of Flaming Gorge."

"Stay put. I've been delayed, but I'll get there."

"Problems?"

Adam gave him a condensed version of the car accident. "I'll see about getting new wheels—"

The blinds at the office parted. Someone watched. The door opened and a man hurried toward him, a hastily thrown-on shirt left unbuttoned.

"Gotta go. I'll call back soon." Adam hung up just as the man reached him.

"If you need a phone, use the one inside the office," the man said. "Best you keep out of sight."

Adam nodded toward Lyle's room. "Has he been up yet?"

The man shook his head. "My niece, Wanda, left about an hour ago and said Lyle was pretty much passed out. She'll be back after work. She said you'd driven all night so I didn't figure I'd see either of you till later this afternoon."

"Actually, I'm supposed to run an important errand for them. Any idea when another car will arrive?"

"I was told to expect you here at least two nights, possibly three, so I wouldn't expect anything till tomorrow. Maybe the next day." The man scratched his chest. "Want me to see if I can scare up something temporary?"

"I'd be obliged."

Adam hurried back to the room. Two more nights? It shouldn't surprise him, given his dealings with the McEdwins thus far. Who knew how much longer Willy would keep up this cat and mouse game? Two days could stretch into another week.

But at least Renata would be gone. In fact, if the man didn't get Adam transportation by this afternoon, he'd see if he could borrow Wanda's car.

Back in the room, he undressed. Renata was awake.

"Anything new?" she asked.

"Not yet." He told her about his call to Zach.

"Eager to get rid of me?" She tried to joke.

"Yeah." He climbed in bed, drew her close. "Go back to sleep."

She snuggled into him. Her hand dipped low, her fingers stroking the swollen ridge of his penis. A soft sound escaped her throat as she grasped him fully. "I don't think I can. Sleep that is."

"Me neither." He grabbed for a condom. Maybe this time, they'd take it slowly.

Slowly never happened. The morning passed in a blur fueled by sleep deprivation. Not the tortuous type of denial, but rather the sweet, delicious muddle born of waking every hour to make love, fast and furious.

Renata felt suspended in another sphere, her sense of time and place discombobulated. With the heavy curtains drawn tight, the room remained dark, shadowy. Yet it was the middle of the day. Which added to her disorientation.

The dramatic change of circumstances with Adam hadn't helped. She'd gone from captive to lover, in the flick of a bed sheet.

What was odd was that she felt no guilt. She'd spent the entire morning in bed—was sore from too much sex. *Not enough.* Where was the regret? The recriminations?

God, what had come over her?

She opened her eyes, not ready to face her thoughts, and found Adam looming over her, his beautiful brow lined with concern.

She closed her eyes, not ready to face him either.

"Look at me, Renata." He ran his finger across her cheek. "I wish our first time had been under different circumstances. But it wasn't. Which doesn't make it any less special. And if—"

A noise caught his attention. A low squeak followed by a scrape. He tucked her behind him and grabbed his gun just seconds before the door burst open. Two men entered.

"Don't move!" Adam shouted.

He recognized the men from pictures he'd seen in the FBI's files: Burt and Tristin McEdwin. The family resemblance was strong. It was like looking at photographs of their father from thirty years ago.

But they didn't know he knew, so Adam kept his gun leveled straight ahead. "Who the hell are you?"

"Jesus Christ!"

"Wrong answer." Adam raised the gun's barrel.

"Don't shoot. I'm Lyle's brother, Burt," one of the men said. "Lyle's pretty sick. Nevin sent us to get the doctor."

"Nevin's next door?"

Burt nodded.

Adam gripped the nine-millimeter tighter. He had two of the McEdwin brothers right in front of him with the other two in the next room. Was it enough? Could he end it right here?

Capturing all four brothers was a hellacious feat. Adam could take them in and leave Willy for another day. Without his sons, the old man would be easier to track down. And if the rumors were true that Willy was retiring and turning the reins over to his sons, then the four brothers were the more dangerous of the bunch.

Except Willy had at least a hundred pounds of plastic explosive, enough to do a lot of damage in retaliation.

Adam was also out-gunned and out-manned. In addition to the McEdwin brothers—and their goddamn pact to not be taken alive—there was at least one of Willy's sympathizers in the motel's office. Maybe more. Those were rotten odds. Especially with Renata to protect.

He lowered his weapon. "What's wrong with Lyle?"

"He's running a fever." Burt stepped forward, angling for a better view of Renata. "And he's puking his guts out."

Acutely aware she was nude beneath the sheet, Adam bared his teeth and leaned up slightly. He felt her hand tighten at his waist. He reached around to draw her even closer behind him, shielding her completely from view. Then he raised his gun again, leveled it at Burt. "Back off."

The other man held up his hands and eased away. "Sorry."

Adam waited a few seconds before lowering his weapon. "How long has Lyle been sick? And why didn't he wake me instead of calling you?"

Tristin grunted. "Lyle didn't call. Nevin found him passed out in the bathroom."

The news about Lyle worried Adam. "We'll meet you over there in a minute."

When they were alone, he pulled Renata into his arms. Holding her tightly against his chest, he pressed his mouth to her ear. "Get dressed."

"What happens now?"

"I'm not sure." Until he knew what the McEdwins' intentions were, he couldn't make alternate plans. Nevin's unannounced return piqued his curiosity.

"Our lives depend on how well we play this game, so remember to play the captive and let me take the lead. Don't take anything I do or say to heart." He kissed her gently, soundly, before releasing her. "I swear I'll get you out of this."

But she stopped him before he moved away. "Swear you'll get us *both* out."

Chapter Eighteen

Lyle's room reeked of vomit.

His three older brothers gathered around the bed, whispering. Adam moved closer, stopping when he glimpsed Lyle. The younger man was as pale as the sheet, his breathing shallow.

Renata tried to move forward. "Let me see him."

That fast, Nevin pointed his gun at her.

"What the hell happened? Did you do something to make him sicker? He was a lot better last time I saw him."

She didn't move, her eyes glued to the gun.

"I knew it," Nevin swore. "I should have killed you sooner."

"Stop." Adam stepped in front of Renata. "Whatever's wrong, he did to himself. Did he tell you what happened in Colorado?"

Nevin snorted. "He's so fucked up on painkillers I can't get a straight answer out of him."

"He drove the car into a ravine." Adam filled him in on what had happened the night before. "We lost all our supplies, the cell phones, and had to steal a truck. Lyle said he banged up his knee, said his girlfriend would take care of it. Obviously, his injury was worse than he let on."

The McEdwin brothers exchanged glances.

"Well, that explains a lot. The cops are all over the place. Which means all those clues we planted on the East Coast just went up in smoke." Nevin looked at Lyle and shook his head. "Shit. I wish he was better so I could beat his ass."

Lyle groaned, muttering unintelligibly.

"Let her examine him while we talk." Adam pushed her closer to the bed.

Renata drew back the sheets. Lyle was nude. A haphazardly taped, bloodstained bandage covered his wound. Moving quickly, she peeled the gauze back, wrinkling her nose at the putrid smell.

The wound had torn open again. It was also packed with dirt, probably from climbing out of the ravine. She wondered if any attempt had been made to clean it . . . or had Lyle just instructed his girlfriend to "throw a bandage on it."

The skin all around was red, swollen, and oozing with pus. She pressed lightly, knew by his reaction that it was tender to the touch.

She glanced at Adam. "I need supplies from next door."

Nevin moved up and glanced over her shoulder, scowling when he saw the condition of Lyle's wound. "Tell Tristin what you need. Burt, we'll be right back. Watch her every move."

Adam followed Nevin outside. "I was told we weren't meeting up until day after tomorrow."

"We got word the Feds are headed this way," Nevin said. "Four agents are on a flight landing in Salt Lake at 8:08 P.M. And I've got a list a mile long of others they're meeting. ATF, Marshals—Christ, they're all involved."

That the McEdwins had access to that level of detailed information exasperated Adam. It also meant the leaks were even more extensive than he'd been told, which made Adam's position trickier.

"So what's the plan?"

Nevin shook his head. "My first priority is to get Lyle out of here. Fast. Pa's got more antibiotics and other medical supplies on standby. And if that doctor needs anything else, we can get it on short notice."

"Wait . . . we're taking her with us?" Adam tried to think of a legitimate excuse to leave her without jeopardizing her welfare. If he couldn't deliver her to a safe spot personally, then leaving her here, at the motel with one of the McEdwins' cronies, was out of the question. They'd kill her.

"We don't have a choice with Lyle this sick again. We'll worry about getting rid of her later."

"Fine. As long as we're straight on one thing: We don't get rid of her until I say so. Got it?" Adam met the other man's eye. "She's a nice diversion. Or at least I think she'll be nice, when we're not getting interrupted. I've had to put up with a lot of her bullshit, so she owes me, big time. So does Lyle."

"Fair enough. But we leave in five minutes."

"Five minutes? I'm supposed to meet my partner today."

Nevin handed him a cell phone. "Call and postpone. Tell him I'll arrange to have him picked up later."

Picked up? Adam tried to think of other options. "If I blow him off again—"

"Tell him whatever you need to, just assure him we're still very interested. Right now, I've got my hands full with Lyle sick and the cops swarming like locusts. Trust me—you're not the only one having to change plans."

It was obvious by Nevin's tone that some of his plans had been foiled as well. Adam wondered if it had to do with the explosives the McEdwins had already acquired.

After all the delays and setbacks, the news that they were finally joining Willy should have pleased Adam. It didn't.

Taking Renata along had never been part of the plan. Neither had getting his brother involved. He needed someone he could trust to pose as his partner, Daniel Montague, and his brother was his only choice. The only good thing about Nevin's suggestion that Adam's partner remain close by was that it could work to his advantage in freeing Renata.

He took the cell phone from Nevin. "How far are we going? Another car trip could kill Lyle."

"Not far. Not far, at all."

Tension encased the motel room like thick coils of rope, heavy and restrictive, as five minutes turned into an hour. It was nearly 3 P.M. Burt and Tristin took turns watching at the window, weapons drawn at all times. Habit? Or did they expect more trouble?

Nevin made two calls, but Adam was unable to determine much beyond the fact that they were waiting on transportation. He had contacted Zach while outside, but with Nevin listening, he'd kept the conversation brief.

Zach played along. Of course, if he'd been reading all the files on Stan's computer, he probably knew as much about the case as Adam. Maybe more.

A vehicle pulled up outside, brakes squeaking. Tristin peeked out, then nodded at Nevin. At the single knock, he opened the door. Adam recognized the man from the motel office.

The man yanked a baseball cap off and wiped sweat

from his brow. "Bad news. Sheriff's deputy found that forest service truck about sixty miles south of here."

Nevin shot to his feet. "How in the hell did that happen?"

"Bunch of damn kids stole it from Pruett's Garage and went joyriding." The man replaced his cap. "Police and FBI are setting up roadblocks at the state line."

"Let's move." Nevin made a terse phone call, then tilted his head toward Renata. "She needs to be bound and blindfolded."

While Adam had expected it, Renata had not. He moved toward her, grasped her wrists. When she resisted, he snatched her close and shook her, aware that they were being observed.

"Cooperate, and this will be easier for both of us. Otherwise, you're likely to be hurt."

The look of terror and betrayal in her eyes was genuine. Working quickly, Adam bound her hands, then blindfolded her and tied a gag over her mouth.

Following the others, he led her out the door and lifted her into the rear of a brown van. He sat beside her on the floor, leaving the back seat for Lyle to lie on.

No one spoke as they pulled out of the lot. Once inside the van, Burt and Tristin holstered their handguns, and took up assault rifles. Crouching near the middle windows, they watched the road. Nevin sat slouched in the passenger seat, his rifle close as he scanned the horizon with high-powered binoculars. They expected trouble and were prepared.

So was Adam. The nine-millimeter in his hand had a full clip. In the event of a showdown, he'd take Burt, Tristin, and Nevin out, rapid fire, with head shots. Two seconds, max.

While the driver hadn't brandished a weapon, Adam

suspected the man was armed. He hoped he would surrender rather than take a bullet.

They traveled for less than fifteen minutes. Lyle groaned as the van lurched to a stop. They were at a makeshift airstrip.

Adam heard the *whoosh-whoosh* of an approaching helicopter. He turned Renata away, sheltering her from the sand and grit the dark chopper kicked up as it landed a short distance away.

As soon as Burt carried Lyle to the aircraft, the van pulled away. Inside the chopper, Lyle was propped up long enough to take the painkillers he'd been moaning for.

Adam frowned. "Is anyone keeping track of how frequently he's popping pills?"

Nevin shrugged. "Keeping him sedated is easier for now."

"Yeah, if it doesn't kill him."

Nevin narrowed his eyes, but checked his watch. "That should last him till we're home."

Home. Growing up, that word had meant the equivalent of hell to Adam. How fitting to think of Willy McEdwin, at home waiting for his sons.

They were in the air for several hours. He'd guess the chopper, stripped down to maximize fuel economy, was one bought as surplus from the National Guard. It probably belonged to one of the militia groups sympathetic to Willy's cause.

The pilot used visual flight rules and a handheld GPS to navigate. They flew low, about three hundred feet above ground level, Adam estimated. By keeping under seven hundred feet—and avoiding major airports—they stayed in Class G airspace. Basically uncontrolled and off the radar.

When they landed at yet another small airstrip,

Adam glanced around and spotted a small sign: GRASSYFIELD, IDAHO—PRIVATE AIRSTRIP. He took Renata into the small bathroom. He loosened her bonds briefly, but had to bind her hands and blindfold her again when she finished.

"If you're gagging me to keep me from crying out, I won't," she whispered.

"Remind me, later, to tell you how much you amaze me." He pressed a kiss to her forehead before opening the door.

They shifted to another van. Adam checked Lyle. He looked terrible. For the first time since the initial shooting, Adam worried the kid wouldn't survive. Once Willy McEdwin saw the shape his youngest son was in, he'd have to recognize Lyle needed a hospital.

This time Nevin drove, heading directly into the mountains. Tristin passed around a sack containing candy bars. "Grab a couple."

As before, they sat on the floor, but this time Renata sat on Adam's lap. He fed her a chocolate bar, breaking off small squares and holding them up to her mouth.

Burt snickered. "They domesticate wild birds that way. Clip their wings, hood them, and make them totally dependent on the hand that feeds them. Makes 'em do anything."

Adam felt her stiffen and pressed a hand to the small of her back, where no one could see. She relaxed slightly. While he'd had second thoughts about telling her the truth, now he was glad she knew. To be held under these conditions, without hope, would be terrifying.

After thirty minutes of winding along a desolate stretch of highway, Nevin pulled onto a road heading up the side of a mountain. For a moment it seemed the van might stall out. It coughed, the idle set too lean for the high altitude, but sputtered and chugged on.

Dusk was falling by the time they came to a gate across the road. From nowhere a man appeared, rifle in hand. He nodded at Nevin and opened the gate—then disappeared back into the trees. A few minutes later they pulled up in front of a two-story building tucked beneath some pines.

Several outbuildings and barns were scattered beneath other trees. From the air, the place would be practically invisible. Adam guessed they were at a secret militia compound. One of the first things he needed to do was find out how many men were here. And exactly where *here* was.

Keeping Renata close, he followed the brothers inside. The interior, while dark, was larger than expected. Tristin and Burt still supported Lyle when their father stepped into the room.

Willy McEdwin's hair was more gray, the lines in his face more harsh than Adam expected. Other than that, the older man looked exactly like the mug shot on his reward poster. Like his sons, Willy had made no attempt to disguise his looks, yet another way of thumbing their noses at law enforcement.

Willy clasped Lyle in a hug. "Good to have you home, son."

The younger man flinched. "Easy, Pa," he slurred.

Willy frowned. "Get him upstairs." Next he turned to Adam, extended a hand. "I owe you for getting my boy out of prison and keeping him alive. Is this the doctor?"

Adam nodded.

"Get her upstairs, too," Willy said. "I don't claim to know a lot about medicine, but if you ask me, he looks like he's got one foot in the grave."

* * *

Renata looked wild-eyed when Adam freed her, but with the McEdwins present, she didn't say anything. She rubbed her wrists and glanced around.

Adam guided her toward the staircase. "You need to check the kid."

Lyle was in the first bedroom on the right. Burt brought in a large footlocker filled with medical supplies and set it beside the bed.

Adam rifled through it, handing her a thermometer, stethoscope, and blood pressure cuff. He checked the rest of the supplies, pulled out several pair of scissors. "We need to control her access to these; but keep them readily available for legitimate use."

Burt nodded and took the scissors.

Except for the hiss of air escaping the cuff, the room remained quiet while she worked.

"His fever is climbing. One-oh-three-point-six," she said. "And he's dehydrated. He'll need IV fluids and antibiotics around the clock."

Tristin looked at her suspiciously. "I thought he's been on antibiotics."

"He was, but only for a couple days; enough to start but not finish the job. The wound's never received proper care. Getting dirt in it certainly hasn't been good." She held up one of the bags of antibiotics that Adam had handed her. "Even this may not be strong enough—"

"Then again, it might," Willy's voice boomed from behind. "And if we need something stronger, by God, we'll get it. Burt, get your little brother undressed while I talk to the doctor."

Grasping her by the arm, Adam tugged her out of the room, and down the hall.

Willy kept his voice low. "Give it to me straight, doc. How's he doing?"

"The truth?" Renata crossed her arms. "He will likely die if he's not taken to a hospital."

"I know that. How long has he got?"

Her mouth opened, closed. "If he doesn't respond to these antibiotics, it's impossible to say. It could be days or weeks. I've seen people linger, going in and out of comas, improving slightly, then getting worse."

"I get the picture." Willy raised a hand and sighed. "Just do what you need to do and keep him comfortable."

"Comfortable? You keep an end-stage cancer patient *comfortable*. There are still options available, still time to save him. But only if we act quickly. Your son needs—"

Adam squeezed her shoulder. "He heard you. So shut up."

To his relief, she lowered her head. To everyone else it appeared she was sulking—expected behavior for a captive. He knew she was madder than a cat on fire.

Willy turned back to Adam. "We need to talk. Downstairs. Tristin and Burt will stay with the woman and help her get Lyle cleaned up."

As soon as Willy had disappeared down the stairs, Adam pulled her close, voice low. "You can't stand up to these men, Renata."

Fury glistened in her eyes. "I can't believe a parent could be so callous about their child's life."

Adam could. "He's not like us. He's blinded by his cause. I have to go. I'll be back up as soon as I can."

"Bet she's not real happy with her circumstances," Willy said when Adam came downstairs. "Abducted by a convict and all."

Adam knew what *and all* implied. Everything from mental abuse to rape. "She doesn't exactly have a choice."

"She's got grit."

"Why do you think I've kept her?"

Willy looked thoughtful then laughed. "Guess it don't matter in the long run. Are you hungry?"

"Hungry. Tired. Wired. Feels like we've been on the road for a month instead of eight days."

They were in the kitchen. A long table was set up, with enough chairs to seat twenty. How many people were here? The room had few windows. Tucked in the far corner of the room was a computer. Adam wondered what incriminating treasures he'd find on the PC's hard drive.

Food and coffee were already on the table. Nevin joined them.

Willy motioned for Adam to have a seat. "Dish up. Chow's hot. And I bet these will be the best chicken and dumplings you ever ate."

Adam spooned a generous portion onto his plate. "After prison, everything's the best."

"I won't beat around the bush," Willy said after they'd both taken a few bites of food. "Lyle said you've made arrangements for my explosives?"

Adam lowered his fork. "I've confirmed availability, but there are a few details to work out, like payment and delivery. And I've had to blow my partner off twice now, which means he'll be jumpy."

"Montague? Can't blame him. I suggest we bring him here. We can complete our transaction. And discuss . . . the future."

"Whose future?" Adam eyed the two men with undisguised suspicion. "And why would I want to discuss it with you?"

"Hear me out." Willy wiped his mouth. "I did some checking on you and your partner, and I think I finally figured out how you two were managing to rip off Uncle Sam."

"Oh?" Adam couldn't wait to hear this.

"Somehow, you managed to hack into the munitions program, arranged for inventory to ship from one warehouse, then you logged it in as received at another, after intercepting it somewhere else. The beauty of it is nobody even knew the stuff went missing since the computer showed it all accounted for. Till your girlfriend ran her mouth, that is."

Adam swallowed coffee, neither confirming nor denying. "And you got this information where?"

"Burt and Tristin figured most of it out. Now, I know I'm missing a lot of the details—for example, you had to have someone helping on the inside—but, to date, the Feds haven't figured out how you did it. So I'm betting your partner went in and removed every trace that you'd been inside the computer. Which means you can go back in, right?"

Again, Adam didn't acknowledge. But he knew by the gloating glint in Willy's eye that the old man assumed he was correct. "Is that what you meant by the future?"

"Yep. And I have a business proposition. You and your partner will make twice what you did before, plus you'll have new identities and transportation to Australia. I hear there's acres of nice looking women down there."

The inference was clear: With so many women, Adam wouldn't bat an eye over losing Renata.

Adam picked up a piece of bread and spread butter on it. "If I'm making twice as much, what's in it for you?"

"Commissions," Willy leaned close. "You know how much U.S. military arms sell for overseas?"

"Yeah. Big bucks. Which surprises me a bit. Doesn't that go against the pro-American doctrine all those groups you belong to embrace?" He knew many of the militia group members professed to be devoted patriots who simply felt the federal government overpowered the little man.

"Over the years I've become pro-Willy. Period. My associations are pretty limited these days, but the Feds still try to link me and my boys to every radical group they can."

Adam dished up more dumplings. "Guess that makes it easier to harass everyone under the guise of searching for you. Kill twelve birds with one stone."

"I hadn't thought of it that way." Pleased, Willy pushed his plate back. "Just give it some thought. For now we need to concentrate on getting that C-4, pronto."

"I'll need access to a phone and—"

A noise sounded from the hallway. Adam turned, saw Burt. Renata hovered behind him. Her hands were cuffed and she'd been gagged and blindfolded again. Seeing her treated like that angered him.

He turned to Willy. "We need to get clear on one thing: The woman can care for Lyle, but her well-being is my affair. I also don't think she needs to be tied up all the time. Where's she going to go?"

Willy looked at him, then nodded. "In here, that's fine. Someone will be with her whenever she's taking care of Lyle. But I'm putting you up in the bunkhouse near the barn, so I insist you keep her handcuffed in your quarters. I don't want to have to worry about her slipping away."

"Fair enough."

Willy nodded at Burt, who untied Renata. "In fact, he can take you out there now, let you get settled. We'll meet again a little later."

As soon as Adam and Renata left with Burt, Nevin turned to Willy.

"Lyle's pretty sick, Pa. He's trying to hide it, but his wound looks terrible."

Willy grew quiet. "I know. I'll have that doctor check him more often."

"Maybe we should move them into the house so she's closer."

"Not just yet. There's something you need to know about Lyle." Willy got up and poured another cup of coffee. "I saw a lot of gunshots like that in 'Nam. Once gangrene sets in, it's all over."

"You think it's that bad?"

"Yep. You never forget the smell of death. And if that infection spreads down his leg—he'll lose use of it."

"Be a cripple?" Nevin's revulsion showed on his face. "Lyle would hate that."

"All of us would. But I don't want to upset Lyle by telling him that. Who knows? Maybe he will get better from those antibiotics." Willy's voice said *I doubt it*.

Somber, Nevin nodded. "Guess I'll go up and visit with him a bit. When will you meet with Duval again?"

"Not sure. I need to make a few calls while he's not around. And I need you to arrange to have the helicopter on standby to pick up his partner."

"You sure it's safe to bring him here?"

"We don't have a choice. Besides, I think Montague's the real brains behind their operation. He may be more valuable to us in the long run."

Nevin's frown deepened. "What if they decide not to join up?"

"We'll kill them. After we get the C-4, that is."

"And the doctor?"

Willy shrugged, nonchalant. "Right now Duval's just looking for a bedmate. Can't blame him after prison, but even he knows she's history."

Stars twinkled in the sky as Adam and Renata followed Burt. Night had fallen, taking the temperature into the fifties, a considerable contrast from the scorching temperatures they'd left in North Carolina.

They passed a rundown barn. Tucked behind it, near the woods, was a small bunkhouse. Inside were two tiny bedrooms and a living area. The air was musty, the rustic furniture coated with dust.

Easing Renata into the closest chair, Adam checked each room even though it was obvious the place hadn't been used in a while.

Burt nodded to Adam's gun. "You always this jittery?"

"Cautious." He tucked his firearm away. "I also want to know the entrances and exits. How many others are staying here?"

"Just you and the doctor. Why?"

"I'd feel bad if I shot someone in the middle of the night, only to find out they were *supposed* to be here."

"No one will bother you. We're the only ones at the house right now. There's two guards stationed at the front, but they have a small trailer. You might see them at meal times."

The news that only two others were at the compound encouraged Adam. Those odds were better.

Burt tossed him the handcuff key, then crossed the

room and opened a tiny closet. It was empty. "Well, that figures. I'll go back and get some supplies from the house. Sheets and towels, too."

"The woman needs food. And I could use some coffee."

When Burt left, Adam motioned for Renata to remain silent. He knew she had a lot of questions; couldn't imagine what she must be thinking and feeling. Hell, he hadn't sorted it out himself yet.

The day had turned out to be one bombshell after another. Willy's interest in a long-term deal with Adam's fictional partner, Daniel Montague, was unexpected, but timely. It also confirmed that Willy believed Adam's cover.

Methodically searching the rooms, he checked for electronic listening devices, even climbed into the small attic space. He didn't expect to find anything, knew Willy kept him away from the main house to protect his own privacy.

A knock sounded at the door. It was Burt again. He carted a box of supplies to the table. "Pa said he didn't realize how late it was. He'll meet with you in the morning."

Adam had no choice but to agree. While he couldn't appear overeager, he was anxious to hear more about Willy's business proposition so he could contact his brother.

As soon as they were alone again, he unfastened one of Renata's handcuffs, leaving the other to dangle at her wrist. He placed his fingers over hers as she rubbed the chafed skin.

Unable to resist, he cupped her cheek briefly. "How are you holding up?"

"I'm scared," she admitted. "Afraid I'm going to do

or say something wrong, something that will get us both killed."

"You won't."

She held up her other wrist. He loosened the second cuff but didn't remove it.

"Willy wants you cuffed out here, so we need to keep one in place," Adam explained. "If we get visitors and I can't get to you, you need to cuff yourself."

"How soon can you get us out of here?"

"Not soon enough. I'll know more in the morning." He led her to the table and unwrapped the plate of chicken and dumplings Burt had brought. "You must be starving. And exhausted."

While she ate, Adam made up one of the beds. When he finished he found her asleep at the table, her meal only half eaten.

He flipped off the lights and gave his eyes a chance to adjust to the dark. Then he picked her up and carried her to the bedroom. She stirred briefly, but relaxed when she saw it was him.

He tucked her in but made no attempt to join her. Yeah, he wanted her. Bad. But he wouldn't disturb her now unless her life depended on it.

He watched her sleep. His admiration for her multiplied as she weathered each new storm. When this was over . . .

What?

What could he possibly do or say to make up for any of this? Thanks to him, she'd been yanked into a nightmare. Was still in it.

Frustrated, Adam slipped outside. The waning moon offered enough light to make out shapes. From the corner of the barn, to see the main house. A light burned in the kitchen. He crept closer, trying to eavesdrop, but heard nothing.

Adam's questions were endless: Where was the first shipment of C-4 and what did Willy have planned for it? What was Ethan up to and would he try to sabotage Adam?

Adam needed help, but who to trust? It wasn't as simple as picking up the phone and calling it in. The leaks . . .

He thought back to Stan's original instructions to Zach: that the data be delivered to Chris Tashley. Tashley was his best bet for now. Adam would have Zach e-mail copies of Stan's files to Tashley, with a message asking for his help in getting backup.

Tense and tired, he headed back toward the bunkhouse. In the morning he'd insist on making contact with his brother and finalize a plan to get Renata to safety and the McEdwins to jail.

Chapter Nineteen

A pounding at the door woke Adam before five.

It was Tristin. "Pa wants the doctor to check Lyle."

Adam grew concerned. "Is he worse?"

"He had a restless night and he don't look so hot. Pa had to leave, but he wanted her to look at him first thing."

The news that Willy was no longer at the compound was also troubling. "When will he return? I have people I need to contact."

"He'll be back before dark. And he's two steps ahead of you; he left a satellite phone at the main house. Nevin's already laying out plans to bring Montague here, too."

"That's presuming a lot."

Tristin shrugged. "You can take that up with him."

Renata was already dressed when Adam returned to the bedroom. He slipped on the handcuffs, felt her shudder. "You have to trust me. Remember: It's part of the act."

She met his gaze. "That doesn't mean I have to like it."

At the main house, they found Lyle's condition had deteriorated overnight. His breathing was labored, his color poor.

"How long has he been like this?" She checked his vital signs.

"I'm not sure," Tristin said. "Pa stayed with him most of the night."

She grabbed the bottle of painkillers sitting on the nightstand. The lid was off, pills scattered on the table.

"Any idea how many of these he's taken?"

"Nope."

She tossed the loose pills in the trash and recapped the bottle before handing it to Tristin. "These have to be monitored and kept out of his reach. He could easily overdose."

"He won't like me taking them."

"Too bad." She checked the IV, found the drip had stopped, the tubing crimped where it had caught in the nightstand's drawer. "Here's part of the problem."

Working to restart the IV, she added yet another antibiotic. "This may be futile. He needs blood work, cultures."

Lyle coughed, his eyes fluttering, unfocused. "No hospitals, Tris. I'd rather die . . . than go back to . . . prison."

"Don't worry. You ain't going back, bro." Tristin turned to Adam. "Nevin's waiting on you. I'll stay and help the doctor."

Nevin was in the kitchen. "Here's what I've come up with," he said. "Call your partner and tell him to drive north into Wyoming on highway 191. We'll pick him up at the Roadside Diner, thirty miles south of Pinedale, in three hours."

"Hold it. I haven't discussed any of this with him. He may have other ideas. His coming here was never part of our plan."

"Plans change. We have a deal to conclude and now all those Feds are massing in Colorado. If we bring him here, it's safer. We can make final arrangements to get the C-4, and you two can talk to Pa, figure out if you're interested in doing more. If not, fine—but you know yourself it's a hell of a lot easier to conduct business in person than on the run."

Adam couldn't fault Nevin's logic. "I may not be able to reach him. If he's gotten wind the Feds are that close, he may have fled."

Nevin checked his watch. "I've got an errand to run. There's a phone in the other room. I'll be back in an hour. If he agrees, we'll take off, then meet the chopper."

"What about the woman?"

"Tristin and Burt will stay here with her and Lyle. Pa should be back by the time we return."

Adam didn't like the idea of leaving Renata. Asking to bring her along was out of the question; would only raise suspicion, especially with Lyle so sick. Having his brother pose as his partner, and getting him here quickly was their best option for now.

Burt was on the computer when Adam went to use the phone, so he kept his call to Zach brief.

"I was getting worried," his brother began.

"There's been a change." He explained his conversation with Willy and Nevin.

"Did you tell him I'd be interested?"

Adam grunted. "I told him I don't put words in your mouth. Can you make Pinedale, Wyoming, in three hours?"

"Might be tight. I'm trying to wrap up a few arrangements here."

"What kind of arrangements?"

"I doubt you want to know. But I've got the merchandise close by."

Adam grunted. The C-4. How in the hell had his brother gotten that? "I need you to forward those files."

"Will do. I'll see you soon."

When Adam returned to Lyle's room, Tristin took a break to get coffee, which gave him a moment alone with Renata.

Adam pulled her away from the bed and lowered his voice. "Nevin and I are going to pick up my brother. I shouldn't be gone long."

Her eyes flared. "Guess that means you aren't taking me, are you?"

"Not with Lyle this ill. I should only be gone a few hours."

"And if you don't return?"

He nudged her chin up. "I'll return."

Footsteps sounded in the hall. Adam moved back to the bed and began discussing Lyle's condition.

Behind them, Burt cleared his throat. "You need to go. Nevin's waiting."

Renata had a strong urge to run after Adam. Even though she knew it was part of the charade, his cold indifference in front of Burt stung. And the knowledge that he'd be gone left her uneasy.

She had no illusions where the McEdwins were concerned. To them, she was nothing more than a temporary caretaker for Lyle. Beyond that, she was a liability. Someone who could lead the police to their hideout.

The morning passed slowly. She remained in Lyle's room, reading old magazines. Tristin or Burt remained just outside the door, the computerized *binks* and *boinks* from a handheld video game a constant reminder of their presence. And their apathy.

At noon Tristin delivered a tray of food. Enough for five or six people—provided they liked it burnt. "It's late for breakfast, but it's all I can cook. The oatmeal's for Lyle."

Ignoring the brown eggs, she forced herself to eat a piece of scorched toast, smearing it first with strawberry jelly. The sugar did little to cover the carbon taste.

Lyle roused enough to take a single bite of oatmeal. "Tastes like . . . shit. Pa must be gone."

"Try a little more," she urged.

"What's the use?" He turned away, drifted back to sleep.

Frustrated, she changed his dressings and bathed him. He looked cachectic—drawn, deathlike—his body so ravaged with infection that it was slowly shutting down.

"Fight," she whispered, pulling a clean sheet over him.

He stirred, barely conscious. "Thanks, doc. I know I don't . . . deserve . . . care . . . like this."

His gratitude surprised her. "Everyone deserves care. It's a basic human dignity."

"I'm not gonna make it, am I?"

"I won't lie. You're quite sick. But I've seen worse." A new idea occurred to her. What if, in his weakened state, she could convince Lyle to ask to go to a hospital? Surely Willy would honor his son's request.

"You'll make it," she urged. "If we can get you to a hospital. Surely your father can pull some strings; get you admitted under an alias."

When he didn't respond, she bowed her head, discouraged.

"My father . . . won't . . . help," Lyle whispered.

She shifted closer. "What about your brothers?"

"Or Adam—" Lyle passed out.

A noise sounded behind her. Burt leaned in the doorjamb, watching her, making her uncomfortable.

"Did I hear Lyle talking?" he asked.

She moved closer to where Burt stood. Lyle had said his father wouldn't help, but he hadn't ruled out his brothers or Adam.

"He asked to go to a hospital." She kept her voice low. "He doesn't want to die."

A shadow crossed Burt's face. "Pa said gangrene's already set in. That he'll lose use of his leg."

"Your father is wrong. The leg could be saved." Renata felt the lie stick in her throat. She'd seen the signs of nonresponsiveness in Lyle's leg, felt the coldness from lack of circulation. Neither boded well. But Burt wasn't a doctor.

He nodded toward the bed. "We took an oath. Not to be taken alive. We take him to the hospital, it'll be as good as turning him in."

"I took an oath, too. To save lives. He's your brother. Doesn't that mean anything? Even if he went back to prison he'd still be alive."

Burt laughed. "You've never been in prison, have you?"

She didn't answer.

"Lyle told us some pretty bad stories about what they did to him. You've seen the marks. Has any one tortured you, Doc? Any scars under here?" Burt inched closer, his hand moving to her sleeve. "Or is it all just creamy skin?"

Renata slapped his hand away and stepped back. "Don't touch me. Ever."

Burt smiled. One of those smiles that didn't hit his eyes. "That was the wrong thing to do, Doc."

The trip was uneventful. The chopper pilot had a car waiting where they touched down in Wyoming. They drove the short distance to the diner, a hole-in-the-wall most people would pass by.

Adam wondered if Zach had made it. He'd spent the helicopter ride second-guessing his choices; now it was too late. He went inside, a stocking hat pulled low on his brow. He scanned the small crowd, not certain what to expect.

The man in the second booth removed his sunglasses and met his gaze. Adam did a double take, scarcely recognizing his own brother.

The blue eyes they shared were hidden beneath brown contacts. Zach also sported a bleached-blond goatee that matched his close-cropped hair. Except for their similar builds—Adam was two inches taller—it was impossible to tell they were brothers.

He shoved aside the twinge of guilt. By nightfall, his brother would be in as much danger as Renata.

"You don't look so bad," Zach said. "Perhaps prison was good for you."

"You'll pay for that crack later," Adam promised. "We don't have long. How's Stan?"

"Unchanged, but stable."

Adam pointed to the duffle bag on the seat. "Anything in there that can't stand scrutiny?"

"It's mostly toys, meant to dazzle. The good stuff's hidden. The C-4's en route to a warehouse in Idaho."

"At this rate, I'll have to include you in the bust."

"News flash: It's not mine. You want to know why Stan had such an easy time creating a believable partner for you? Daniel Montague is the alias Ethan Falco used in the past to front arms deals and further his cause by boosting some of the militia groups. It also made him a little money on the side. Guess he's still up to the same old tricks. Stan had even tracked down a warehouse of stuff Falco has cached. The man could have supplied a small army. I helped myself to everything I thought we could use."

"Nothing surprises me anymore. Guess I owe you an apology. Did you hear from Chris Tashley? Did he get the files?"

"He got them and confirmed a few of the facts Stan gathered. Enough to convince him it's all legit. He's working through the proper channels to assemble a team in private. But he wants you to locate that first shipment of C-4 before taking the McEdwins down."

Adam didn't like the thought of one hundred pounds of C-4 floating loose either. "I'll try to find out tonight, but I'm prepared to close it down without that info. Lyle needs a hospital and Renata's in constant danger. Besides, the longer we wait, the greater the chance of one of the McEdwins slipping away." The fact that Willy had disappeared already bothered Adam. What if the old man didn't return?

Adam kept quiet as the waitress approached. He waved her off. "We're leaving."

Zach stood. "Where's the woman now?"

"At the compound. That's why I'm in a hurry to return." Adam threw a twenty on the table.

When they approached the car, Nevin climbed out and pointed to the bag Zach carried. "Tell him to drop it."

"He drops it, something's liable to break," Adam said. "Or explode."

Nevin eyed the bag with undisguised interest. "I'll still need to search it."

"No problem," Adam said. "But let's get away from here first. Being out in the wide open makes me nervous."

Renata backed away. Her foot brushed a stool. She glanced down, checking the path for other obstacles.

"You're a spunky little thing," Burt taunted. "I see why Duval's been so hot to keep you for himself."

Without warning, he rushed her. Renata had a split second to react. She swung her fist, but only grazed his chin.

They crashed to the ground, Burt on top. He easily pinned her.

She screamed and kicked, fighting.

"Yeah, that's it," Burt snarled. "Remember to buck just like that when my dick's inside you—"

His words were cut off as he was physically lifted off her. Renata saw Willy McEdwin standing over them.

"You idiot! Leave her be!"

Burt snorted. "What's the bitch got that everyone's so concerned about? A fucking golden pussy?"

"I gave Duval my word she wouldn't be harmed. Besides, your brother still needs her."

Renata scrambled backwards and climbed to her feet. She knew by the contemptuous look Willy gave her that the only reason he'd intervened was because he didn't want to risk jeopardizing his deal with Adam.

"She claims Lyle wants to go to the hospital," Burt said.

"I don't believe that," Willy said. "Take her downstairs,

tell Tristin to get her some decent food. I'll stay with
Lyle until Nevin and Duval get back."

It was almost comical how friendly both Nevin and
the pilot became once they searched Zach's bag and
saw the weaponry. Even Adam was impressed. Most
intriguing was a mini-machine gun with a grenade
launcher. The compact grenades came in incendiary
and fragment models.

The pieces had all been customized and looked
state-of-the-art. Where in the hell was Ethan Falco getting this kind of hardware and what was he doing with
it?

"Are these the Star Wars prototypes I keep hearing
about?" the pilot asked.

Adam knew the man's question was sincere. He also
knew a stupid question when he heard one. That the
government was secretly developing futuristic spy
satellites and revolutionary weapon systems was a favorite conspiracy theory.

"You think I'd carry those around in a bag like this?"
Zach joked. Then he winked, leaving just enough
doubt to fuel the pilot's imagination.

It was late afternoon when they returned to the
McEdwins' compound.

Willy met them at the door. He eyed Zach's gold
hoop earrings quizzically before extending a hand.
"You must be Daniel Montague."

Zach shook it. "My partner says you have an interesting proposition."

"All business, eh? I like that. Come in."

Nevin nodded toward the staircase. "How's Lyle?"

"Not good. His kidneys may be shutting down. The

doctor thinks it's as easy as loading him into a car and taking him in for dialysis." Willy shook his head.

"Is she with him now?" Adam asked.

"Tristin's with her, too. She and Burt had a little tussle earlier; guess she got a little mouthy. You need to speak to her about cooperating."

Adam scowled. He'd be eager to hear Renata's version of what happened. "She's okay?"

"Yep." Willy motioned them to the table; then set a large pot of coffee in the center. "How soon can I get my hands on that C-4?"

"Within hours," Adam said. "We have it ready for pickup."

"After payment, of course," Zach added.

Willy turned to Nevin, who left the room. He returned moments later and set a cardboard box on the table.

"Count it for them," Willy said.

Nevin withdrew stacks of worn hundred dollar bills. Twenty-five of them. "There's a hundred bills in each one. Ten grand per stack."

Zach reached forward and thumbed through the stacks. "Looks like a quarter million to me."

Willy met Adam's gaze. "I need to check on one thing first, then we'll discuss specifics on delivery. You can take half the money now, with the rest on receipt. Fair enough?"

Adam nodded. "I need a little notice myself, to make a call."

"That settles that," Willy said. "What about my proposal on other items?"

Zach looked from Adam to Willy. "At double what we were getting before? I'm interested, but I won't yank your chain. A lot depends on what kind of merchandise you're looking for."

"And the time frame," Adam said. "Getting the C-4 on such short notice was a miracle. That can't be the norm."

Willy agreed. "As far as resale opportunities go, I can use any kind of weaponry. Nevin mentioned Montague's brought some fancy hardware along. Naturally, the high tech stuff gets top dollar. I have a personal interest in remote relay systems if you can get any fast. The ones I get from overseas are crap."

Zach frowned. "Are you talking about remote detonators for the C-4 we're getting?"

"Guess it's no secret that I've got an ax to grind."

"Remote relays are a dime a dozen," Adam said.

"Not the kind I want," Willy said. "These have to trigger simultaneously, at five different locations."

"What kind of distance are we talking?" Zach asked.

"Several hundred miles."

"You've considered cell phones that could be auto-dialed by a computer?"

"The reliability's spotty. Damn dropped calls."

"What about satellite phones, from a secure tower?" Zach continued. "With locations transmitted by GPS coordinates?"

Willy shook his head. "That sounds complicated."

Adam refilled his coffee. "For someone like you and me, it's impossible. But for someone who knows electronics and can access the right database, it's easy."

Zach sighed. "He makes it sound so simple."

"Then spare me the details and give me a simple answer," Willy said. "Is it doable?"

"Not under all circumstances," Zach replied. "I would need a few more details on the type of application—and the locations—before I can give you an answer."

"Let me think about it," Willy said.

"As far as the other stuff," Adam said. "I propose

you let us check what weaponry is available. Then you tell us what we can unload quickly to turn some fast cash."

Zach nodded. "I'll also check on those remote relays. Do you have an Internet portal and a place my laptop can sit uninterrupted for a while?"

Willy pointed to the corner of the room where his computers were hooked up. "We can run a line from over there."

Nevin, who'd finished splitting the cash into two piles, turned to Zach. "I gotta tell you, I'm curious as hell how you managed to crack the defense department's system. It's supposed to be hack-proof."

"That's why we go in through the manufacturer," Adam said. "Government's contracted most inventory management back to them and—"

Zach cut him off. "You're giving away my secrets."

Nevin whistled. "Slick."

"But not easy." Zach reached into his bag and withdrew a laptop and a small black box. "They change passwords regularly and have elaborate security sequences that I have to debug first."

"What's the black box?" Nevin asked.

"A scrambler. And it has to be close to where the line comes in, next to the wall."

"Let me see that." Willy held out his hand. "What are all these for?" He pointed to the line of phone jacks and cable connections across the back.

"Careful. That's a one-of-a-kind piece of technology." Zach said. "I can run up to four units through here. Phone, fax, desktop, laptop. The box scrambles the signal and sends fake transmission info. Then it boomerangs from phone system to phone system, changing its own trail, so it can't be traced."

"Mind if I try it out while you're here?" Willy asked.

"Go ahead. Just don't get too attached to it. It's not for sale."

"Everything's for sale." Willy moved to watch Nevin help Zach get the laptop connected. "You can leave it there. I'll see that it's not touched."

Zach cracked his knuckles and then started hitting keys rapid fire. A dialog box popped up. KEYGUARD ACTIVATED. Behind the box, strings of symbols began flashing.

Willy looked back at Adam. "He can stay with you in the bunkhouse. I'll have Tristin bring the woman out shortly. Let's meet again for supper in two hours."

When they were out in the bunkhouse, Zach completely emptied his duffle bag. Beneath the equipment Nevin had seen was a hidden cache of smaller arms, ammo. And some electronics. "Here, catch."

Adam examined the small flat disks in the plastic bag his brother had tossed. "Listening devices?"

"If we need them. The laptop I left inside also has a listening device. We can monitor it with this." Zach held up a second, smaller laptop.

"Did all that come from Ethan's stash?"

"Nope."

"Is any of it legal?"

Zach tossed him a cell phone. "This is. The rest belongs to a friend. Which means I didn't steal it, if that's what you're asking. I am trying to be cognizant of your position. Besides, it did the trick. Convinced them I'm an arms smuggler. You saw Nevin drooling."

Adam crossed his arms. His brother had a point. "So what's with the black box you had inside?"

"It's a ruse. It will copy Willy's hard drive to my laptop."

A knock on the door sounded. Adam gave Zach a few seconds to stash his gear before opening the door. It was Tristin with Renata.

"Pa said to bring her back with you later."

No sooner had Tristin left than Adam spotted the small bruise on her cheek. He swore violently. "Who did that?"

"Burt. His father intervened before he could do anything." Renata hugged herself. "But if we had been alone . . ."

"I'll make damn sure he pays for this," Adam vowed.

Zach cleared his throat. "And when will you introduce me?"

"Renata, this is my brother. You need to remember him as my partner, Daniel Montague."

"My pleasure." Grasping her fingers, Zach kissed her hand. "And I'll protect you as my brother would."

His courtly action made her smile. She looked from Zach to Adam and back again. "It's difficult to tell you're related."

"That's exactly what we want," Adam said. "How's Lyle's condition?"

"There's no real improvement." She looked at him. "Restarting the IV has helped, but I'm struggling to keep him stable."

"By this time tomorrow, it should be over." He saw the relief on her face. "But I need to make a phone call."

Adam's phone call to Chris Tashley had been fruitful. Chris was working behind the scenes getting backup lined up, under the guise of busting a counterfeit ring. To avoid leaks, the arresting agents would

have no idea they were going after the McEdwins.
Ethan Falco would be arrested and charged later.

When they met with Willy again, Adam got another
unexpected surprise. Willy disclosed his target to Zach
as they ate.

Willy was targeting presidential candidate Richard
Barrington. Or actually, Barrington's VP nominees. Barrington had plans to barnstorm the Midwest the
following weekend, appearing at rallies in the home-
towns of the four potential vice presidential candidates.
Barrington would end up in his own hometown of Tulsa,
where he'd finally announce his choice.

Willy planned to set off bombs at all five stops.

"My reasons are personal," Willy said. "I've finally
tracked down a very old enemy."

Adam knew immediately which potential VP he was
after: Ethan Falco. The irony was sickening. Ethan had
been after Willy. Willy was after Ethan. If they only
knew . . .

Zach scratched his goatee. "Sounds like you could
use those new detonators soon."

"Only if I can get them within forty-eight hours. If
not, I'll stick with my original plan." Willy turned to
Adam. "I'd like you, Nevin, and Burt to pick up the C-4
in the morning, and transfer it so the bombs can be finished. I'll stay here and work with Montague."

"Sounds perfect," Adam said. Perfectly insane.

"We're scheduled to be on a freighter heading to
Honolulu in three days." Willy looked at Adam. "That
means the woman's got to be dealt with."

"I'll handle it after I get back tomorrow."

Chapter Twenty

It was late when the three of them returned to the bunkhouse.

Zach excused himself. He had surreptitiously swapped the disk from the black box. "I want to see what it copied from Willy's hard drive."

"Whatever it is, send copies to Tashley," Adam said.

He tugged Renata into the bedroom. It was the first time they'd been alone all day. And if all went as planned, it would be their last night together.

The bruise on her cheek distressed him. Willy had blown off the incident, blaming Renata, and in his current position, Adam couldn't contradict him. But before this ended, Burt would pay.

Taking her in his arms, he simply held her. He'd never been one to contemplate the future. Now it loomed large with only two options: A life with her. Or a hell without her.

"It's ending, isn't it?" she whispered.

"You'll be safe. I have to leave again but my brother will be here. You have to do everything he says, Renata. He'll get you out and keep you safe until I return."

"Will you be in danger?"

"No more than we've both been in all along."

"How long do we have?"

"Till morning."

Moisture shimmered softly in her eyes. "Then let's not waste a moment."

Adam picked her up and laid her on the bed. He took his time undressing her, trailing his mouth over every inch of her skin. Tonight he'd take it slow, try to prolong each second; treat it like the precious gift it was. Tomorrow she'd be gone and who knew what lay beyond? Life had a way of being generous one moment and cruel the next.

He removed his clothes before moving over her, careful to keep his weight on his elbows. That first touch of bare flesh was startling. He caught her lips, swept his tongue deep. Her hands speared through his hair, drawing him closer as she opened her mouth.

She boldly took over the kiss, ravishing him. His desire swelled as she pressed a line of kisses along his jaw, down his neck, brushing his throat with her teeth before tenderly biting the soft flesh at the top of his shoulder. "I want you."

Her erotic bite, those three simple words, were Adam's undoing.

All thoughts of going slow fled as he pressed into her with one stroke, his way eased by wet, welcoming heat.

Maybe next time.

He got up once during the night to talk with Zach. The black box had copied some incriminating data from Willy's hard drive. Names of contacts, domestic and abroad.

And a whole file on Ethan Falco. It had taken Willy nearly ten years, but he had finally traced the origins of the money that funded the antigovernment group he'd belonged to years ago.

Ethan Falco had run the funds through overseas accounts in an elaborate maze of money transfers. He'd also skimmed hundreds of thousands in interest and kickbacks, diverting it to secret personal accounts.

Adam shook his head. In the end, Willy had flushed Ethan out by emptying Ethan's secret accounts via Burt and Tristin's hacking talents. Ethan couldn't report the money as stolen without showing his hand.

And Willy had been using Ethan's funds to finance his vengeance. Small wonder he hadn't blinked over paying a quarter million for the C-4.

Next, Adam called Chris Tashley. It was settled.

Adam gave Tashley the warehouse address where Zach had stored the C-4. Tashley promised that homing devices would be hidden in the shipment before morning. FBI and ATF agents would trail Adam, Nevin, and Burt from the warehouse to the final delivery spot, in hopes of getting all the C-4 at once.

As soon as Adam delivered the C-4, he'd call his brother, pretending to confirm all was fine. That was Zach's signal to get Renata away from the compound and hide in the woods until law enforcement and FBI agents arrived. Tashley would have a second team ready to overtake the compound and arrest Willy, Tristin, and Lyle. A chopper would be brought in to ferry Lyle to the closest trauma hospital. To circumvent the leaks, Tashley wasn't disclosing locations or names until the last moment.

"Any addenda to your will?" Zach joked.

"See that she's taken care of. No matter what."

"Do you love her?"

Adam grunted. "I've never loved anyone. Don't even know what it feels like."

"It's rather nasty. And arbitrary." Zach shook his head. "Close your eyes and imagine her dead. How do you feel?"

Adam didn't have to close his eyes. The thought sickened him.

He had endured more physical pain in his life than most. Yet nothing—not even being shot—equaled the burning grief of imagining Renata gone. He didn't like the implications.

He stood. "Make damn sure she's not harmed."

Adam, Nevin, and Burt left the compound before dawn, flying the short distance to the warehouse by helicopter. Adam learned that they'd fly back to a different location in Montana once they had the C-4.

Leaving the pilot behind with the chopper, they climbed in a car and drove to the warehouse address Zach had furnished. The abandoned building had plywood covering the windows with dozens of faded FOR SALE signs tacked up.

"Pull around to the rear," Adam said. "I have a key."

His thoughts flew back to Renata. Zach's litmus test—*close your eyes*—had haunted Adam's sleep. He'd kissed her before leaving, but refused to say goodbye. "I'll see you later," he'd promised instead.

In retrospect, he realized what a fool he'd been. And hoped he hadn't missed the chance to tell her . . . he loved her.

Renata spent the day with Lyle. His condition was unchanged from the night before which was heartening since she had expected worse. Perhaps he was responding to the antibiotics.

Her mind kept drifting to Adam. Where was he now? Were things going as planned? He didn't tell her specifics about what he'd be doing, but she knew that once Zach received a call from him, they'd leave.

She thought back to their night of lovemaking, tried not to overanalyze it. There'd be time for recriminations later. Time, too, for examining her feelings for Adam. They weren't simple. And they weren't all nice. But the not-so-nice ones were easier to contemplate than the ones that made her feel like she was losing control.

Yes, she cared for him, but they'd been thrown together under extreme circumstances. Were still battling those circumstances. Now was not the time to . . .

"How's he doing?"

Renata whirled around at the sound of Willy McEdwin's voice. "He's stable. I hope it means this combination of antibiotics is working. But he's still gravely ill, so—"

"So he could still die. I understand."

"His chances for recovery could drastically improve at a hospital."

Willy cut her off. "You remind me of a bulldog I once owned. Damn dog got kicked chasing the neighbor's mule. Almost killed him. Thought for sure he learned a lesson, yet whenever that mule was out, the dog would chase it and get kicked again. One day he didn't come home and I found him stomped to pieces in the neighbor's field. I hope you're smarter than that."

Renata lowered her head and began putting away the supplies she'd used earlier.

"You can leave that," Willy interrupted. "I'm gonna sit a while with the boy. Tristin will take you out to the bunkhouse with Montague. If I need you, someone will fetch you."

Tristin hovered at the door. As soon as they were gone, Willy moved closer to Lyle's bedside. For several minutes he just stood, lost in memories.

His wife had nearly miscarried twice with Lyle and practically bled to death giving birth.

"No more babies," Willy had sworn. But she'd laughed, teasing about how she wanted a girl. The morning she died, she'd told Willy she thought she was pregnant again. "And it feels like a girl."

It would be twenty years ago next week that she'd died and it still hurt.

But he'd finally found the man responsible for her death. Willy had dreamed of this for years . . . and nothing—not even his own flesh and blood—would stand in his way.

He stared at Lyle. Nevin, Tristin, and Burt were the spitting image of Willy. They remembered their mother dying, their father going to prison while their mother's murderer roamed free. Their grief and bitterness had bound them to Willy. Yeah, they had their moments, but their obedience was unquestionable.

Lyle had never really shared that bond. There'd been a time when Willy thought the boy had changed. He'd helped them on a couple jobs. Kept his mouth shut, too. But then he'd broken the pact. Let himself be taken alive.

Willy fingered the control on the IV, shutting off the flow. No one but the doctor would notice, and she wasn't coming back in.

Lyle's eyes fluttered open. He could hardly speak. "Pa."

"Easy now." Willy patiently held a glass while Lyle drank. Most of it dribbled down his chin.

"Sorry." Lyle coughed. "I fucked up again, didn't I?"

Willy nodded, grabbing the corner of the sheet to wipe Lyle's mouth.

"How long . . . have . . . have I got?"

"Doc says you could linger for days. Maybe weeks."

Lyle let out a cry. "Can't do anything right, can I?"

"You know we can't stay here after tonight."

"I'll only slow you down. Leave . . . me."

For a long moment, Willy was quiet. Then he placed a hand on Lyle's shoulder and squeezed gently.

When his son's eyes fluttered open again, Willy laid a pistol within reach on the bed. "There's one bullet. Do what you gotta do."

Adam unlocked the door and entered the building. According to Zach, the C-4 was in a locker in a corner.

"This way," he said as soon as the door closed behind Nevin and Burt.

He'd barely taken three steps when bright lights flashed on, blinding them. Adam stiffened, tried to look away.

"Freeze! This is the FBI. You are under arrest," a voice boomed over a loudspeaker. "Put your weapons down, and keep your hands in the air."

"Run!" Nevin aimed for the lights. He'd barely gotten off a shot before falling to the ground, blood oozing from his head.

Burt stopped when Nevin fell. Adam acted swiftly, taking advantage of Burt's shock to yank the rifle from his hands and knock him to the ground with a fist. Burt sprawled unconscious on his stomach.

"That's for Renata."

"Lie down and place your hands behind your head," a voice shouted.

Not certain who the players were—and what had gone wrong—Adam tossed Burt's rifle aside and raised his hands as he dropped to his knees, prepared to identify himself as an FBI agent. What the hell had happened to the plan he'd discussed with Tashley?

Two men came out of the shadows. Both had handguns drawn. Adam recognized one of them. It was the same man he'd locked in the trunk . . . Ethan's man.

Without a word, the man moved up behind Burt and fired two shots to the back of his head.

Adam braced, expecting the same.

Tristin took Renata to the bunkhouse and released her to Zach's custody. "Keep her handcuffed."

"Have you heard from Adam?" she asked when they were alone.

Zach motioned her into the bedroom and pulled the laptop from his bag. "Not yet. But Nevin and Burt haven't called in either, so I'm not concerned. And our being left out here may work to our advantage when the call does come in. We can slip through a back window."

Renata hugged herself, feeling cold. "I'm worried."

Zach shrugged. "If you knew my brother better, you wouldn't be."

"How well do you know him? I got the impression you two weren't close."

"Have a seat," Zach pointed to a chair. "I was six years old when our parents split. Up till that point my brother was mother, father, savior. Most nights, I slept under his bed, hiding from the rampages. When I'd start crying he'd whisper stories. They were awful. The three bears ate Goldilocks, then went looking to barbeque the three little pigs."

"Did it distract you?"

"Yeah. When I was four and he had to go to school, he'd drag me along, make me hide behind the lunch-room dumpster. Threatened to kill me if I left. If we couldn't scrounge food there, he'd steal it." Zach leaned forward. "I may not know a lot of particulars about his adult life; we've been estranged. But I know he's a good man, Renata."

She dashed away a tear, confused by her emotional response. "I don't even know his real name."

"Now that I can help with. It's Jake. Jake Ryan—"

A pounding at the door, brought Zach to his feet. He shoved the computer under the mattress and drew a gun.

Tristin was at the door, breathing heavy. "We need the doc. Fast!"

Zach lowered his gun, motioning for Renata to pre-cede him. But the moment she stepped out the door, a man grabbed her and pressed a gun to her throat.

"Throw down your weapon. Or watch her die."

Zach dropped his gun.

Another man stepped forward. He wore a suit and tie, and looked completely out of place. "I take it you're Jake's brother, Zachary. I know some people at Interpol who'd like to talk with you."

"You must be Ethan Falco," Zach said.

Tristin had retrieved Zach's gun and now pointed it at him. "I can't wait to show you how the McEdwins deal with traitors."

Ethan held up a hand. "Not yet. He has something of mine—Stan Beckwith's computer. Search this place."

Ethan's man kept a gun on Renata, while Tristin kept his weapon trained on Zach. They found the laptop hidden in the bedroom.

"That's not Beckwith's," Ethan's man said. "Wrong brand."

"Come on," Ethan said. "We'll continue this at the house."

When they reached the main house, Willy was waiting.

"We don't have a lot of time," Ethan said to Zach. "So I'll cut to the point: Where's Stan's laptop?"

"In a safe place. Where's my brother?"

A helicopter circled overhead. "That's probably him now." Ethan turned to Willy. "As soon as I get the computer, you can dispose of them. I'll throw the woman in for free."

Zach looked at Willy, all pretense dropped. "You're working together? I thought you wanted him dead?"

"I do." Willy scowled, clearly unhappy. "But we've struck a deal. He did me a favor, tipping me off that your brother is an FBI agent. I'm ashamed to admit he fooled us. As soon as Nevin and Burt get in, we're taking off." Willy tipped his head toward Ethan. "He gets what he wants and the McEdwins live to fight another day. Too bad I can't say the same for you."

Footsteps sounded on the porch. Tristin checked the front door, opening it to admit two more of Ethan's men. They dragged Adam between them. He appeared unconscious, blood dripping down from his scalp.

Renata tried to rise, but Ethan kept a hand on her shoulder.

"He's hurt," she said. "Let me check him."

"He tried to jump the pilot," one of the men explained to Ethan. "Had to cold-cock him."

"Where are Burt and Nevin?" Willy asked.

The two men dropped Adam. "There was a problem—"

"They killed your sons, Willy." Adam's voice was raspy. "Executed both of them. Head shots."

Behind Willy, Tristin let out an anguished cry. "You motherfucking bastards!"

Tristin started firing, catching everyone off guard. He shot the two men standing over Adam. Both men fell, dead, as pandemonium broke loose.

Adam grabbed one of the men's guns and rolled behind a chair. He struggled to sit up, his head throbbing. *Renata.* He had to save her.

Almost as quickly as it began, the shots ceased. Easing forward, Adam peered around the chair. On the floor, in pools of blood, were the bodies of Ethan's other man and Tristin McEdwin. Willy had disappeared. So had Zach.

Ethan stood in the center of the room, one arm around Renata's neck, his gun pointed at her. "Throw your gun out, or she gets it."

Adam complied. "Let her go."

"Stand up where I can see you," Ethan ordered.

"You mean shoot me?"

"The choice is yours. I can shoot you . . . or her."

Adam stood. Now he saw Zach, sprawled on the ground, his blood staining the floor red. "You'll never get away with this."

"Wanna bet? I'll be a hero," Ethan laughed. "I killed all the McEdwins—"

A shot rang out. Renata screamed as Ethan staggered forward.

"Not all of them," Tristin rasped.

"Renata, drop!" Adam shouted, but she'd already moved away, giving Adam a clear view of Tristin.

He was propped on his elbow, his gun now pointed at Adam. Blood oozed from his shoulder. "That was for Burt. This is for Nevin."

Tristin swung his gun toward Renata.

Adam lunged toward her, pulling her down, shielding her. Behind him another shot rang out. He braced.

"I got him." It was Zach's voice. He sounded weak.

Adam tugged Renata to her feet and rushed to his brother's side.

Zach waved him back. "Go after Willy. He went upstairs."

"I'll help him." Renata was already ripping open Zach's shirt. Adam could see his brother had been shot in the side.

Pausing just long enough make certain all the others were indeed dead, Adam raced up the stairs. He heard voices coming from Lyle's room and eased up to the door.

"It's over, Willy," Adam shouted. "Give up peacefully."

"You can come on in," Willy replied.

Cautious, Adam stayed behind the wall, and shoved the door open. Angling slightly, he saw Willy standing next to Lyle's bed.

"Lay down your weapon and put your hands where I can see them," Adam ordered.

Willy nodded, but didn't move. "Where's Tristin?"

"He's been shot, too."

Willy's shoulders dropped, shook with noiseless sobs. Moving slowly, he stepped away from the bed. Then he put his gun on the dresser and raised his hands. "Were you telling me the truth down there? Nevin and Burt . . . they're really gone?"

"Yes."

Now Willy's voice cracked. "They were good boys. They kept their word."

Behind him, Lyle moaned. "That . . . fucking . . . oath. McEdwins . . . never get taken alive."

Adam watched in surprise as Lyle drew a gun from beneath the sheet.

"Drop it, Lyle!" Adam quickly took cover. But instead of pointing the gun at him, Lyle had pointed it toward his father.

Willy's mouth gaped. "What are you doing?"

"Helping you keep your word, too." Lyle fired once and dropped the gun. It slid to the floor.

Clutching his chest, Willy fell.

Cursing, Adam moved quickly, kicking the gun away before kneeling beside Willy. The old man gasped, then closed his eyes and simply quit breathing.

Lyle had passed out. Checking him for more weapons, Adam collected the firearms and raced back downstairs. Zach was propped up, Renata beside him talking quietly into a cell phone.

"She called 911," Zach groaned. "I heard a shot. You get Willy?"

"Lyle did. You okay?"

"Okay? I was shot. That's never okay."

"He'll survive. I've stopped the bleeding." Renata hurried to Adam's side. "Your head is bleeding, too."

"Lucky I've got a thick skull."

"The police are on the way," she said. "I told them we need ambulances, preferably medivac helicopters. Is . . . Lyle dead?"

"No. But he needs immediate transport."

"So it's over?" she asked. "And you'll tell me everything?"

"Everything." Including how much he loved her.

Epilogue

Six months later

"I . . . can't . . . breathe." Renata's ribcage felt dangerously compressed.

"Don't use your diaphragm; inhale through your nose," Janet advised.

"But my liver—"

"You know, I never took you for such a whiner. And I'm almost finished. There. Now turn around and look."

Renata gasped. The woman in the mirror looked like she'd just stepped out of an X-rated magazine. The black lace corset, with its lace-up boning, had her waist cinched tight, which in turn thrust her breasts up and out at an unnatural angle. Beribboned straps of satin snaked down her thighs to grasp silk stockings. And the four-inch stilettos . . . hurt.

"I can't do this," Renata began. "It's too out of character for me."

"Duh! That's the whole point of role playing, girlfriend. And there's no time for second thoughts. We have five minutes. Hold still!" Janet fastened an elaborate jet and black crystal choker around Renata's neck, then handed her matching dangling earrings. "Put these on and do your lipstick. I'll finish lighting candles on my way out."

"Wait! Tell me again what Zach said." Adam's—*Jake's* brother had called while Renata was in the shower and left a cryptic message with Janet.

"He said your package would be delivered at seven," Janet said. "Which means now you've only got four minutes."

Renata panicked. What had seemed like a wonderful idea a week ago now seemed harebrained.

Jake had been on the west coast the last four months, working undercover out of the Seattle office. She understood it was what he did, but still she'd been glad to hear the job had ended.

After returning from Willy's compound, they'd stayed in touch, talking mostly by phone. The awkwardness, the anger, she had expected to feel toward him never surfaced. And while Jake lived in Baltimore, he'd flown to Durham several times. For dates. He'd brought her roses. Taken her to dinner. And was a perfect gentleman.

"We'll take it slow this time," he insisted. "To make certain your feelings are real."

Then he'd been temporarily assigned to Seattle. The distance, the time apart, indeed made her heart grow fonder. She'd counted hours until he came back to Baltimore, secretly determined that his days as a gentleman were over. And then he'd called, wanted to fly to Durham to see her.

Renata had enlisted Janet's help in planning a special night. Janet had come up with a role-playing, kidnap-your-lover-for-a-night-of-ecstasy idea. *Turnabout's fair play* had been her logic. "He kidnapped you first, right?"

Janet had offered to meet Jake's plane and abduct him, but at the last minute, Renata had decided to ask

Zach for help with the actual *faux* kidnapping. To keep it a surprise. Jake would have suspected something if Janet had showed up at the airport. Zach had agreed to have his brother picked up in a limo, then blindfolded and brought to her door.

"I owe you a favor," Zach had said. "Remember?"

Renata had stayed with Zach after he'd been shot in Idaho. Fortunately, his wound had been minor. And she hadn't said anything when he'd slipped away from the emergency room before authorities could question him.

She understood that Zach's background was checkered, his past dark. Jake promised to explain it some day. *Some day soon,* she thought, recalling the news she'd received earlier in the week.

Lyle McEdwin, the only surviving member of his family, had recovered and ended up accepting a plea bargain to avoid the death penalty. He'd been given a life sentence, with no chance of parole, for murdering his father. There would be no trial.

Thanks to Stan and Willy's files, Ethan Falco's tangled past was neatly documented. With Falco dead, more people came forward with accusations, prompting a congressional investigation. An ugly chapter of history was about to be closed.

All that remained now was for her to convince Jake that she truly cared for him. The circumstances of their meeting be damned.

"I'm out of here," Janet shouted from the living room. "You've got thirty seconds!" The front door slammed.

Renata walked—carefully—into her living room. She didn't recognize it. With the help of a hundred strategically placed candles, and four miles of thumb-tacked gossamer netting, Janet had converted her apartment into a gauzy fantasy.

"God, what was I thinking?" She grabbed a piece of the netting and yanked it down just as the doorbell rang. "Great!"

There was no turning back now. Squaring her shoulders, she went to the door, glanced out the peephole.

And nearly died. Two men stood outside, one with a bouquet of flowers. The bell rang again. Damn it! She needed to get rid of them before Jake arrived.

Grabbing a trench coat from the hall closet, she threw it over the corset and yanked open the door. The wind blew snow inside. It wasn't supposed to start snowing until later, which gave her hope that Adam's plane would be delayed.

"Renata Curtis? We got a delivery for you. From a Zach Ryan."

Puzzled, she accepted the flowers.

The man nodded his head to one side. "Where do you want this?"

She looked around the corner, saw a rolled up carpet. A very large carpet . . . lumpy . . . complete with bare feet sticking out one end.

"Oh no! Get him inside. It's freezing out here!"

The men picked up either end of the rug, and carried it inside.

"Get him out of there. Now!"

"Yes, ma'am." The men held the edge of the rug and let the rest drop. Jake hit the ground and rolled across the floor, his hands and feet bound, duct tape over his mouth.

Renata dropped to her knees, and tried to pry the tape loose. One of the deliverymen bent over and ripped the tape free in a single yank. "It hurts less that way."

"The hell it does," Jake growled. "And quit looking at her!"

Renata glanced down, noticed the front of her coat had come open. She snatched the edges together.

"If you don't mind, we'll leave before you untie him." Grinning, the men took the carpet and left. "Zach sends his regards, by the way."

"Tell my brother to watch his back," Jake snarled at the slamming door. "Untie me."

Renata grabbed a kitchen knife and began sawing through the cords. "This was not supposed to happen."

The gold flecks in his eyes glittered dangerously. "Don't tell me you're dressed like that for someone else?"

She shook her head. "It was for you. I was . . . trying to get you here for a romantic fantasy, but I see now it wasn't such a great idea."

Free of the rope, Jake stood. Grasping the lapels of her coat, he opened it and stared. "Anything that involves you in black lace is a great idea. So exactly what was this fantasy?" He looked around her apartment, seeing it for the first time. "And what's burning?"

Renata caught a whiff of smoke and turned. The piece of netting she'd torn loose had blown too close to a candle and was now going up in flames, melting and crackling like spun sugar.

Jake reacted swiftly, vaulting over the sofa and yanking the netting down from the ceiling. Blazing pieces dropped to the carpet. Renata took off her coat and smothered the flames just as the smoke alarm started beeping.

Swearing under her breath, she wrenched open the French doors that led to the small second story balcony and began fanning her arms. Her apartment smelled like burnt nylon, the smoke thick and acrid.

"Come on," Jake pulled her outside, onto the balcony. "Flames are out but those fumes will kill us."

Renata sucked in frigid air, coughing as the corset hampered her ability to draw a deep breath.

In the distance, sirens echoed.

"The smoke alarms. They're wired into the alarm system," she said. "I need to get dressed before they— tell me you didn't shut the door all the way."

Jake hovered close, caught her chin. "Why?"

She reached behind him, tried the doorknob. "Because it locks automatically."

Fire trucks roared into the complex, their sirens growing louder. They'd be there any moment. Mortified, Renata closed her eyes. "Do you have any idea if Mercury went retrograde today?"

Jake laughed and brushed snow from her hair. She had no business being outside, dressed like this. *Dressed like this,* she should be in his bedroom.

"I can't believe you did all this for me."

She frowned. "Well, believe me, it won't happen again."

"God, I hope you're joking." He ran a hand along the top of the corset, his fingers brushing the swells of her breasts.

Removing his shirt, he pulled it over her shoulders. It went to her knees. He would have preferred it went to her ankles, but it would do until the fireman freed them. He tugged her into his arms.

"I don't know about retrogrades, but my horoscope said I'd find love today. I always thought those columns in the paper were kinda lame . . . until now. I love you, Renata."

A ladder crashed against the side rail of her balcony. A moment later a fireman appeared. "You folks okay?"

She smiled. "We're perfect."